"Perhaps you did not realize that this is my private chamber, milord," Gillian said, her tone cold.

"You must also be unaware that 'tis most unseemly for us to be here unchaperoned." She met Rannulf's eyes, tried to ignore the heat she saw smoldering there. "I suggest you leave at once, before my guardian discovers you here. I am certain he wouldn't approve."

Rannulf closed the space between them and leaned close, his breath warm against her cheek. "You never used to mind us being alone together, Gillian. Indeed, I think you welcomed it...welcomed me."

Jerking back from him, she said, her voice little more than a croak of sound, "You, sir, are no gentleman."

"And you, milady, knew that already." He drew closer as his hand crept nearer her chest. "I believe 'twas one of the things you liked best about me."

Dear Reader,

Welcome to Harlequin Historicals—stories that will capture your heart with unforgettable characters and the timeless fantasy of falling in love!

Sharon Schulze returns this month with the fourth book in her popular L'EAU CLAIR CHRONICLES, *The Hidden Heart.* Since Sharon's debut in our 1997 March Madness Promotion with *Heart of the Dragon,* critics have hailed her work as "rich" and "satisfying." In this medieval novel, a beautiful noblewoman must guard her heart from the only man she has ever really loved—the Earl of Wynfield, who has returned to her keep on a dangerous secret mission. Watch love begin anew!

Fans of Western romance will no doubt enjoy *Cooper's Wife* by Jillian Hart, the heartwarming tale of single parents—a lonely sheriff and a troubled widow—who marry to protect their children, but find a lasting love. And in *The Dreammaker* by Judith Stacy, also a Western, two people who are swindled by the same man go into business together to recoup their losses and realize their dreams—when love, the dream of a lifetime, is right in front of them! Award-winning author Gayle Wilson's latest Regency-style historical, *Lady Sarah's Son,* is the heart-wrenching tale of sweethearts, torn apart by tragedy, who come together again in a marriage of convenience and can no longer deny their enduring love....

Enjoy! And come back again next month for four more choices of the best in historical romance.

Sincerely,

Tracy Farrell, Senior Editor

P.S. We'd love to hear what you think about Harlequin Historicals! Drop us a line at:

Harlequin Historicals
300 E. 42nd Street, 6th Floor
New York, NY 10017

THE HIDDEN HEART

SHARON SCHULZE

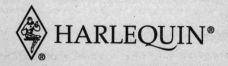

HARLEQUIN®

TORONTO • NEW YORK • LONDON
AMSTERDAM • PARIS • SYDNEY • HAMBURG
STOCKHOLM • ATHENS • TOKYO • MILAN • MADRID
PRAGUE • WARSAW • BUDAPEST • AUCKLAND

ISBN 0-373-29084-5

THE HIDDEN HEART

Books by Sharon Schulze

Harlequin Historicals

* *Heart of the Dragon* #356
* *To Tame a Warrior's Heart* #386
* *The Shielded Heart* #442
* *The Hidden Heart* #484

* l'Eau Clair Chronicles

SHARON SCHULZE

began writing romances while pursuing her first career as a civil engineer, and discovered that confirmed day-dreamer/bookaholics can practice their craft anywhere, even somewhere as unromantic as a wastewater treatment plant. In her writing, she gets the chance to experience days gone by—without encountering disease, vermin and archaic plumbing!

A New Hampshire native, she now makes her home in Connecticut with her husband, Cliff, their children, Patrick and Christina, and her "lovely assistant"—Samantha, a miniature dachshund. In her ever-shrinking spare time she enjoys movies, music and poking around in antique shops.

Readers may contact her at P.O. Box 180, Oakville, CT 06779.

With love and appreciation to my husband,
Clifford—
ever and always my hero.

Prologue

The Welsh Marches, spring 1213

Gillian de l'Eau Clair leaned over the curtain wall of l'Eau Clair Keep and stared down at the new grass covering her father's grave. Nigh two months gone, yet the pain of his loss had scarce eased. And now to find this among her father's papers! She crushed the unsigned betrothal contract clasped in her hand with all the strength of her aching heart and cursed the man who'd scrawled his stark refusal where his acceptance should have been.

Rannulf FitzClifford—once the friend of the child she'd been, later her heart's desire. As she had been his, so he'd led her to believe. The date on the agreement remained etched upon her brain—her seventeenth birthday, more than two years past—not long after his visits to l'Eau Clair had suddenly ceased, as if he'd vanished from her world forever.

It seemed her father hadn't allowed that fact to prevent him from trying to further his plan to see her and Rannulf wed.

She raised her arm to toss the useless document away, then paused and let it fall to her feet. She dropped to her knees and pressed her cheek against the uneven stones as she fought the despair threatening to overwhelm her.

She'd sent word of her father's death to her godfather, the earl of Pembroke; her kinsman, Prince Llywelyn of Wales; everyone she thought might help her fight off the unknown foe who had harried her people and her lands since her father's passing. She stifled a bitter laugh. By the Virgin, she'd even sent a messenger to her overlord, King John, though she hadn't a bit of hope he'd bother to fulfill his duty.

Though it had been two months, none had bothered to reply.

In her desperation, she'd thought to put aside her wounded pride and contact Rannulf. She had searched through the documents stored away in her father's chamber for some hint of how to reach him.

What she'd found destroyed that plan, for 'twas clear by his words he wanted naught to do with her.

The icy wind beat against her, whipped her unbound hair about her face and sent the crumpled missive skittering toward the edge of the wooden walkway. "Nay," she cried, and lunged to grab it. The parchment grasped tight in one hand, the edge of the crenel in the other, she rose to her feet and let the cold, powerful gusts blow away the fear and cowardice she'd allowed to beset her.

She smoothed out the contract and forced herself to read the hurtful message once more. She'd keep it as a reminder, lest she forget yet again that the only person she could depend upon was herself.

Chapter One

Rannulf strode through the dark and silent streets of London, taking care to avoid the noisome puddles, more easily smelled than seen in the fitful moonlight. He'd rather have waited till morning to obey his over-lord's command, but judging from the message he'd received upon his arrival in the city, Lord Nicholas would be put off no longer.

He'd managed to escape meeting Nicholas Talbot for nigh two years, sending his men under the able command of his lieutenant whenever Talbot required his aid. He'd served Talbot's uncle, the previous lord of Ashby, long enough to know he'd no desire to deal with another Talbot if he could avoid it.

Raking his hand through his still-damp hair, he paused before the prosperous-looking merchant's house Talbot had hired to billet his troops. He'd not arrived too late, alas, for light still showed golden through the shutters. 'Twas past time to learn if this Talbot would prove to be another branch of the same twisted tree as his uncle had been.

The servant who answered his summons led him through the barracks set up on the ground floor—full of men tossing dice and swilling ale—and up a flight of stairs at the far end of the room. The lackey thrust aside the curtain covering the doorway at the top and motioned Rannulf into the room. "'Tis Lord Rannulf FitzClifford, milord," he said.

The tall man who rose from the settle before the fire and turned to face him wore the look of both warrior and courtier—a dangerous combination seen all too often in King John's court. Rannulf bit back a groan and shoved his travel weariness aside. It seemed Lord William Marshal, the earl of Pembroke, had the right of it when he warned Rannulf he'd best be on guard in his overlord's presence. Nicholas Talbot would bear watching.

Rannulf stepped into the chamber and bowed. "My lord."

"FitzClifford." Talbot motioned him to a chair before the fire. "'Tis a pleasure to meet you at last." He picked up an intricately chased ewer from a nearby table. "Wine?" he asked as he poured a measure into a silver goblet.

"Aye, thank you." Rannulf took the drink, casting a swift look about him while Talbot poured himself wine and resumed his seat on the settle.

The lord of Ashby enjoyed his comforts, from the look of it, for his garments appeared as costly as his surroundings. Gold threads shimmered in the fanciful design embroidered about the neck and cuffs of his deep green tunic, and his boots and belt were the finest leather. Rannulf sipped his wine—a vintage worthy of the cup, he noted without surprise—and glanced down at his own much simpler garb. Though the soft wool and well-worn leather were of good quality, he'd never felt the need to adorn himself in the vivid colors and elaborate embellishments so popular at court.

Besides, why should he bother? He'd no desire to draw attention to himself, be it from his peers—or from women.

He'd no place for either in his life.

Why, then, did the mere thought set up a deep yearning for all he'd lost?

He quashed the hint of weakness and buried it once again. He deserved nothing more than this new life he'd fashioned for himself—one of duty, of honorable toil, of atonement for his sins.

Though it would never be enough, he could do naught but try.

Rannulf forced himself to sit back in the chair and bring the chalice to his lips, to savor the wine and smile with pleasure at finally meeting his overlord.

"I'm pleased you're able to join me at last, FitzClifford. I've need of your men, 'tis true, but I'll be glad of your company as well." Talbot's mouth curved in a wry smile as he shook his head. "Especially in this latest venture the king has set me upon."

Interest piqued, Rannulf straightened. "And why is that, milord?" He raised his cup and took his time draining it, watching Talbot closely all the while.

"It seems I've angered the king yet again." Talbot thumped down his goblet on a side table and leaned forward.

"Yet again?" Rannulf asked. "'Tis a habit, I take it?"

"So it seems," the other man muttered. "Although perhaps 'angered' is too strong a word. Our liege finds me more of an annoyance, a fly buzzing along the fringe of his notice." He grimaced.

"'Tis dangerous to upset the king, milord, no matter the degree. Best pray he doesn't decide to slap away the annoyance with the blade of his sword." It wouldn't be the first time their liege had dealt thus with his own nobles. But Talbot must know the king well enough to realize that fact. "I'm surprised you're still here to tell of it."

Talbot sighed and glanced up, meeting Rannulf's curious gaze. "I'll not be here for much longer," he said wryly. "Nor will you. By the king's decree, we've been banished to the hinterlands—at least until his anger abates, or he grows bored and calls me back."

By Christ's bones, was he to be tarred with the same brush as Talbot? Rannulf bit back a groan of frustration. While 'twas his intent to stay close to Talbot for the nonce, he'd no desire to draw King John's attention.

Though he had no intention of sharing that bit of information.

"Where are we bound, milord?" he asked, though the answer mattered to him not a whit. He had his orders and his obligation to his overlord to consider as well. 'Twas idle curiosity that brought the question to his lips, nothing more.

Talbot rose and crossed to the table to pour more wine, then set his cup aside untouched. "I've the writ here someplace," he muttered. He opened a plain wooden box—conspicuous in its simplicity—that sat next to the ewer of wine, and shuffled through the jumble of scrolls before drawing forth a beribboned parchment. "The king leaves little to chance," he said, moving closer to the fire. "My orders are set forth here, couched in such terms as to make it appear that I deserve congratulations on my good fortune. I'm to be warden of a keep, and guardian of its lady." He unrolled the missive and scanned it. "Of course, judging by the king's mood when he bestowed this upon me—" he brandished the parchment in the air "—'tis just as likely that condolences would be appropriate." Scowling, he cast another glance at the decree, then held it out to Rannulf. "What do you think this means?"

Rannulf rose and took the scroll, turning the document into the light as he held it open to read.

The words shone dark and clear to his disbelieving gaze before the shadows he'd thought locked deep within his heart broke free and jumbled the letters into a meaningless scrawl.

But that one brief glimpse had been time enough to etch the image upon his brain—and his heart.

Talbot had become guardian of the lady of l'Eau Clair….

Gillian.

Rannulf could have sworn his heart ceased to beat for a moment from the shock of seeing her name. It took several attempts before he could force his voice past his lips. "Congratulations, milord," he said, his hearty tone at odds with the sense of panic rushing through his veins. "A Marcher keep, it says." He reached for his drink and brought it halfway to his mouth before he remembered 'twas empty. Biting back a curse, he pretended to drink, then set the cup aside and scanned the words again. He'd best proceed with care, lest he reveal more information than the brief missive contained. "And a noble lady." He glanced up at Talbot, who stood poised by the fireplace, worry—or was that confusion?—written on his handsome face. By sheer force of will Rannulf curled his mouth into a careless grin. "Just think of the possibilities."

"Believe me, I have." Talbot sat down abruptly, slumping into the chair, his fingers clasped tightly on the carved arms. "Given the king's mood, l'Eau Clair Keep is likely naught more than a crumbling ruin, and its lady a crone stooped and withered with age." He grabbed his wine from the table and gulped it down. "Or a babe still wrapped in swaddling bands. Either way, 'tis no prize I've won, FitzClifford. Of that I have no doubt." He stared into the flickering fire, his expression grim.

Rannulf's mind reeled. If Talbot knew the truth of the situation, they'd have left London already. He could only be grateful for his overlord's ignorance.

But such good fortune couldn't last. Talbot could scarce avoid the king's command for long. Rannulf considered ways to elude this trap before Talbot was ready to set out for l'Eau Clair, but even as his frantic brain sought shelter from his predicament, he knew there was no escape.

He had his orders, to stay with Talbot at all costs, to observe this crony of the king's. 'Twas a stroke of luck that the man was his overlord, giving him the perfect opportunity to obey Pembroke's command. Even if it were possible to send word of the situation to Pembroke, Rannulf knew his orders would not change. Indeed, he could well imagine Pembroke's pleasure that fate had placed Rannulf in the perfect position to not only keep a close eye on Talbot, but on Pembroke's godchild as well. Pembroke could not have arranged the matter better had he set it up himself.

Had Pembroke arranged it thus? He bit back a curse. Nay, his foster father would have told him of Lord Simon's death, warned him that Talbot was bound for l'Eau Clair. Besides, wouldn't Pembroke have arranged the wardship for himself, had he any say in the matter? Despite his quarrels with the king, he was Gillian's godfather. Who better to protect her, after all?

By Christ's bones, he sought plots where there were none! He closed his eyes for a moment, then blinked them open again to dispel the image of Gillian that rose to fill his mind. The mere thought of her held the power to addle his wits. Time and hard-won maturity had not changed that fact, it seemed.

He glanced at Talbot, still enthralled by the fire. His displeasure at his fate would be short-lived, Rannulf had no doubt, for once Nicholas Talbot arrived at the mighty stronghold of l'Eau Clair and caught sight of his beautiful ward, the man would count himself twice blessed.

And Rannulf would be cursed to a purgatory worse than Satan himself could devise.

'Twas his lot in life—why expect change now? He'd a job to do. He stood, poured himself a generous measure of wine, then topped off Talbot's goblet and held it out to him.

"Come, milord, drink to your good fortune."

Talbot looked up, his strange violet eyes still troubled, and accepted the wine. "Easy for you to say," he muttered. "You're not the one who might be saddled with a child, or an old woman past her prime."

Aye, but I'd gladly be burdened with the lady of l'Eau Clair. 'Twas all Rannulf could manage to hold back the words. "It cannot be any worse than you've surmised," he said instead.

Talbot rose. "I pray you're right, FitzClifford." He raised his goblet. "To Lady Gillian," he said. "May she be a beauty beyond compare, a paragon among women...." He drank.

Rannulf brought his wine to his lips and sipped the heady brew, then nearly choked at Talbot's next words.

"...a meek, sweet, silent dove with not a thought of her own." Grinning now, Talbot quaffed the rest of his wine and slammed the goblet down on the table.

Rannulf set his own wine aside. Unless Gillian had changed—drastically—in the past few years, his overlord could not have been more wrong about the woman who would be his ward.

He'd not have a moment's peace between here and the Marches, he could see that clear enough. And once they arrived at l'Eau Clair... Rannulf shook his head. It appeared his time in purgatory had already begun.

Chapter Two

The distant thunder of hoofbeats beyond the castle walls captured Gillian's attention as she crossed the bailey to the keep. "Riders approaching!" cried a guard. "Close the gates!"

Several women shrieked and hurried toward the stairs to the hall, while the men in the bailey clustered near the gatehouse. A man-at-arms stepped into the narrow doorway beside the gate to urge several villagers up the path to the castle, then slammed the door closed behind them as the portcullis began its ponderous descent.

Heart racing, Gillian gathered up her skirts and headed back toward the curtain wall.

She cast a swift glance at the heavy wooden gate—already barred against intruders, she noted gratefully—before mounting the steep stairs to the guardhouse atop the wall.

"What do you see, Will?" she asked the guard when she reached the top.

"'Tis a party of riders, milady," he replied. "They've got no engines of war, but I can see the sun shinin' off their armor." He stepped back from the arrow slit so she could join him. "They rode straight by the village."

"Praise God." She breathed a sigh of relief at that blessing. Though many of the villagers had moved within the castle wall since the attacks on the outlying farms of her demesne, still the fields needed to be tilled and the cattle and sheep pastured outside. Unless faced with a direct attack, life beyond the walls of l'Eau Clair must go on, lest they all starve come winter.

Gillian turned to slip farther into the slit, accepting Will's help to kneel within the deep embrasure. Bracing herself with one hand, she raised the other to shade her eyes against the bright spring sun. "Holy Mary save us," she whispered when the breeze snapped open the pennon atop the lead rider's lance.

She could not mistake the raven blazoned stark and bold upon the shimmering silver cloth.

The device of her Welsh kinsman, Steffan ap Rhys.

What could he want with her? She feared she knew the answer to that only too well. A shudder swept over her as she recalled the last time they'd met, the feel of his heated gaze, foul and possessive, creeping over her from head to toe. Nay, she'd not permit him to worm his way within these walls by accepting so much as a crust of bread from him.

"Milady?"

She slumped back against the cold stones and closed her eyes for a moment. "Keep the gates barred, Will, and man the walls." *Why him—and why now?* Hadn't she enough troubles to deal with?

"Shall we heat stones and oil, milady?"

She opened her eyes at the eagerness in Will's voice. "I doubt that will be necessary." Straightening, she slid from the slit unassisted, shook out her skirts and adjusted her veil. "Much as I'd enjoy seeing my cousin's reaction to such a greeting, 'tis no way to welcome him to l'Eau Clair." She brushed past Will and headed for the door leading to the battlements. "Of course, he doesn't deserve much better than that as a welcome, either, the arrogant knave," she muttered to herself. She stepped through the portal, then turned to the guard at the door. "Send for Sir Henry to join us, if he's within."

"Aye, milady." He bowed and left.

"Will, come with me. Steffan's so thickheaded, it just may take a show of force to convince him to leave."

Will chuckled. "I remember Lord Steffan well," he said. They left the gatehouse, and Gillian led the way to a spot where they'd have the best view of the track to l'Eau Clair. "Do you recall the time, milady, not so many years past, when we crept into his chamber and hid all his fancy clothes while he was in the bath?"

Heat flooded Gillian's face. "I do, though it does neither of us credit." She stared out over the treetops. "Lady Alys was sorely disappointed. She thought she'd made a lady of me."

Will snorted.

Gillian jabbed at his ribs with her elbow—a reaction left over from their childhood—then groaned as she connected with his mail hauberk.

He somehow contrived to look wounded. "You might have had the look of a lady by then, but inside you were still Gilles, the brave lad who used to join in all our schemes."

"Steffan thought I was a lady even then, unfortunately.'' She couldn't keep a trace of bitterness from her voice, but she thought she at least hid her fear.

Will had the right of it, though she'd never admit it. Her transformation from ''lad'' to lady had taken far longer than she'd ever imagined it would. And there were times—few and far between, 'twas true— when she wished it had never happened. ''The miles of thread I spun and wove as punishment for that jest cured me of the last of my old ways,'' she said. ''Gilles disappeared many years ago, by my choice.''

Steffan and his men rode out from the trees between the village and the castle and trotted up the last rise at a decorous pace, casting her thoughts of the past to the back of her mind where they belonged.

She'd trouble enough to face in the here and now. Gillian squared her shoulders and moved into the opening of an embrasure where she'd be visible from the area across the moat.

Steffan and his party—eight men-at-arms and a standard-bearer—halted on the bank of the moat. He slipped off his helm and placed it on the high pommel of his saddle.

Still atop his mount, he bowed with all the finesse of a French courtier, his handsome face alight with pleasure from the look of it. Straightening, he scanned her face with a piercing look. ''My dearest cousin.''

''Milord,'' she called down to him, her voice cold as death. 'Twould take more than that display to impress her! ''What brings you here, so far from home?''

''Once I heard your sad news, I had to come at once to offer my condolences—and my support. You and I have much to discuss. May we enter l'Eau Clair and take our ease?'' he asked, including his men with a sweep of his hand.

Take his ease? He'd want more than that, of that she had no doubt. "I thank you for your sympathy, milord. 'Tis much appreciated. But I fear we cannot permit you—or anyone,'' she added lest he question her choices, "to come within.''

Steffan drew in a deep breath and his face went still and cold—a remarkable transformation, but one that did not surprise Gillian in the least. He concealed his true self behind the veil of elaborate manners and fine clothes, but she'd been in Steffan's presence often enough over the years to know him for a sly weakling. He was all talk and little action.

She'd no desire to waste her time listening to the likes of Steffan ap Rhys jabber on about nothing.

Especially not now.

Before she could draw breath to speak, Steffan's expression had regained its usual urbanity. He tossed his helm to the man beside him and slipped from the saddle, bowing once more.

Did he truly believe his airs would change her mind?

"Cousin, I must speak with you.'' Another motion of his hand and a sharp nod sent his men riding a short distance down the trail toward the village. He headed toward the door beside the gate with a confident stride.

"Hold, milord,'' Gillian called.

Steffan stopped and stared up at her, the expression on his handsome face still pleasant, but his dark eyes glowing with some other, fiercer emotion.

At the sound of firm footsteps on the stairs, she glanced over her shoulder. Sir Henry, the captain of

the guard, crossed the guardroom and joined her and
Will. "I wondered how long 'twould be before yon
popinjay dared show his face here again," Sir Henry
muttered, scorn etched deep upon his bearded visage.
"Especially now that your father's not here to send
him on his way yet again—"

Gillian cut him off with a hand on his mail-clad
arm. "Fear not—he'll find no welcome here," she
assured the grizzled warrior. She smiled. "I know just
what to do to send him on his way," she added, low-
voiced. She clasped her fingers tight about Sir
Henry's arm for a moment, taking comfort from the
strength tensed beneath her grip before she released
him and turned her attention back to Steffan.

"Milord, we've sickness within the keep. Surely
you noticed the graves outside the wall." 'Twas no
effort to imbue her voice with sorrow for those words,
but to strengthen her tone for the next…aye, that was
a chore. "I would not have you risk your health—
perhaps even your life—merely to speak with me,"
she said, eyes downcast. "Nothing could be that important."

Sir Henry snorted, turning the sound into a cough
when Steffan eyed him suspiciously.

A look of distaste—nay, fear—crossed Steffan's
face, so fleeting she could almost believe she'd imagined it.

Almost. She fought back a smile.

"I must speak with you, cousin," Steffan demanded. "Is there not some way we can talk privately?"

Will gestured for Gillian to move back from the
wall. "A moment, milord," she said, then stepped
behind the cloaking mass of a merlon.

"He'll not leave until he gets his way, milady. You know it as well as I." Will glanced down at Steffan. "Look at him. The fool's nigh hopping with impatience."

"Aye, the lad's right," Sir Henry added with disgust. "Lord Steffan's got something stuck in his craw. The sooner you meet with him, find out what he wants, the quicker you can send him on his way."

Gillian nodded. "All right. Best to take care of this now." Her mood brightened. "Mayhap after this, I'll never need to see Steffan again."

She returned to the embrasure. "I'll speak with you, but you cannot come within. Wait for me by the door," she said, then turned away.

She passed through the guardroom, Will and Sir Henry on her heels, and came to a halt at the head of the stairs. "My shadows," she muttered. "You need not accompany me. He cannot harm me if I stay within, and he remains outside."

"Who's to say he'll obey you?" Will growled. "He's ne'er shown any inclination to listen to anyone but himself, so far's I've seen. You need one of us there to make certain he behaves himself."

Though she didn't believe Steffan meant her any harm—and she knew the threat of sickness would keep him from entering l'Eau Clair—Will could be right. Steffan seemed more determined than she'd ever seen him.

But she'd no desire to prolong the agony of holding a conversation with him, either. "Sir Henry, come with me. If it looks as though Steffan plans anything too dangerous, I'm sure a glare from you will put him in his place." She chuckled. "Your presence alone, especially once he sees the scowl on your face, should be spur enough to speed him on his way."

As Gillian and Sir Henry made their way through the now-silent bailey, Gillian kept her expression relaxed, nodding to the group of villagers milling about near the stairs to the keep. Steffan was no threat to any of them—to anyone, most like. No sense adding more fuel to the already smoldering tension tearing at her people.

Sir Henry dismissed the man guarding the doorway and unbolted the heavy portal himself. He swung it open just far enough to reveal Steffan standing nigh upon the doorsill, one hand resting against the frame.

He straightened and reached for Gillian's hand as she stepped into the narrow opening.

"None of that, milord," Sir Henry growled, making as if to move in front of Gillian.

She stood her ground. "Nay, Sir Henry. I'm sure Lord Steffan knows I've been caring for the sick. If he wishes to risk illness himself, 'tis his affair."

'Twas almost beyond her to stifle a laugh at Steffan's swift retreat. Once he stood several paces away from the doorway, he bowed once more.

Face composed, she curtsied. "What did you wish to speak with me about?" she asked with more haste than grace.

He took one step closer to her, then glared past her at Sir Henry. "I wished to be private, cousin," he hissed.

She permitted herself a faint smile. "We are private, milord."

"As private as you'll get," Sir Henry muttered.

Gillian silenced the knight with a glance over her shoulder. "Sir Henry is privy to all my business, milord, for 'tis *his* business to protect l'Eau Clair and all who dwell here.'' She gathered her skirts in her hands, prepared to leave. ''Speak or remain silent, it matters naught to me. But you'll say your piece before us both, or not at all.''

She could practically hear Steffan's teeth grinding, though his frustration showed only in his eyes, not upon his face. ''I've come to offer my hand and heart, Gillian, to claim you as my bride.'' He swept a hand through his dark curls, sighed heavily, then held both hands out to her in supplication. ''You must see, 'tis a perfect match. With the two of us ruling l'Eau Clair as one, our blood—the blood of Welsh princes—joined together in our sons, our dynasty will be a force to be reckoned with in the Marches. Welsh and Norman both will cede to us the power we deserve.''

She could scarce draw breath after his outrageous words, could barely restrain herself from grabbing for the glossy hair swinging to his shoulders and wrenching his throat back for her blade.

Instead she used her body to block the doorway and hold back a cursing Sir Henry, though her fingers closed tight around the hilt of the dainty jeweled eating knife at her waist. ''Sir Henry!'' she snapped when the knight clamped his hand about her arm and tugged her from the doorway. He released her at once. ''One madman is all I can deal with for the moment.''

She stepped back into the doorway just as Steffan whipped a dagger from the sheath on his sword belt and held it toward Sir Henry. ''You dare lay hands upon your lady?'' Steffan snarled. Gillian drew her own blade and raised it threateningly when he would have lunged past her at her man. The unmistakable sound of Sir Henry's sword slipping free behind her sent a chill through her.

"Enough, both of you!" She glanced from the naked steel glinting in the sunlight to the fire raging in Steffan's eyes, then sighed. "We've all gone mad, it seems." She lowered her knife. "Have done, both of you. I'm no piece of meat for you to fight over."

Steffan rammed his dagger home, scowling his displeasure. Gillian feared 'twould take little to push him past reason.

"Sir Henry?" She peered back at him and saw that he'd sheathed his sword, but hadn't bothered to hide his temper. Hot color tinted his cheeks, and he looked ready to burst.

This had been a bad idea from the start; she'd best end it now, before the next flash of steel—and she'd no doubt they'd come to that point again, should she attempt to converse with that lunatic Steffan.

Gillian raised her chin and looked Steffan in the eye. "I'm honored by your offer, milord." How she forced those words past her lips, she'd no notion. "But 'tis not for me to say who I must wed," she murmured. "My hand and inheritance are King John's to give." She lowered her gaze, then glanced up at him through her lashes. "You are welcome to apply to my liege, if you truly wish to marry me."

Steffan's expression didn't appear so pleasant now, she noted with a secret smile. And his bow was so abrupt as to be insulting. "What of your father's wishes in the matter? When last we met, but a few months ago, he led me to believe he thought us well matched."

The hint of amusement she'd felt at taunting Steffan fled as swiftly as it had arrived. "Indeed?" she asked, her curt tone matching his. "Since my father's death I've looked through all his papers. I've found nothing to indicate he ever thought of you at all."

She couldn't be certain whether 'twas her words, or Sir Henry's muffled snort that overset Steffan's fine manners. Whatever the reason, she could only offer up silent thanks.

"You've not heard the last of this, Gillian," he sneered, all trace of the handsome courtier gone. He stared long and hard at her, then shifted his gaze to Sir Henry. "I'll go to your king, if need be." He reached for her arm, then evidently thought better of such a foolhardy act and let his hand drop just short of her. "You *will* be mine." He turned on his heel and headed for his mount, pausing a few paces from the showy beast. "And once you are, I swear you'll never mock me again."

Chapter Three

The look Steffan gave her just before he spurred his horse into a gallop haunted Gillian through the rest of the day. She'd never cared for him in the slightest; indeed, she'd felt nothing but scorn for him for as long as she could remember. Her other Welsh kin—her distant cousins Ian and Catrin, especially—were dear to her. She welcomed their rare visits to l'Eau Clair. Her father had respected them, had encouraged her to nurture these ties to her mother's family.

Now that she was seated at the table in her solar to tally the accounts, she could hold back her thoughts no longer.

She tossed aside the quill she'd been using and settled back in her chair, tugging off her veil and un-plaiting her tightly braided hair. The thought of taking Steffan as her husband disgusted her. Had Rannulf FitzClifford spoiled her taste for all other men? When she thought back to his last visit, to the closeness they'd shared...

How could she ever hope to have that with an-other?

And to abandon her as he had—without warning,

without reason. Had he gained all he wanted from her, and desired her no more? Or had he found her lacking?

The answer was beyond her ability to understand. She'd never have an opportunity to learn the answers from him, that much had been clear from the message he'd penned upon the betrothal contract.

She fought the urge to draw the crumpled parchment from the box where she'd locked it away. In the week since she'd found the missive, her mind refused to set her free of it. Her thoughts circled, distracting her as she sought some way to protect her people, her home.

Was she doomed to mourn his loss yet again?

Rannulf FitzClifford did not deserve her attention or the time she'd wasted upon the lost cause he represented.

Matters of far greater import weighed heavy on her. How to provide for her people, to protect them, to uncover the miscreants who seemed set upon destroying all her father had established. She raked her hands through the trailing mass of her hair and pressed her fingers against the throbbing ache at her temples.

The sound of footsteps pounding up the stairs to her solar provided a welcome distraction. She rose and opened the door.

Will reached the top of the spiral stair and hurried to her. "Riders approach, milady," he said, his urgent tone matching his expression.

Gillian drew the door closed behind her and sighed. "Not Steffan again?" she asked, already racking her brain for another way to keep him outside the gates.

"Nay, milady. 'Tis far worse." Will motioned for her to precede him down the stairs. "'Tis a war party,

Lady Gillian, nigh a hundred strong. They're armed to the teeth and provisioned for siege, to judge from the size of their baggage train.''

Her heartbeat raced, increasing the sense of urgency flying through her veins. Was this the attack she'd feared since the raids began? She'd known 'twas but a matter of time before l'Eau Clair itself became the target!

Her boots clattered on the stone risers as she hastened down them, snatching up her hem and running once she reached the great hall. ''Muster anyone who can fight in the bailey at once,'' she told Will, who followed hot on her heels. ''And send the older women and the children to wait in here.'' Her maid met them near the door. ''Ella, you'd best prepare to care for the wounded in here as well,'' she said.

''Aye, milady,'' Ella said, then snatched at Gillian's arm as she made to pass through the door Will held open. ''Here now, where are you going?''

Gillian drew a deep breath. ''To the walls.''

''Nay, child, 'tis no place for you.''

Gillian reached down and took Ella's hand in hers and lifted it, freeing herself. She gave Ella's fingers a quick squeeze before releasing her. ''Where else should I be? I command l'Eau Clair now. 'Tis my place to lead my people.'' She pressed a kiss to Ella's wrinkled cheek and gathered up her skirts again. ''I'll be fine,'' she said before she turned and left the hall.

''Where is my sword?'' she asked Will as they hastened through the crowd already gathering in the bailey.

Will stopped in his tracks. ''You've no need for that,'' he said, his voice more stern than she'd ever heard it. "Do you think to lead us in battle? By Christ's blood, Gil—"

"Bring me a sword, Will. Now." Not waiting to see if he'd heed her command, she continued on and raced up the gatehouse stairs.

A lad dashed after them, calling for Will, and entered the gatehouse in their wake. "A moment, milady," Will called as Gillian headed for the wall walk.

He took her sword from the boy and handed it to her, his lips twisted into a rueful smile.

"You know me too well," she said as she slid free the blade and set aside the scabbard. Fingers clenched tight about the hilt, Gillian drew a deep breath to settle herself and stepped out onto the walk. Still not ready, she moved past the first merlon, catching a glimpse of what awaited them below.

She paused for a moment, scarce able to breathe, then forced herself to turn and look over the wall.

"Holy Mary save us," she whispered. She leaned into the crenel, her free hand braced on the low stone wall as she gazed, transfixed, at the army spread out across the crest of the hill.

They were doomed.

Rannulf sat atop his stallion before the familiar gray walls of l'Eau Clair Keep and fought back the wave of memories threatening to flood his mind. He could not permit his heart to reign over his head, no matter the provocation.

He would not allow himself close to Gillian again.

A flash of red—Gillian's hair, no mistaking it— moved swiftly past the crenels of the gatehouse tower, making his heartbeat trip and falter for a moment.

He doubted the battle between heart and mind

would ever cease. The moment he'd dreaded since the night he met Talbot had arrived, and he felt no more in command of himself now than he had the last time he'd seen Gillian.

He took a deep breath and reached up to tug his helm lower over his brow—a more comfortable position, true, but also a way to hide his identity from Gillian's keen eyes for a little while longer.

By the rood, his reaction to her this time was stronger than ever before, and he'd yet to face her.

'Twas all he could do to stay put, and not spur his mount far away from the one woman he'd prayed he would never have to face again.

Nicholas nudged his mount closer to Rannulf's. "How long do they expect us to sit here before someone comes to answer our summons?" Nicholas asked, low-voiced.

"There's some movement on the wall," Rannulf said, just as Gillian came fully into view between two tall crenels.

The sight of her traveled from his eyes to his brain, and then to land like a blow from a mailed fist to his chest.

How could he have forgotten how lovely she was? Her unbound hair framed the pale alabaster glow of her face, the wavy mass hanging past her waist to disappear behind the wall.

"By the Virgin," Talbot declared, his expression as awestruck as his tone. "Please let that be my ward." He urged his horse forward and whipped off his helm. "Milady," he called. He bowed so low, Rannulf noted with disgust, 'twas a wonder he didn't fall from the saddle.

Gillian straightened and moved nearer the edge of

the wall, revealing the sword she held in her left hand—and the full beauty of her form, outlined against the deep blue sky. Rannulf bit back a smile of admiration at the sight of her courage. His heart sank at Talbot's obvious appreciation, although Talbot had yet to notice the blade of Gillian's weapon gleaming in the sunlight, he'd wager. He doubted armed women were Talbot's style.

However, 'twas Rannulf's misfortune that Gillian, armed or no, was all the woman he could ever desire.

If she'd changed since he'd last seen her, 'twas only to become more beautiful.

And more stubborn? a voice in the back of his mind mocked. *Her sweet temper turned bitter by your betrayal?*

"Milord." She responded to Talbot's greeting with a curt nod—the perfect accompaniment to the sharpness of her voice—and no smile of welcome brightened her face. "Who are you, and why are you here?"

Talbot's shoulders stiffened. "I am Lord Nicholas Talbot of Ashby, sent by King John to protect Lady Gillian and her lands. Have I the honor of speaking to my ward? Pray open the gates at once, that I might meet you."

"To any preening fool who rides up to the door? I think not." She leaned forward. "What proof have you of your claim?"

"The king's writ, signed and sealed by our liege himself," Talbot replied, his tone as cold as hers.

He turned to Rannulf and motioned him forward.

Rannulf rode up to join him, careful to center his attention on the man beside him, not the siren poised above him. Would she be able to feel his presence, as he was all too aware of hers?

"Milord?" he asked, pitching his voice low.

Talbot reached into a leather pouch on his saddle and drew forth a rolled parchment. He held it out toward Rannulf. "Will you permit my vassal to carry the writ within?"

Gillian stared down at Lord Nicholas Talbot. He appeared far too self-assured and handsome—and arrogantly aware of the fact, 'twas easy to see—for her to trust him any more than she'd trusted Steffan that very morn.

She eyed the vassal, who had yet to take the scroll from Talbot. Did the fellow await *her* permission? Somehow she couldn't imagine that was the case, but who knew what his hesitation might mean? She could not judge him by his expression, with his face hidden by his helm, but that he was a warrior she could readily see by his strong build and well-worn armor.

She tugged Will aside. "What think you?" she whispered.

He shook his head.

"Aye, why allow a fox amongst the chickens?" A few more whispered words sent Will on his way.

She stepped back toward the crenel. "Your vassal may remain where he belongs, milord—by your side," she called to Talbot. "Have one of your lackeys bring the writ to my man who awaits him below." She pointed to the door in the wall beneath her. "He will bring it to me."

Talbot frowned, then called to a man in servant's livery from among the mounted men ranged behind him. "As you command, milady," he replied with ill grace. He handed off the scroll to the manservant who approached him on foot and settled back in the saddle to stare up at her.

Gillian fought the urge to glare back as she waited while Talbot's man gave the parchment to Will and Will hurried to her side, Sir Henry following hard on his heels.

"I was watchin' from the other tower, but I figured you'd want me over here," Sir Henry said.

"Aye. I'd appreciate your counsel." She set aside her sword and reached for the message Will held out to her.

She stood behind the bulk of a merlon to read the scroll, out of sight of Talbot and his men, for she'd no desire to provide a show for their enjoyment, depending upon her reaction to what the parchment revealed.

Her hands remained steady as she unrolled the writ, examined the seal—King John's, that much at least was true—and began to scan the words scrawled boldly across the page.

She finished reading, then closed her eyes for a moment before handing the king's writ to Sir Henry. "He has the right of it," she murmured. "We're to welcome Lord Nicholas Talbot, such vassals as he's brought along and all their men, to 'aid in the defense and protection of the keep of l'Eau Clair, and specifically the person of its heir and lady—'" She drew in a deep breath. "Me."

Scowling, Sir Henry looked up from perusing the document. "We've no choice but to let them in." He gave back the parchment. "Though I must admit, all those men'll come in handy, should we be attacked again."

Will glanced over the wall. "That they will. Most

of them look as though they know how to fight.'' He nodded. ''And I'd rather fight with 'em than against 'em.''

Both of them were right. And wasn't this what she'd hoped for? Help for her people, protection for l'Eau Clair—it seemed her prayers had been answered after all.

How could she regret giving up command of the keep, when it would benefit them all?

''Tell them to lower the drawbridge and raise the portcullis,'' she ordered. Once Will left to relay her command, she took up her sword once more. The scroll clasped tight in her right hand, her sword in her left, Gillian left the merlon's protection and composed herself to be hospitable. ''My lord Talbot.'' She curtsied. ''You and your men may enter l'Eau Clair and be welcome.''

Gillian used the brief time it took for Talbot and his party to enter l'Eau Clair to twist her unruly hair back into a rough braid and cover it with a piece of veiling. Emma had just settled a copper circlet upon the finely woven linen when the pounding of booted feet on the stairs heralded Talbot's arrival.

She dismissed her maid and, heart racing, settled back into the commodious seat of her father's great chair and reached out to clasp the carved armrests in her hands. The appearance, at least, of command. The chair held pride of place on the dais at the far end of the great hall from the stairs, providing her with a clear view of the entire chamber. It also placed her on display.

Talbot led the way, the sunlight streaming through the tall windows gleaming off his blond hair and the silver embroidery adorning his surcoat. Some might count him handsome, but to her he appeared too polished, too finely turned out for a true warrior.

Gillian lowered her gaze lest he find her staring, and remained seated when he stepped up onto the dais and swept a low bow before her. "Lady Gillian." He reached for her right hand and raised it to his lips, allowing her a glimpse of his unusual violet eyes before she glanced past him at his men. "Rumors of your beauty did you scant justice, I fear."

"Milord," she murmured. She bit back a snort of disgust at his empty flattery and sought to look more closely at his retinue where they stood grouped before her on the main floor of the hall, for something seemed familiar....

"Permit me to introduce my men," Talbot said as he moved aside, allowing her a clear view of them. "Chief among my vassals is—"

Gillian rose to her feet when the man stepped up onto the dais and swept her a bow so low, it seemed almost a mockery. It took all her control not to lash out with her hand to strike his beloved, lying face.

Only the faint negative shake of his head kept her from saying the name before Talbot did, that and the fact that her shock at the sight of him was so great, she doubted she could force a sound past her lips.

Talbot's words sounded in her muddled brain, echoed loud over the confusion reigning there.

Rannulf FitzClifford.

Chapter Four

She'd never thought to see him again.

Now that he was here, what should she do?

Force of will alone lent Gillian the strength to remain on her feet, to jolt her heartbeat back to its familiar rhythm, to steady her hand and allow her to rest her fingers upon Rannulf's battle-hardened palm. "I am honored, milady," he murmured. The low, rough timbre of his voice, combined with the heated glance he sent her way, sent a traitorous ache throughout her body even before he brushed his lips over the back of her hand.

His gaze returned to her face, his eyes widening for some reason before they fixed upon her. The questions she saw within the deep brown warmth of his eyes startled her from her reverie.

How dare he stare at her thus? She looked away and focused on a point just past the breadth of his shoulders.

"Milord," she said, giving a terse nod.

The urge to snatch her hand free was nigh impossible to fight, but she eased her fingers from Rannulf's grasp and tried to ignore his presence as Talbot pre-

sented the lesser of his vassals. Calling upon Lady
Alys's training, Gillian remained polite but cool, her
welcome no more than courtesy demanded.

Once Talbot had finished, she motioned Sir Henry
and Will forward. She made them known to the others, wondering all the while if they'd reveal, through
word or deed, that Rannulf FitzClifford was no
stranger to them. But neither man betrayed by so
much as a scowl any reaction to his sudden presence.

Gillian felt her ire—and her confusion—rise to
even greater heights. Did no one but she wish to rant
and scream, to show some response to the traitor in
their midst?

Her men knew nothing of Rannulf's betrayal, she
reminded herself. She drew in a deep breath and
willed herself to calm. They knew the man, even
though they were ignorant of what he'd done. Why
didn't they…?

Sir Henry leaned close. "Milady, you don't intend
to keep 'em standing about in here much longer, I
trust," he whispered, his tone dry. He urged her to
turn slightly away from the others. "You'd best bring
this audience to an end soon, else your guardian's apt
to start slavering like a hound down the front of that
fancy surcoat of his."

She glanced over her shoulder at Talbot. Indeed,
his eyes held the look of a man much taken with what
he saw. And she found the smile lighting his handsome face far too arrogant to acknowledge. Stifling a
shudder, she nodded and resumed her seat in the great
chair.

"Sir Henry will show your captains to their lodgings," she told Talbot. "And you may trust Will to
settle the remainder of your troops in the barracks."

Curling her fingers about the carved armrests, she drew comfort from the memory of her father's hands lingering in the selfsame spots. "You and Lord Rannulf are welcome to stay within the keep, of course."

Talbot's grin widened at her words, and he accepted with a nod.

While her men led the others away, Gillian rose with as much grace as she could muster and motioned Ella forward. "If you would care to bathe now, Ella will show you to the bathing chamber and assist you. I will have food prepared for you, and your rooms readied, while you refresh yourselves."

Ella stepped down from the dais and curtsied. "If you'll come with me, milords?"

Talbot bowed to Gillian. "I'll see you at supper, then, milady, if you'll deign to join us?" he asked.

"Of course," she murmured.

His smile broadening, he bowed again and turned to follow Ella.

Rannulf stepped forward and reached for Gillian's hand once again. She gave it reluctantly, fuming while he pressed his lips to her fingers, then grasped her hand more tightly when she would have pulled free. "I would speak with you later, milady," he told her. His dark brown eyes held hers captive. "When we've a chance to be private."

"I think not, milord," she said, her voice as cold as her heart.

"FitzClifford," Talbot called. Gillian took advantage of Rannulf's start of surprise to free herself. "Leave my ward alone," he chided, his tone amused. "Else you'll frighten her off with your ardor. At least allow us a chance to know her." He paused near the door. "Are you coming?"

"Later, Gillian," Rannulf repeated, his voice too low for Talbot to hear. He straightened. "I beg your pardon, milord," he called as he turned on his heel and crossed the hall. "'Twas not my intention to disturb the lady." He joined Talbot and Ella. "I was much struck by her beauty, 'tis all."

"Indeed?" His unusual violet eyes alight with amusement, Talbot sent yet another bow her way. Seething, Gillian nodded in return, polite but cool, and stood watching, waiting for them to leave, but it seemed Talbot wasn't finished yet. "I cannot fault your taste, FitzClifford," he added as he turned to leave the chamber. "But see that you keep your distance. I find that I'm feeling protective of my ward...."

Gillian remained on her feet as Talbot's voice trailed away. As soon as the sound of their boots upon the stairs faded, however, she slumped into the chair. Hands shaking, she reached up and slid the veil and circlet from her head and dropped them into her lap.

Blessed Mary save her, how could she bear this? She closed her eyes, but all she could see was her new guardian's well-tailored clothes, the fantastic, elaborately embroidered design covering his surcoat from neckline to hem. The man had journeyed from London into the fastness of the Marches, yet he appeared more finely turned out than anyone she'd seen in her life. Did the king honestly believe that a man like Talbot—naught but a showy popinjay, from what she'd seen thus far—could protect her people?

She drew her hand over her face and opened her eyes, erasing the image. 'Twould serve her better to send word to Prince Llywelyn...nay, even to her cousin Steffan himself, to come take command of l'Eau Clair, than to believe Lord Nicholas Talbot competent enough at the art of war to defend them against the most meager of threats.

Could that be why he'd brought Rannulf with him? No matter what she thought of Rannulf—and what did she think of him? she asked herself—she could not deny he was a fierce warrior, strong and well trained. Her father had believed Rannulf capable of holding l'Eau Clair, had offered him her hand and all that went with it—the keep, the lands, her heart....

Her fingers tightened about the metal band in her hand until the jeweled cabochons bit into her palm. To see Rannulf here, once again within these walls, was a situation she'd given up all thought of ever having to face.

Gillian looked down at the circlet and felt her heart falter. It had been months, perhaps years, since she'd last seen it. Why today, of all days, had Ella placed this circlet upon her head?

Giving vent to the rage welling up from deep inside her, she leapt to her feet and hurled the offending item across the room. It clattered against the stone wall and fell to the floor, the puny sound in the cavernous room doing little to satisfy her.

Weariness weighting her movements, she left the dais and crossed the rush-strewn floor, the sharp scent of mint rising from beneath her boots serving to clear away her anger.

She stooped to pick up the circlet, smoothed her fingertips over the flowers etched into the soft copper as she'd done so often in the past. How many times over the years had she sat staring out the window, the copper and jade band clutched in her hands while she stroked the beautiful design and turned her thoughts upon the man who'd given it to her?

A tear trickled down her cheek as she smoothed her fingers over the misshapen circle, then pressed the cool metal to her lips.

'Twas as battered as her heart, she thought, choking back a mirthless laugh. And her heart was like to become more bruised yet, the longer Rannulf remained within her sight.

Gillian dabbed at her wet cheek with the trailing end of her sleeve and straightened her shoulders.

'Twas no wonder Rannulf had stared at her—she could only imagine what he'd thought, to see that circlet upon her head.

But how could Ella have suspected Rannulf FitzClifford's presence in Talbot's party?

Rannulf followed Talbot and Ella to the bathing chamber near the laundry, his mind brimming with confusion. He went through the motions of bathing, his brain registering Talbot's continuing commentary about Gillian's beauty even as he silently berated himself for a fool.

If he kept on as he'd started, 'twould be no time at all before Talbot discovered far more about Rannulf FitzClifford than Rannulf had ever planned to reveal. By the rood, once he'd noticed the copper circlet Gillian wore—his gift to her the day she'd given herself to him body and soul—it had been all he could manage to keep from sweeping her into his arms, Talbot be damned!

He drew in a deep breath and ducked his head beneath the steaming water, drowning out Talbot's voice and allowing himself a few moments to clear his thoughts. He could not continue to remind himself of the past. 'Twas long gone, taking the dreams of his youth—and any hope of a future with Gillian—with it.

He could scarce afford to jeopardize all that he had accomplished for Pembroke, simply for the gift of Gillian's presence in his life.

Not that she'd have aught to do with him at any rate, to judge by her attitude toward him and Talbot both. The Gillian he'd come to know would have welcomed guests to l'Eau Clair with warmth and a genuine smile.

The cold, imperious woman who had greeted them from the dais was a stranger to him, the circlet notwithstanding.

Rannulf popped his head up out of the water and took a gulp of air. He'd be naught but a fool to read anything into the fact that she'd worn his gift. She'd no way of knowing he was part of Talbot's party. 'Twas a coincidence, nothing more.

Though 'twas surprising she'd kept it after his defection, he mused.

He rubbed his eyes. At least she'd no knowledge of the hateful words he'd penned upon the betrothal agreement. Otherwise he'd never have escaped the hall intact.

He accepted the towel Ella held out to him and wiped his face, then glanced up at the old woman in surprise once her stern glare made an impression upon his befuddled brain.

"My lady is a virtuous maiden, milord," she said, indignation lending her voice an arrogance not usually heard from a servant.

In his shock, he barely resisted the urge to snap out

a response—any response—to her words. Did she think to take him to task here? *Now?*

And did she suspect...?

Her scowl deepening, Ella looked past him to Talbot, settled into a tub nearer the fire, and he realized she'd spoken to his overlord, not to him. What had Talbot said that he'd missed?

"I care not what the custom is elsewhere, milord, but at l'Eau Clair 'tis not proper for a young lady, innocent and unwed, to bathe a man." Ella drew a length of toweling from the stack draped over her arm and fairly snapped it into Talbot's outstretched hand.

"'Innocent' and 'unwed' don't necessarily go together," Talbot pointed out with a grin. Ella drew herself up and stared down her nose at him. Talbot sat up straighter and held out a placating hand before she could say more. "Though I've no doubt your mistress is pure as the Blessed Mother herself, of course."

Rannulf watched Talbot carefully; the other man's apparent sincerity lightened the burden of concern he carried. He'd troubles enough to deal with already, without having to worry that Talbot might see Gillian as tainted goods, fair game for his obvious attraction to her.

And if Talbot ever discovered the full truth of Gillian's purity or lack thereof—and Rannulf's part in it...

No sense wandering down that peril-strewn path unless they must.

He knew of no reason why the subject should ever arise, so long as he found a chance to speak with Gillian as soon as possible.

Assuming she agreed to do as he asked.

"Indeed, you'd better believe it." Ella gave a rude snort. "And as for the bathing, I care not whether the guest be King John himself! My lamb'll not be helping any man with that chore, not while I'm here to stop it," she added with a decisive nod.

Stifling a chuckle at Ella's vehemence, Rannulf rose, wrapped the towel about his waist and climbed out of the tub. He turned to face Talbot, curious about how the arrogant lord reacted to the maidservant's words.

He didn't seem to have taken offense. Indeed, he appeared at his ease as he slicked back his hair with his free hand and swiped the towel over his face. "I'm pleased to see that my ward has so staunch a champion." He settled back against the padded edge of the tub with a sigh. "'Twill make my task easier, for I know little about protecting a lady's virtue."

Ella bobbed a brusque curtsy in response and turned away, muttering under her breath all the while. "Too busy relieving 'em of it, most like," Rannulf heard her say as she walked past him, crossed the chamber and knelt by the hearth to tend the fire.

Talbot's servant, Richard, swept into the room, one arm loaded with Talbot's clothes, Rannulf's saddle-bag clutched in the other. "These lodgings are not so fine as those we left in London, milord," the man said with a sniff. He cast a measuring glance about him, his lean face twisted into a frown. "Though I suppose they'll be sufficient for the nonce."

Ella rose and turned to face them. "Lord William Marshal, the earl of Pembroke, has broken his journey behind these walls and counted himself well lodged," she said, her wrinkled visage alight with pride. "They're more than enough for the likes o' you, I trow.'' She nodded toward Talbot. ''No offense, mi-lord.''

''None taken,'' Talbot replied as he climbed from the bath and wrapped himself in a towel.

Richard's scowl more pronounced, he dumped the pack at Rannulf's feet, then scurried across the room to place his master's belongings carefully on a table near the hearth. ''It's not as if we have any choice in the matter, at any rate.'' He began to sort through the garments, shaking his head and continuing to mumble beneath his breath.

''Cease your prattle, you fool,'' Talbot commanded, although his lazy tone lent little weight to the order.

'Twas no wonder he'd taken no insult at Ella's words, Rannulf decided, for he tolerated an amazing amount of insolence from his own servant. 'Twas yet another example of how little he understood his over-lord. The longer he spent in Talbot's company, the more confused he felt. He'd thought to get to know the other man on the long journey into the Marches, but Nicholas Talbot remained a mystery he'd yet to unravel.

'Twas an annoyance, and a hindrance, too, for how could he decide how to deal with Talbot—how to work around him to carry out Pembroke's dictates—when he never knew from one moment to the next which facet of the man he'd encounter?

Talbot accepted another towel from Ella and dragged the linen over his chest. ''Lord knows how your last master stood your rantings without relieving you of your tongue, Richard. If you'd turn your en-ergies to your duties, instead of finding fault with everything, I might be dressed and out of here before Lady Gillian has the tables cleared away.''

Rannulf shook his head and turned his attention from the fractious servant. Mayhap if he left now, while Talbot lingered here, he might find a way to speak with Gillian before everyone gathered for supper.

'Twould be best to find her and get it over with, before they had to rub along in Talbot's presence. Spurred on by his eagerness to see her again, even though the encounter was bound to be unpleasant, he snatched his bag from the floor. He pulled out a shirt and drew it over his head, muffling the sudden sound of raised voices.

He tugged down the shirt in time to see the towel-clad Talbot lunge across the chamber and grab Richard by the shoulder. He gave the wiry little man a shake like to set his teeth clacking and lifted him till his feet cleared the floor. ''Enough, you fool. If you *ever* speak of the lady so foully again, I'll see you suffer for it.'' Richard still held in his grasp like a terrier with a rat, Talbot turned and thrust the servant toward the door. ''Get you gone from my sight,'' he added, nudging him on his way with a cuff aside the head.

Talbot stalked over to stand by the blazing fire while Richard stumbled from the room. ''By Christ's bones, where did he come up with such filth?'' he asked, dragging a hand through his hair. ''Scarce arrived, and already running his mouth.''

What could Richard have said in so brief a time? Rannulf wondered. To judge by his master's reaction, it must have been vile. A swift glance at Ella showed that the old woman appeared shaken; he'd ask her for the details later.

Despite his ignorance of the offense, he'd best make some response. "Mayhap the journey addled his wits," he suggested. He stepped into his braes and knotted the drawstring at his waist.

"Who knows?" Talbot shrugged. "I'll not put up with any more of his foolishness, I assure you." Draping the towel he'd used to dry his hair around his shoulders, he rubbed his hand over his chin. "And now I've sent him off before he could perform any of his duties." He grimaced. "Mayhap that's his game. 'Tis hardly the first time he's angered me enough to send him away with his work undone, the clever bastard."

Ella stepped toward him. "If 'tis a shave you're wanting, milord, I can do it, and trim your hair as well, if you wish. I helped care for Lord Simon in his last months, and I've a careful hand with the blade."

Precisely the opportunity he needed! Rannulf shoved his feet into his boots before Talbot had finished agreeing to Ella's offer. He grabbed the first tunic he found in his pack and didn't even bother to put it on, slung his belt and sword belt over his shoulder, and headed for the door.

"FitzClifford, where are you going in such a hurry? Come, take your ease, let Ella shave you. We've journeyed hard and fast to get here—there's no need to rush about now that we've arrived."

"Nay, I thank you. I wish to speak with my captains, and I thought I'd seek out Sir Henry, see what he can tell me of the situation here. I trust there'll be some work to occupy us, else our men will grow fat and lazy."

Shaking his head, Talbot took a seat on the stool Ella pulled up for him near the hearth and waved a dismissal. "Go, then. But there's no reason to hurry. We've plenty of time yet before the evening meal, haven't we, Ella?"

"Aye, milord." Ella moved to stand behind Talbot and adjusted the towel draped round his shoulders. "I'm sure that Lady Gillian is still busy seeing to your chambers and arranging for a fitting meal for your lordships." She motioned for Rannulf to go. "We'll not dine until dusk tonight, I venture, and 'tis still full light. You've time to spare to attend to your duties, sir."

He sketched a brief bow. "Until this evening, then," he said. His step light, he headed off to seek out Gillian.

Chapter Five

Rannulf paused halfway up the spiral stairway to peer out a window into the bailey. Troops, servants and children bustled about, filling the courtyard with life and sound. The scene reminded him of his first visit to l'Eau Clair as a squire in the earl of Pembroke's service. The bailey had been more chaotic that day, and more exciting when he faced off in a contest of arms against a lad purported to be one of l'Eau Clair's better swordsmen, according to the youths gathered round.

And Gilles had been a good fighter. Though he was slight of build, his reach was long, his movements swift and sure. The wooden practice swords had clattered together many times before Rannulf slipped beneath Gilles's guard and knocked him to the muddy ground. Even then, Gilles had managed to take him down with him. They'd landed together in a tangled sprawl of arms, legs and long red hair.

Gillian stared up at him, her green eyes wary and confused.

And thus Rannulf had met his fate.

Mayhap she'd met her fate that day as well, for she

remained unwed. And was not spoken for, either, else her betrothed should be here by her side.

The sight of Gillian leaving the stables and heading for the keep roused him from his reverie. He'd gain nothing by lurking about, woolgathering and delaying his meeting with her.

He hurried up the stairs to the second floor and down the corridor that led to her solar. She was bound to end up there, or in her nearby chamber, before the evening meal. He didn't mind the wait.

The hallway and stairwell were empty, the servants no doubt busy settling in l'Eau Clair's newest residents. She wouldn't realize he was here until 'twas too late for her to do anything about it—the only way he'd manage to see her, for he knew she'd refuse him an audience should he ask again.

He slipped into the solar and shut the door.

Little had changed since his last visit here. The chamber reflected its owner—the Gillian he'd known and loved, not the icy woman he'd met today. A large embroidery frame stood before a cushioned bench near the hearth, and a book held pride of place upon the table next to it. Gillian was both lady and scholar, skilled in housewifery, as well as languages and history—and in the healing arts, he recalled, taking note of a tray of herbs set out near the simple fireplace.

A warrior, too, he reminded himself, catching sight of her sword in its scabbard leaning against the wall near the door. Gillian de l'Eau Clair was a woman of many talents, some of them unusual, all of them intriguing. She was all the woman he could ever want, and far more than he deserved.

He'd do well to remind himself of that fact, now that he was near her once more.

A chill permeated the air and the afternoon light had begun to fade. Rannulf set his tunic and belts on the bench and stirred up the banked fire in the hearth before kindling a taper from the growing flames. After lighting a branch of candles on the table, he closed the shutters and settled on a stool near the door to await Gillian's return.

As warmth filled the chamber, Rannulf relaxed back against the smooth plaster wall, surrounded by a sense of comfort and welcome he'd not felt in far too long. The scent of lavender and roses—Gillian's scent—mellowed by the smoke of the fire, enveloped him until he could almost imagine 'twas four years past, and that he sat waiting for his love to join him once again.

The door creaked open, dispelling the illusion, and Gillian entered the room, thumped the door closed and went directly to the fire.

She dropped to her knees upon the hearthstones and reached up to slip off her veil, then slumped down and lowered her head into her hands. Rannulf rose and turned the key in the lock in one swift motion, the quiet click of metal against metal bringing her head up and around before he had time to move away from the door.

"I suggest you try locking it with yourself on the other side, Lord FitzClifford. You are not welcome here." She rose and turned, tripped over her skirts and pitched backward toward the fire. Rannulf lunged and caught her, swinging her away from the fireplace and setting her on her feet in the middle of the floor.

"Are you all right?" he asked, maintaining his grip on her arms.

Gillian shrugged free of Rannulf's firm grasp and

took a step back, all her shaking legs would permit. She couldn't be certain if 'twas her near-mishap or Rannulf's touch that set her nerves aquiver. Whichever the cause, she'd best lock her knees and stiffen her spine, for she refused to back down—to sit and look up at him—in her own solar.

Nay, she'd not allow him the slightest opportunity to believe he held any power over her, in any way.

She shook out her tangled sleeves, straightened her bliaut and found the strength to move another step away. "Perhaps you did not realize that this is my private chamber, milord," she said, her tone cold. Lowering her hands to her sides, she resisted the urge to tighten her fingers in the fabric of her skirts. "You must also be unaware that 'tis most unseemly for us to be here unchaperoned." She met his eyes, tried to ignore the heat she saw smoldering there. "I suggest you leave at once, before my guardian discovers you here. I am certain he wouldn't approve."

Rannulf closed the space between them and leaned close, his breath warm against her cheek. "You never used to mind us being alone together, Gillian." He raised his hand, brushed his fingertip along her chin. "Indeed, I think you welcomed it." Tracing his finger up to her mouth, he outlined her lips, sending a tingle of awareness thrumming through her. "Welcomed me." She began to breathe again when he lifted his finger from her lips, then nearly gasped as he moved his assault upon her senses to the flesh of her throat.

Jerking back from him she said, her voice little more than a croak of sound, "You, sir, are no gentleman."

He reached toward her again, capturing the end of one of her braids and winding it slowly around his hand. "And you, milady, knew that already." He drew closer as his hand crept nearer her chest. "I believe 'twas one of the things you liked best about me."

"Enough!" She tried to pull free, but he refused to release her. "Rannulf, please," she whispered, reaching up to cover his hand with her own.

To her surprise, a flush of color rose to stain his face. "I beg your pardon, milady." He unwound his hand from her hair and stepped back from her, then turned and went to kneel at the hearth and tend the fire.

Gillian took the opportunity to catch her breath while he faced the leaping flames, settling herself upon the bench and smoothing her skirts about her, taking up a small piece of embroidery simply for something to occupy her trembling hands. Why was he here?

Finally he stood, brushed off his hands and turned to face her. "I'm sorry I startled you, milady. And I apologize for trespassing upon your privacy, but 'tis imperative I speak with you alone, without Talbot's knowledge."

Gone was the imploring tone, the heated glance, in its place a cool, impersonal courtesy.

'Twas what she wanted, was it not?

Why, then, did she feel a wave of sadness sweep over her, and moisture begin to pool in her eyes?

Blinking back the tears, she laid her needlework in her lap and gazed unseeing at the pattern of vines outlined on the linen scrap. "I see now that I should have agreed to your request, milord, rather than summarily refuse to speak with you." More composed now, she risked a glance at his face.

He appeared no more willing to look at her than she to watch him. Perhaps they might get through this interview without further mishap, emotions intact.

Emotions hidden, 'twas what she really meant, she reminded herself. Her emotions, at any rate.

What Rannulf might feel, she no longer cared to know.

"Please, tell me what you wished to speak to me about. The hour grows late, and we must go down for supper soon."

Rannulf paced the length of the solar, coming to a halt in front of her and clearing his throat. "Talbot doesn't know I've been here before."

"Does it matter if he does?"

"It might." He resumed pacing, sending her nerves jittering.

"Sit down," she told him. She waited until he drew the stool away from the doorway and took a seat. "You'd best explain yourself—and quickly, for we mustn't linger here much longer."

"Your godfather, Lord William—"

"I know who my godfather is," she cut in. His voice sounded strange. Could he be nervous?

"Lord William asks that you and your people forget they ever saw me or knew aught of me. He does not wish Talbot to know I have any ties to l'Eau Clair."

Her heart skipped a beat before settling into a faster pace. If only it were that easy to forget him! She drew in a deep breath and willed her pulse to slow to its normal rhythm, bit back the bitterness welling from deep within her before she spoke. "You have no ties to l'Eau Clair, milord. You saw to that yourself already."

Rannulf glanced up sharply. "What do you mean?"

"You know very well, milord." She tossed aside her sewing and clasped her hands together in her lap, restraining her own desire to leap up and pace the room.

She'd not give Rannulf the satisfaction of seeing her agitation. 'Twas bad enough to admit she'd seen—

"What do you mean, Gillian?" he demanded.

Her movements slow, as steady as she could manage, she stood and went to the large table pushed against the wall on the far side of the room. She fumbled with the ring of keys hanging from her belt, found the one she sought and unlocked the small, iron-bound coffer set near the back of the table. Reaching inside, she pulled out the betrothal contract.

The parchment clutched in her hand, all pretense of calm gone, she spun and hurried to stand before him.

"Mayhap I should ask you what *you* meant, milord," she snarled, tossing the crumpled roll into his lap. He looked down at it and picked it up, but made no move to unroll the document. Instead he simply looked up at her, his dark eyes as blank, as emotionless, as his face. "But there's no need to ask. Your words state your feelings clear enough."

He glanced away for a moment, but when his gaze returned to her face, 'twas as expressionless as before. "The past matters not. Will you do as I ask?"

How could he say that? The past *did* matter. But now was clearly not the time to discuss it. So be it.

"I grant your request, Lord FitzClifford. I know not the reason, nor do I wish to know why we must

keep our knowledge of you secret, but it shall be as
Lord William requires. None here shall admit, or
show by their actions, that they have ever seen you
before. For the love and respect I bear my godfather,
I shall do what you ask.'' She picked up his tunic and
belt from the bench and held them out to him. ''Will
you send Sir Henry to me immediately? It might be
too late to inform my people, for they may have already revealed your secret.''

''We'll simply have to hope all will be well.'' Rannulf rose slowly to his feet and bowed. ''I thank you
for your generosity, milady. No doubt 'tis more than
I deserve.'' He took his belongings from her and
slipped the tunic over his head, then buckled his belt
about his waist. ''May I have my sword belt?'' he
asked, raising his left eyebrow. ''Or did you plan to
keep me weaponless until I leave l'Eau Clair?''

Temper seething at his baiting tone, Gillian peered
behind the bench and found the sword on the floor.

He reached past her and picked it up by the scabbard. ''I am no danger to you and yours, Gillian,'' he
said quietly. He straightened and took her hand. It
took all her will not to snatch it free, especially when
he captured her gaze with his. ''I swear to you I am
not.'' He raised her hand to his lips and, turning it
over, pressed a kiss to her palm.

He bowed, released her and turned to leave before
she realized he'd not returned the parchment, but held
it still in his left hand. ''I'll have that back, milord,''
she said, pointing to the roll.

'''Tis of no value,'' he said quietly. ''I thought to
be rid of it.''

She held out her hand. ''It has meaning for me,
milord. Pray return it.''

Rannulf set the parchment into her outstretched hand, but he would not meet her challenging gaze.

Clearly he must recall the words he'd written there.

Sword clutched in one hand, he made a formal bow. "I thank you for your patience with one who does not deserve it," he murmured. "Adieu."

He slipped from the room and closed the door before she could respond. 'Twas just as well, for his last statement had left her uncertain what she would have said.

Rannulf hurried down to the barracks in the ground floor of the keep, securing his sword belt around his waist as he went. He guessed he'd find Sir Henry there, or someone who'd know where the crusty old soldier might be. Gillian's request dovetailed nicely with his own plans, as it happened.

He hadn't lied when he'd told Talbot he needed to settle his men, either, though he'd scant time to take care of business before the call to supper.

Several of his men had been to l'Eau Clair with him years ago. While he'd warned them before they set out on this ill-favored trek that they must pretend 'twas their first visit to the place, it would do no harm to remind them, now that they'd arrived, that they must be especially careful not to slip up in front of Talbot's men when they encountered their old friends among the castle troops.

Actually, his men didn't concern him so much as keeping Gillian's people quiet did. He'd brought along a select cadre of his vassals on several of the tasks he'd performed for Pembroke, men he trusted. He knew he could count on them to guard their backs—and their tongues—no matter what the situation.

Fortune favored him for once as he discovered Sir Henry preparing to leave the barracks when he entered them. He met the other man's respectful nod with one of his own. "A moment of your time, Sir Henry?"

"Aye, milord," the soldier said, motioning for Rannulf to precede him into the corridor outside. "How can I be of service?"

"Lady Gillian wishes to speak with you at once in her solar," Rannulf told him as they walked away from the barracks door.

"Does she now, milord?" Rannulf felt his face start to color beneath Sir Henry's speculative gaze. "And how did you come to be her message boy, eh? You being a stranger here and all," he added in a low voice, a spark of amusement lighting his sharp blue eyes.

"I'm merely doing a favor for her, nothing more."

Sir Henry led Rannulf deeper into the shadow-filled corridor. "I know not what your game is, milord, but I'll not give it away for the nonce."

A relief to hear, though not completely a surprise. "I appreciated your silence earlier, 'tis true. Though I didn't expect it."

"Man'd have to be a half-wit not to realize something's going on. You'd never greet my lady thus, so cold and indifferent, without a damned good reason. Christ's bones, lad—" he nudged Rannulf in the ribs with his elbow "—you ran tame behind these walls for far too long to be treating us like strangers now, unless there's some plot afoot." When Rannulf didn't respond, his stare became more intense. "You *do* have a reason, don't you?"

"Aye. Several, though the only one that truly matters is that Pembroke wishes it so." Of a certainty, that was the only reason he planned to give Sir Henry. Details of the situation between him and Gillian had remained private for this long—he had no intention of delving into them again now.

And certainly not with the man who'd been a mentor to him, and Gillian's protector all her life.

At the least that way would cut short his stay at l'Eau Clair, if it didn't bring his very existence to an abrupt end, he thought wryly.

"That Pembroke asks is reason enough for me," Sir Henry said. "'Tis a shame he's at odds with the king. Is that why John gave my lady into another's keeping?"

"Aye," Rannulf replied shortly. "Though I cannot tell you more now."

"I'd be glad to hear more about it once we've a chance to share a pitcher of mead and the details."

That he could do. "You shall have them as soon as we're settled," he agreed. He glanced out the narrow window above them and saw that the light was nearly gone. "You'd best hurry if you're to see Gillian before supper."

Sir Henry nodded. "Aye, I'll get to it right away, milord. Though I've already warned our people to treat you and your men as strangers in our midst, same way we'll treat Lord Talbot's men till we come to know 'em better. Seemed wise to do so until I had the chance to hear just what was going on."

"I thank you," Rannulf said. "I know that's one

thing Gillian wanted to speak with you about. There
could be more, so I'll let you be on your way.''

To his surprise, Sir Henry clapped him on the back.
'''Tis glad I am to see you here again, milord. I don't
mind telling you, you've been sorely missed these
years past. Your lady needs you now that her father's
gone, more than ever before. 'Tis good to see you
where you belong.''

Before Rannulf could respond, the older man gave
another nod and headed for the stairs, whistling under
his breath.

Rannulf shook his head and tried not to let his ever-
growing burden of guilt weigh him down further.
''Ah, Sir Henry, if you only knew the truth,'' he muttered. He turned back toward the barracks. *Though
I'm more glad than I can say that you do not.*

He paused for a moment outside the door, reaching
into the pouch on his belt, drawing forth a heavily
embroidered riband and holding it up to the flickering
torchlight.

Copper threads shimmered, their brightness untar-
nished by years of handling. Gillian had done such a
fine job of copying the circlet's design, the resemblance was truly remarkable.

Although he knew the scent had long ago faded
beyond detection, this time when he raised the favor
to his lips he could almost imagine he smelled the
essence of rose and lavender…Gillian's fragrance.

He tucked the favor back into the pouch, but he
could not elude the truth it represented.

No matter what he might say or do, or that he could
never claim her, Gillian remained his lady, ever and
always, the one truth hidden deep within his heart
where it could not fade away.

Chapter Six

Gillian dragged the crude stool across the hard-packed dirt floor of the cotter's daub-and-wattle hut and set it down next to her patient's straw pallet. Rowena had given birth to a stillborn child the week before—the second child she'd lost—and despite Gillian's best efforts to build up her strength with an elixir of healing herbs and good food from the castle kitchen, Rowena remained weak and pale upon her bed.

"How long, milady, 'fore…you know, 'fore I can try again?" Rowena asked, her pale cheeks tinged pink. She peered into the cup of tonic Gillian handed her.

Although Rowena was no more than a year her senior, Gillian's cheeks heated. She'd never had a female friend her own age to talk with about such things. But Rowena depended upon her to give her aid and advice, so she'd offer what she could.

"You know 'tis too soon to even be thinking of *that*," she cautioned.

"'Tis easy to see you're a maiden still, milady,"

Rowena said, her pale lips curled into a faint smile. "Else you'd know the men think o' little else."

"True as that may be, 'tis much too soon. Allow your body to mend, at least." She stood and concentrated on gathering her simples together in her basket. "It may better your chance of carrying a live babe next time, if you've regained your strength beforehand."

What must it be like, to carry a babe beneath your heart, tangible proof of the love you'd shared with your husband—your lover?

And to lose a child... Mayhap she was better off than she knew, to be yet unwed.

And like to stay that way, if her luck held. Lord Nicholas seemed unlikely to pledge her elsewhere, now that he'd seen what a fine holding he'd the governing of. He'd be a fool to let it slip from his grasp.

So long as he didn't decide she should wed him herself, she thought with a grimace. Despite his handsome face and form, he didn't appeal to her in the least.

Rannulf's reasons for refusing her hand rose to her mind yet again. The mere image of his words upon the page sent a chill of loss and dread through her heart.

Perhaps she was not fit to be wife or mother at all.

She took up the basket of simples and rose to leave. "I'll come again tomorrow," she said, pausing by the door. "See that you take care of yourself."

"I thank you for your help, milady," Rowena said. "'Tis a fine mistress you are, to make time to care for such as me." She settled back onto the pallet. "May God bless you and keep you safe."

Touched, and uncertain how to respond, Gillian nodded and left the hut.

Many duties awaited her within the keep, especially now that their numbers had increased so dramatically. Evidently the king had received her request for aid, for Talbot had brought a sizable train with him—and supplies to help feed them, she'd been grateful to learn. But it was bound to take some time before they all settled into the new regime.

Her step lagged the closer she drew to the track leading up to the castle. Gillian stood and stared at the hum of activity, the people everywhere she looked, and knew she could not face them yet.

The pool in the nearby forest gave the castle its name. There, as she'd done so often in the past, she could escape for a little while, clear her mind and dream her dreams. It was exactly what she needed.

She turned and set off through the greening fields until she reached the edge of the forest. Her step growing lighter by the moment, she settled her basket of simples upon her arm, kilted up her trailing skirts to avoid the underbrush and wove her way through the trees.

Eventually she came to a clearing nestled deep within the older trees, an island of peace and beauty not visible from the castle walls. 'Twas a sylvan glade straight from ancient lore. A sparkling waterfall emptied into a small, flower-bedecked pool, blending its restful murmur with the solitude of the forest.

A smile upon her lips, Gillian set aside her basket under a towering fir and made her way over the smooth carpet of new grass and spring flowers to the moss-covered stones scattered around the edge of the water.

Perhaps here, in her childhood retreat, she might regain her composure, settle her thoughts.

She settled onto a mound of rocks beside the pool that formed a seat of sorts, and stared down into the water. Clearing her mind of all thought, all fear, she let it roam where it would.

But the journey she took in her mind's eye was not one she'd have chosen to relive. 'Twas Rannulf she saw there, a Rannulf younger than the man who'd arrived at l'Eau Clair the day before.

Younger in more than years, for that other Rannulf FitzClifford bore the glint of laughter in his eyes, and an expression of joy upon his handsome face. They'd been so happy that day, carefree and innocent. They'd escaped Lady Alys's vigilance and gone seeking adventure and privacy. Closing her eyes, she felt again the warmth of his hand holding hers, heard the laughter in his voice as he led her headlong through the forest to this very glade.

The sun had shimmered on the water that day, sparking rainbows from the mist at the base of the falls, lending a magical glow to the air. How could she forget the cool water lapping against her body as she waded, clad only in her thin linen shift, into the depths of the pool, the heat of Rannulf's gaze as he joined her there all she needed to warm her?

Opening her eyes, she reached down and trailed her fingertips through the water, sending ripples coursing over the smooth surface and distorting her reflection. She stared at the wavy surface until the water stilled, then started at the new image mirrored there.

"Rannulf!" she gasped, whirling to see if he was there behind her in truth, or naught but a creation of her imagination.

"Good day to you, milady." He stepped away from her, but reached out a hand to steady her when she wavered on her rocky perch. The touch of his fingers on her arm was firm, impersonal...and lingered a moment too long for her peace of mind. "I didn't mean to startle you. I thought you would have heard me coming through the forest," he said with a glance to where his huge chestnut warhorse stood tethered to a tree.

'Twas a wonder she hadn't noticed, a measure of how deeply enmeshed she'd been in the past.

"What do you here, milord?" she asked, her voice as cold as she could make it, given the heated memories still lurking in her brain. "Are you lost?"

"Nay, Lady Gillian. I sought you in the village. When I couldn't find you there, a lad told me he'd seen you head this way."

"Are you following me, milord?" If that was his plan, for her own sanity she must set him from that path at once.

For how could she survive his constant presence, the continual reminder of what had been?

And what could be, whispered a taunting voice within her traitorous mind.

He raised an eyebrow in inquiry. "Following you? Why should I do that, milady?"

Gillian felt her temper flare. "I know of no reason, sir, none at all." The trembling that had beset her since she noticed him behind her disappeared, replaced by a wave of determination.

She'd show him his error! She would not permit him to torment her any longer.

Her legs firm beneath her, she stood, shook out her

skirts and threw back her shoulders in a deliberate display of bravado.

Rannulf held his ground in the face of her show of spirit, not out of any desire to flee, but rather to fight the urge to leap more fully into the fray. Dear God, but she was magnificent!

His arms ached to reach out to her, to enclose her in their grasp, to pull her flush against him and appease the hunger burning for satisfaction. Four years of yearning howled for appeasement, and though he knew 'twas impossible, his body refused to accept that answer.

He wanted her, not just to gratify a physical hunger, though his body throbbed with wanting. Nay, simply to feel the joy of Gillian held tight within his arms, to know he'd never have to give her up again… 'Twas a pleasure worth any price.

Except that of his honor.

And her safety.

Taking his time, he glanced about the glade, not permitting his gaze to linger anywhere, lest the memories of this place etched within his memory take control of his reason and destroy his will to resist them.

When his wandering attention returned to Gillian, he shrugged. "And why would I follow you here of all places, milady?" he asked. Though he kept his tone light, he added a taunting edge to his voice that sent a flush of color into Gillian's pale cheeks. "Your guardian sent me to fetch you back to the keep, 'tis all."

"Does he think to lock me away within the castle walls like some helpless damsel?" She stirred into motion, pacing away from him, her fingers going to the hilt of her eating dagger. She looked as though she'd like to draw the blade and spit someone with it—himself, most like.

He suppressed a chuckle at the image. Aye, that would be a sight to stir any man!

And why not rouse her anger further? He found Gillian de l'Eau Clair difficult to resist under any circumstances, but when she had that soft, remembering look in her sparkling green eyes as he'd peered at her reflection in the pool, 'twas all too easy to give in to the compulsion to join her there. They'd both be better off sniping and snapping at each other.

And that way, there'd be no chance he'd give himself away before Nicholas Talbot, as he'd so nearly done too many times the day before.

At least if Gillian were angry with him, she'd do her best to avoid him.

Aye, he could not ask for a better plan.

"You, a helpless damsel?" he mocked. "How could he ever make that mistake?" Taking his time, he joined her at the water's edge, then followed her when she stalked past him toward the trees. "You're about as helpless as a she-wolf. If the king had known anything about you, he'd never have bothered to send you a guardian."

He'd swear her eyes glistened with tears before she turned her back to him, her knuckles white as they tightened about the dagger.

It felt as though she'd stabbed that blade deep into his heart, but he kept at it.

"Did you know that Ella took Talbot to task yesterday when he asked why you had not come to help us bathe?" The morning sun fell on her hair where it hung below her veil, igniting the fiery locks with warmth, momentarily distracting him from his purpose. He shook his head and forced himself to forge on. "She told him you were an innocent maiden whom she'd protect to the death, most like, should he seek to change your state." He gave in to temptation and reached for the end of her braid, tugging until she turned to face him. "Interesting that she doesn't know the truth."

"What truth is that, milord?" Gone was any hint of tears, her eyes instead alight with righteous anger. "That you took my innocence—here, in this very spot?"

He nearly glanced over his shoulder to the grassy bank she referred to, but that would be an act of monumental stupidity. Better he keep his eyes fixed upon Gillian's face, Gillian's anger, for 'twould serve to remind him why he'd led them down this path. Instead he released her hair and folded his arms across his chest. "Did I?"

Rannulf leveled a measuring look upon her, till she wanted to squirm beneath that cool, dark gaze. She realized her fingers had nigh gone numb from clutching her knife, and eased her grip. Did he realize, she wondered, how close she'd come to drawing the blade? Merely to keep him away, of course.

'Twas a mistake to let down her guard, she saw at once, for he stepped nearer to her, forcing her to retreat. "Did I indeed?" he asked.

She pressed her back against the rough trunk of an ancient oak and raised her chin in challenge. "Do you deny I was a virgin when you took me to your bed?"

He gave an aborted laugh and reached out to tug once again on a lock of her hair hanging loose over her shoulder. "My *bed?*" He wound the end around his wrist as he'd done the day before, bringing his captive hand ever closer to her breast, even as his eyes held hers hostage. He leaned so near, his words brushed her lips.

Though she knew she should try to free herself, Gillian could not make her reluctant body obey the dictate of her mind, could scarcely draw breath for fear of pulling him nearer still.

"There was no bed involved, as I recall, save the one we fashioned from my tunic and your bliaut." His stubbled cheek grazed her face from temple to chin, sending a shiver down her spine. "I'll never forget the sight of your hair glowing in the sun—" He released her hair and trailed his freed hand along its length, his knuckles coasting over her shoulder in the barest of caresses. "And the shadow here..."

She jerked away before his wandering fingers could settle against her bosom, but he trapped her hand in his.

His fingers intertwined with hers and he tugged her into his arms. "Gillian," he breathed against her lips. His touch gentle, he wrapped her into his embrace.

He'd slipped off her veil before she realized what he was about, and buried his fingers in the mass of her hair, loosening her braid and sliding his hands up through the wavy mass to cradle her face.

Her eyes drifted closed, her breath caught on a sob as he nuzzled her cheek, pressed his body against hers in a caress devastating in its tenderness. Force she might have withstood, but this gentle assault proved beyond her will to resist.

She opened her eyes to stare into the familiar brown depths of Rannulf's questioning gaze, lost herself in the web of desire he wove around them so effortlessly, watched as he lowered his lips to hers slowly, so slowly she could feel his touch before their mouths met.

Warmth flowed from his lips to her heart, set up a sense of loss so deep it spilled over into tears that flowed down her cheeks even as her lips clung to Rannulf's.

He gasped against her mouth, his hand sliding up her cheek to capture a teardrop, then slowly stepped away. He fixed his gaze somewhere beyond her shoulder and drew in a deep breath. "Forgive me. I hadn't intended to touch you."

Before her disbelieving gaze he cast off the languor of desire and resumed the mantle of warrior—or tormentor. Somehow all emotion drained away from his features, leaving behind a shell of the man she'd seen.

The man she'd known so long ago.

"You've grown even more lovely these years past, milady. I don't suppose you'd care to pick up where we left off back then, would you?" he asked, his mouth curved into an insolent grin. "If we're careful enough, Talbot need never know."

She had the knife free of its sheath before her stunned brain could form the words to curse him straight to hell where he belonged.

Grin still intact, Rannulf eased away from her, one hand held in front of him as though to ward her off. "No one need know you're no longer a maiden. I wouldn't want to harm your chances of making a decent marriage, although with a dowry such as yours, combined with your beauty, I doubt most men would care."

Gillian drew in a gasp of air and, knife upraised, snatched her skirts into her free hand and charged after him. "Whoreson knave," she growled, stalking him as he backed through the trees toward his mount. "Get you gone, else I'll gut you where you stand."

He believed her threat, it seemed, for he spun on his heel and leapt into the saddle. "Let me know if you change your mind, milady," he called, gathering the reins and nudging the stallion into motion. "At any time."

She gave a scream of outrage and let the dagger fly, sending it to land, quivering like her shaking limbs, in the thick tree trunk near where they'd kissed.

Though she knew 'twas foolish, she watched him guide his mount through the trees, listened to the hoofbeats fade away, before she roused herself to motion. Not until she knew he'd gone beyond her reach did she dare to relax her guard.

Then, her thundering heart the only sign of her anger and pain, she gathered her disordered locks together and began to fashion them into a neat braid.

No one must know, she reminded herself. Not only that she and her servants knew Rannulf, but especially all that had happened between them.

In both the past and the present.

She settled her veil on her hair, then tugged the dagger free and slid it into its sheath.

She picked up her basket and set off for the track back to l'Eau Clair.

Her step faltered when she walked past her father's grave, and she paused to say a prayer. He'd never have suspected the kind of man Rannulf had become, she thought as Rannulf's parting words echoed in her mind. She knelt beside the grave and laid her hand atop the tender grass, then dashed a traitorous tear from her cheek. He'd never have offered her to Rannulf otherwise, she knew. What had gone through his mind when he'd received the betrothal agreement, with its detestable message, back from Rannulf? Often these past few weeks she'd wondered why her father hadn't told her what he'd done. Perhaps he'd sought to spare her the pain he knew she'd suffer if she knew how Rannulf had responded to the offer of her hand.

'Twas no use thinking of what she'd lost yet again, although with Rannulf there as a constant reminder, how could she ever forget?

Chapter Seven

Rannulf stood on the battlements and observed Gillian's progress. He'd spurred his mount hard so he might avoid her as she headed back, yet he felt compelled to watch over her, if only from afar. A stiff breeze tugged at his hair and whipped his tunic snug against his body, but it could not scour away the sickness roiling in his belly and stabbing at his heart over his cruelty to Gillian.

He greatly feared 'twas beyond him to maintain that pose for long, so he'd taken the cowardly way and run from her. The blade she'd brandished nigh in his face had not threatened him—by the rood, he'd permit her to have at him with her sword, knowing full well she might spit him with it—if he thought 'twould help promote his ruse.

But after holding her in his arms, 'twas almost beyond him to let her go.

He saw her pause near a grave in the fields alongside the path to the castle—her father's, perhaps?—drop to her knees beside it and reach out to place her hand on the mounded soil.

Lord Simon de l'Eau Clair. An honorable man, decent and true, who had never done him ill. Who had made him welcome here. A far better man than his own sire, he thought bitterly—in every way.

And what had Rannulf done to repay Lord Simon, when he offered Rannulf his greatest treasure, his daughter's hand? It shamed him to recall how he'd repaid his generosity, for not only had he refused his gift, but insulted him and his daughter with his heartless words, made a mockery of so many things—hospitality, love, honor.

'Twas no doubt he was indeed his father's son. How else could he have done the things he'd done—said the words he'd forced from his lips this very day, smiling all the while like the most false-hearted knave at court?

Who would ever believe he had reasons for what he'd done? And to his shame, he continued to believe his reasons valid and true.

He continued to watch as Gillian rose and brushed dirt from her bliaut, then raised her hand and swiped at her cheeks as well. Her tears were all that had saved him from insanity by the pool this morn, jarring him from his selfish greed as he stole from Gillian— her taste, her touch, the priceless gift of peace he felt within her arms.

His brief respite over, Rannulf descended the stairs and went to the bailey to await Gillian's return. He'd told Gillian one truth this morning, for Talbot did wish to see her.

Supper the night before had been a strained and stilted affair, the presence of Talbot—and himself, he had no doubt—at the high table seeming to rob Gillian of her appetite and her conversation. Perhaps Talbot was more observant than Rannulf gave him credit for, since he excused Gillian from attending him after the meal, instead postponing his meeting with her until today.

But the time of reckoning—if that was what Talbot intended—had arrived. Since Rannulf was still attempting to establish himself with his overlord, he'd best do as he was bid and bring Talbot his ward.

He walked up to her as soon as she passed through the gate, reaching for the basket she carried on her arm and calling for a servant to come take it for her.

She refused to release it. "No, milord," she said, waving away the maid and tugging on the handle until Rannulf let go of it. "What's inside is far too valuable." She turned her face away from him. "And you, sir, are far too high-handed. How dare you order my servants in my presence?"

He took her by the arm and turned her toward him. "Your guardian wishes to see you at once, milady. I suggest you come with me now."

"You didn't seem to be in such a hurry earlier. Nor as considerate of me, either. What's brought about this change? Were you distracted from your duty, perhaps?" She shook her head. "Nay, that couldn't be the reason. I haven't the power to divert your attention from anything," she snapped. "Though it appeared to me that your master's command was the last thing on your mind then." She met his narrowing gaze fully, her own expression thoughtful. "I wonder what he'd have to say if I were to tell him—"

"Enough!" he snarled. His fingers tight about her forearm, he resisted the urge to haul her along after him and instead led her in a calm fashion to a sheltered spot beneath the wall and blocked her from view with his body. But his voice when he spoke again was far from calm, though he spoke in a whisper. "Are you mad, Gillian, to even consider telling him about this morn? About everything?" He eased his grip, though he did not release her. "Because you'd have to confess it all before you were through, I have no doubt. He's already your guardian by the king's order. How much power do you want him to have over you?" he demanded. "I don't even know how much control he has over me." He raked his fingers through his hair. "By the rood, you make me daft! Neither of us knows what he's capable of doing."

"He's *your* overlord. Don't you know?" she asked, her eyes sharp with curiosity.

He shook his head. "I managed to avoid meeting him until I was ordered to come here with him. I know little of Talbot, save that he's King John's crony." Absently smoothing down his hair, he added, "That alone is cause for concern, wouldn't you say?"

She lifted his hand from her arm, her face pale. "There is much going on here that you've not told me, Rannulf, of that I'm certain." She shook out her skirts and adjusted the basket on her arm. "I'll go with you now to see Lord Nicholas, but only if you swear you'll explain this situation to me more fully later." She grasped his arm. "And soon. I'll not be put off for long, or I'll be forced to reconsider going along with your initial request." Leaning closer, her gaze holding his as surely as her hand held him there, she added, "I mean it, Rannulf. You owe me that much, at least."

He weighed her request—and her sincerity. She'd follow through, he knew, for once set upon a course,

Gillian seldom wavered. "You've my word, if you'll trust it."

"I will, so long as you give me no reason to change my mind."

"Agreed."

His mind awhirl, he took her by the elbow, as custom dictated, and led her through the bailey and into the keep. They discovered Sir Henry and Will seated at a table in the hall, a pitcher of ale between them.

Sir Henry turned on the bench and eyed them as they trod sedately across the room. "Now isn't this a pretty sight?" he murmured when they halted by the table.

Rannulf released Gillian at once; she sent Sir Henry a look fit to slay a lesser man.

Will sloshed the last of the ale into his cup and chuckled. "'Tis milady Gilles, I vow, finally come to enchant her guardian," he teased, saluting her with the ale before downing the draft. He glanced up at Rannulf, a frown replacing his grin. "Took you long enough to bring her back, milord. Mayhap you should have sent someone who knows the lay o' the land to seek her out."

"Since I found her, I'd say I know it well enough." Rannulf couldn't quite keep a menacing note from his voice. Will hadn't wanted to go along with the ruse that Rannulf was a stranger to them; only the fact that Sir Henry—and Gillian—had ordered it so could compel his obedience.

'Twas clear to Rannulf that the other man suspected him of something—exactly what, he could not say. If he hadn't known better, he might have believed that Will, Gillian's lifelong friend, was jealous.

But he knew, better than any of them, that there was nothing to be jealous *of*.

For despite any lingering feelings he might harbor for Gillian, Rannulf knew just how unlikely it was that Gillian felt anything for him but hatred.

He'd certainly done everything he could think of to ensure that end.

Sir Henry thumped his mug down on the table and stood. "Come along, then, children." He hitched up his braes and settled his belt around his middle with a sigh. "We've kept his lordship waiting long enough, I'd imagine. We don't need him growing too curious about the goings-on here, now do we?"

After asking where her guardian could be found, Gillian led the way to the small, well-appointed chamber that had been her father's sanctuary, her expression tinged with sorrow, to Rannulf's mind. It must be difficult for her to see another in her father's place.

She knocked, and Talbot bid her enter. Rannulf, Sir Henry and Will trooped in after her, her two men ranging themselves on a bench by the door while she and Rannulf took seats at the narrow table in the middle of the room.

Gillian arranged her skirts about her, folded her hands in her lap and waited.

The perfect picture of a lady, Rannulf thought, hiding a smile. Ah, if Talbot only knew the truth of the matter....

Gillian glanced at her guardian, standing at the table's head—her father's place—and forced her sense of resentment deep. Lord Nicholas was only doing his duty, she reminded herself, as his overlord—*their* overlord, in fact—had ordered him to do. For all she knew, Talbot had no more desire to command l'Eau Clair, to be saddled with a ward, than she had for him to do so.

He'd already commandeered her father's chair, she noted when he resumed his seat after gifting her with a polite bow. Though Talbot stood as tall as her father had, he lacked her father's bulky frame and did not present her father's imposing presence.

And certainly not as impressive a presence as 'twas clear—to her, at least—he thought he did.

Or perhaps he *hoped* he did. Though she'd had scant opportunity as yet to observe him, what she had noticed about her guardian thus far led her to a rather strange, and no doubt completely false, conclusion.

To her it appeared that Lord Nicholas was playing a role.

He wore his fine clothes with a natural grace, and carried himself with an almost challenging arrogance—as if he dared anyone to think him less than what he seemed. But she'd watched him carefully at supper the evening before, and it looked to her as if he observed everyone else nigh as closely as she did him.

It could be natural curiosity, she supposed, or a suspicious nature, but...she didn't know him. She'd do well to guard herself and her secrets in Lord Nicholas's presence.

In his vassal's presence as well, she reminded herself as she glanced across the table at Rannulf.

"I'm sorry for the delay, milord," Rannulf said. "Lady Gillian was busy in the village when I ran her to ground." *Ran her to ground*—did he think her his quarry? She resisted the urge to grimace. "I brought her back as soon as her tasks were finished."

Gillian darted another look at Rannulf when he uttered that patent falsehood, but his face, his eyes, bore an expression of complete sincerity.

Interesting, the skills he'd acquired in recent years.

It seemed that Talbot believed him, at any rate, for he nodded his acceptance. Leaning forward, he picked up a map from the stack of parchments littering the table and pushed it toward them. "Come join us," he told Sir Henry and Will, then waited while they dragged the bench to the end of the table opposite him and resumed their seats. "I understand from what the king told me that you've had trouble with raids and attacks about the demesne?"

"Aye, milord," Sir Henry said. He squinted down at the map. "Here—" he pointed to a small farm high in the hills on the far western edge of her lands "—and in several places along the northern border here," he said as he drew his finger over a dark, winding line near the top of the drawing.

"They never do much damage," Will added. "But enough people have come to harm—two injured badly enough that they died of their wounds—that 'tis difficult to work the lands away from the castle itself. We haven't enough men to mount guards everywhere we've work to do and our people are fearful whenever their duties take them away from the keep."

Talbot stood, pulled the parchment closer and turned it about to study it. "Did you take any guards with you to the village, milady?" he asked.

Startled by his question, she glanced up at him. "Of course not." His violet gaze held an unexpected look of censure. "'Tis just down the track. What harm could come to me there, in my own village?"

Placing his hands palms down on the pile of documents, he leaned toward her, his handsome visage set in stern lines. "I doubt you so ignorant that you're unaware of your worth, Lady Gillian. All it would take to threaten your safety—and that of all who dwell here—would be for a few brawny men to drag you from the road and haul you into the forest. No one would even know you were gone till the ransom demand arrived, most like—a demand that we turn over l'Eau Clair in exchange for you." He straightened and settled his hands upon his hips. "I have no desire to explain to the king why I traded this holding to ensure your safe return because of your imprudent behavior. From this moment on, you're not to leave these walls unescorted."

Gillian rose to her feet and met his eyes. "That is impossible, milord," she said low-voiced, not bothering to disguise her outrage. "I am lady of this keep. I have a duty to my people, and I will not allow you to keep me from it."

"Lady Gillian," Sir Henry said, his tone sharper than she'd ever heard him speak to her. Unwilling to cede control to Talbot for so much as a moment, she kept her gaze fixed on her guardian. "He's the right of it, child. You know that as well as I."

"And how am I to go about my duties, then? Drag a troop of guards down the hill to the village every time I've a sick child to attend in the middle of the night? Or never go beyond the castle walls?" She dared a glance over her shoulder at her men, both of whom refused to look at her, and spun on her heel to confront them. "You agree with him, don't you?" It was obvious they did. Swallowing her disgust—and her hurt—she moved away from the table and turned her back on them all. "I'm surprised you've tolerated my command these past few months, for I'm clearly not fit to lead.''

''You've not done so bad,'' Will said quietly. ''But you cannot do everything, milady. Your father never expected that of you. Lord Nicholas speaks truly. You cannot continue to take such risks.''

Gillian closed her eyes for a moment, glad they could not see the pain on her face. Aye, her father had had other plans for her, plans that included a husband to share the welcome burden of l'Eau Clair. Why he'd never sought beyond the man sitting silently behind her for her mate, she could not say.

Or perhaps he had, but had left no proof of his quest.

Whatever her father had in mind for her, she could guess he'd not intended to leave her so unprotected.

Wondering about her father's plans solved nothing now, however. She'd be better served to face her guardian and discover what he had in mind.

Drawing in a deep breath, Gillian spun and returned to her place at the table, although she remained on her feet. ''Have you a plan to solve this problem, Lord Nicholas?''

Talbot sat down and leaned back in the chair, his expression pensive. ''Aye, Lady Gillian, I believe I do.'' He toyed with the map, turning it about and staring at it for a moment before raising his gaze to Rannulf. ''FitzClifford shall be your guard when you wish to leave the keep, if I'm not available.'' Stifling a gasp, Gillian dropped onto her seat lest her shaking legs betray her completely. ''You need not fear for your safety when he's about, milady, for he's a prodigious fighter.'' For the first time since they'd entered the room, Talbot smiled. "What say you, Lady Gillian? Will that meet with your approval?"

Under Lord Nicholas's questioning gaze, what complaint could she possibly raise? It seemed she had no choice but to accept.

But she didn't have to like it, nor did she have to remain in Rannulf's presence for another moment.

Gathering her skirts, Gillian rose and curtsied to her guardian. "Aye, milord, your plan should solve the problem. Pray excuse me," she added, then headed to the door without waiting for permission to leave.

Once she'd shut the portal behind her, she slumped back and pressed her cheek against the smooth wood.

She'd never leave the keep again till they were gone, she vowed, for how else could she avoid being alone with Rannulf FitzClifford?

Chapter Eight

The next few days presented Gillian with plenty to occupy her within the keep as Talbot's company and the people of l'Eau Clair settled into a new routine—and into the command of a new regime. The adjustment proved tumultuous at times, for Gillian had reigned over the castle as chatelaine for several years, and since her father's death had been the sole and final authority at l'Eau Clair.

'Twas a blessing she'd remained so busy, for it left her with little opportunity to ponder the consequences of Lord Nicholas's command—and thus far, no reason to leave the confines of the castle walls.

But such good fortune could not last forever, she knew. Sooner or later she would have to face Rannulf FitzClifford alone again.

They met every day—every meal, at least—for 'twas impossible to completely avoid each other. It seemed to Gillian, however, that Rannulf was no more eager to be in her company than she to be in his.

If Talbot but knew it, he could not have devised a

more effective way to keep her within the confines of l'Eau Clair.

Under Sir Henry's direction, her guardian and his men rode the boundaries of her property, familiarizing themselves with the area and examining the defenses. This, too, kept her tied to the keep, for Talbot could scarce leave behind one of his best warriors simply to provide her with an escort.

Of the raiders they found no sign. She hoped the addition of Talbot's forces to her own would prove sufficient deterrent to whoever had been attacking them, and permit them the freedom to get on with their work.

After a week's time, Gillian felt as restless and frustrated as if she'd been living under siege. If she couldn't escape the castle walls soon, she'd go mad. But when she asked for Lord Nicholas to accompany her, she was told he was too busy to do so. As much as she wished to avoid Rannulf—to avoid asking him for anything—she needed to go to the village to visit the sick. Though she cursed her ill luck, some tiny part of her couldn't help but yearn to be with him again.

Coward that she was, she sent Ella to request Rannulf's company. Determined to prove to herself that he mattered not a whit to her, she wore her oldest tunic, drab but comfortable, and bundled her hair beneath a linen headrail. He'd find no haughty noble lady here—not in appearance, at any rate.

She awaited him by the gate, her basket of simples slung over her arm. Though she'd been sorely tempted to don her sword, she couldn't decide if he'd interpret that act as an attempt to mock his ability to protect her, or simply as something she'd do as a matter of course. There'd been a time not so long past when she had worn her sword regularly—and used it, too—and he knew it.

But she'd rather not have to explain why she wore a man's sword to her so-proper guardian. She doubted Lord Nicholas would understand that deviation from maidenly behavior, and he *did* seem to be a stickler for propriety.

The sound of hooves against the flagstones roused her from her thoughts as Rannulf rode toward her on his chestnut stallion. He reined in beside her, forcing her to crane her neck to look up at him. "Where is your mount?" he asked. He peered back toward the stables and frowned. "I thought Ella said you were ready to leave."

She bit back a sigh. "The village is so near, I've no reason to ride there. It's not worth the bother to saddle a horse. Besides, when I go by myself, there's usually no one to hold my mare while I'm busy."

He shrugged. "Suit yourself." Leaning from the saddle, he reached down and hooked his arm about her waist. "My mount is strong enough to carry us both," he added, then swept her up in front of him in the commodious saddle with surprising ease before she could do more than gasp in protest.

'Twould serve no purpose to oppose him, she thought, the memory of how his muscled arm felt clasped round her middle disturbing in ways she'd rather not explore. Even now, the heat of his body pressed to her side, the slow, steady rise and fall of his chest against her back, caused an odd flutter beneath her heart.

Blessed Mary save her, she could not bear to feel these feelings once again....

Especially not with Rannulf FitzClifford as their cause.

But he'd not let her dismount, of that much she was certain. Best to present a calm front, go along with him and bring this torture to an end all the sooner.

Resolved to endure, she shifted to sit more comfortably across the saddle bow. She had an excellent view of his handsome visage, of the freckles—faded now that he was a man grown—scattered over his lightly tanned face. She turned her attention to arranging her basket in her lap, lest she be tempted to gaze once more into the dark eyes she knew had focused on *her* face.

He nudged the stallion into motion. They passed through the portcullis and over the drawbridge in a silence broken only by Rannulf's greeting to the guard stationed at the top of the road leading down to the village. Once they'd passed the man, Rannulf spoke to her. "I suggest that the next time you ask me to accompany you, you bring your own mount." He shifted in the saddle, managing to enfold her closer in his arms in the process. "Unless, of course, you'd prefer to ride with me again," he added, something in the low timbre of his voice sending a ripple of awareness vibrating through her.

It compelled her to turn her head to meet his gaze, a mistake, she realized at once, for his deep brown eyes held a warmth nigh impossible to resist. Her senses seemed suddenly magnified—the feel of the sun's heat beating down on her clothing, the smell of the greening earth in the fields around them, the faint, exotic scent of sandalwood and leather enveloping the man who held her pressed against him.

Her heart beat faster in response and her mouth grew dry; she wet her lips with her tongue, even that innocent motion suddenly invested with a new, sensual awareness.

Rannulf drew in a deep breath and willed his hands to remain light and easy on the reins instead of grabbing Gillian and lifting her to meet his yearning body, his aching mouth. The feel of her weight against him, the sight of her so near him, was almost more than he could bear. Dear God in heaven, he thought, closing his eyes on the sight of temptation personified, how could he have been so misguided as to believe he could sit here with Gillian practically riding in his lap and remain unaffected?

He nudged March to a faster pace, eager to reach the village before he came to the end of his endurance. At the edge of the wide main street he brought the stallion to a halt, nearly leaping from the saddle. He reached up and grasped Gillian about the waist and lowered her to the ground with more speed than grace.

Her basket tumbled from her hold and fell into the muddy road, scattering dried herbs and small parchment packets across the puddled surface. "No!" she cried, dropping to her knees in the muck and gathering up what she could.

Feeling lower than a snake, he stooped to help her. Despite his ignorance about healing, he could tell that what had spilled from the basket had been ruined through his impatience. Once he'd retrieved the last small bundle, he straightened, holding out the befouled items he'd collected. "I'm sorry, Gillian," he murmured. "I should have been more careful."

"Wait." She pulled a piece of linen from the basket and held it spread open so he could place everything in it. After wiping the worst of the mud from her hands on the edge of the material, she tied the corners together and looped the parcel over her wrist.

Her gaze lowered, her face pale and solemn, she took up the basket in one hand, clutched the linen packet firmly in the other and started to walk away. Rannulf caught hold of her arm, his touch gentle but insistent. "Gillian, wait."

Since he gave her no choice but to stop, she halted, but continued to look ahead, not at him. "Will you still have enough medicines to care for the sick?" he asked, unable to mask his concern.

"I don't know," she said, her voice flat. "I'll need to look everything over, see what's been spoiled." She met his gaze now, her green eyes glowing with some strong emotion—anger, most like, righteous anger. How could he guess what harm he might have done? "Some of the simples I carry are not easily come by, or must be compounded and left to blend before they can be used. I may not be able to replace them any time soon."

Rannulf felt his face heat. Someone might be harmed by his carelessness...nothing new about that, unfortunately. "Then I pray you'll have no need for any of those medicines." He released her arm and stepped back to let her go on. "I'll do whatever I can to help you restore what you've lost. Give you coin to buy what you need, help you gather plants and such or assist you in the stillroom...." He met her gaze and held it with his own, so she'd not doubt him in this. "Simply tell me what you want of me, and you shall have it."

Gillian watched his face, his eyes, to judge if he

meant what he said. His regret, and his offer, seemed sincere, and she'd hold him to his word.

Beginning now.

"Indeed, milord? Then I accept your apology, and thank you in advance for your help." She started toward Rowena's hut, glancing over her shoulder when she heard no sounds of movement behind her.

He stood in the road, his stallion's reins held loosely in his hands, his expression pensive. "What are you waiting for, milord? Come along. We've much to do, and scant time to waste by standing in the street talking about it." Not lingering to see if he obeyed, she resumed walking. The creak of saddle leather and the quiet rattle of Rannulf's scabbard soon followed her. "If we finish here quickly enough, we might have time to stop by the pool before returning to the keep. Many healing herbs grow near the water."

She could only pray the blessed Virgin would protect her, and keep her from wishing to indulge any of her foolish desires while they were there.

As soon as they reached Rowena's, Gillian took a moment to spread out her simples and assess her losses. She'd been fortunate, for most of what had ended up in the muddy street had been powders compounded from local plants, and herbs she grew in the castle gardens. Replenishing them would take some time and effort on her part—and Rannulf's, she thought with a smile—but they could be replaced.

Before they were through, he might be sorry he'd offered to help.

She frowned. So, perhaps, might she.

She left him standing guard outside Rowena's hut while she examined the village woman, then had him do the same at the next three places she visited to treat the sick. At her last stop, she enlisted his aid in setting the dislocated shoulder of a young lad of five who'd taken a tumble from a tree.

He soon held the boy enthralled with tales about the wild exploits of a strange Irish creature called a leprechaun. While she couldn't prevent the boy feeling some pain when she reset the joint, Rannulf's stories distracted the lad from the worst of it; she was glad he was there to help.

The sun had not yet reached its zenith when they left the boy's home, his mother's grateful thanks sending them on their way in a far better state than they'd arrived in the village earlier that morn. Casting a glance at the sky, Gillian smiled. "Good—we've time enough to go looking for plants before dinner."

Rannulf, adjusting the girth on his saddle, paused. "You know that Talbot doesn't wish you to be gone from the keep for long."

"The plants grow nearby. 'Twill take no time at all to gather them."

He finished tightening the strap and stepped toward her, hand outstretched to take her basket. "Despite the fact that it's been quiet here of late, you still shouldn't be wandering through the woods," he cautioned.

"Lord Nicholas simply said that I should take my guard with me whenever I leave the keep. Sir Henry is keeping him busy plotting ways to improve our defenses—they'll have no need of my help." She set aside the basket and adjusted her skirts so Rannulf could boost her into the saddle. "You're here." Pointing to the sword and wickedly long dagger on the belt strapped around his waist, she added, "And well armed, I see.'' She waited until he met her gaze. ''Do you doubt you can protect me?''

''You know I can,'' he muttered. Shaking his head, he clasped his hands about her waist and lifted her into the saddle, then passed her simples to her before swinging up behind her. ''Come along, March,'' he said, nudging the stallion with his boot heels.

''What did you call him?''

''March.''

Gillian ignored the shiver his voice in her ear sent skittering down her spine and, seeking a distraction, sought to satisfy her curiosity. '''Tis a strange name for a horse.''

He leaned over her right shoulder to peer at her face. Unfortunately, the action also brought his lips even nearer to her ear. ''Not so strange, if you realize I gave him a Welsh name.''

Eyes fixed on the track in front of them, she laughed. ''You're not serious?'' His nod of agreement tapped his chin on her shoulder. ''You named him Stallion.''

''Aye. It seemed a fine idea at the time.'' He shifted a bit, and she'd have sworn he nestled her more snugly into his arms. ''Besides, I have an abiding fondness for all—nay, for some, at any rate—things Welsh.''

His chuckle caused his chest to vibrate against her back.

What did he mean by that? Or did she imagine a hidden meaning where none was meant? She was Welsh—half Welsh, at least. But he couldn't have meant anything by it... By the Virgin, he could not. 'Twas the taint of her Welsh blood he'd referred to in that accursed betrothal agreement...

Or was it?

'Twas nigh impossible to think clearly while cuddled so closely to him. Frantic to dismount and drag her reluctant body away from temptation and confusion, she noted that they'd reached the path into the forest and gave silent thanks. "We cannot ride through the trees, can we?"

"Of course we can," he replied, and gathered her more firmly into his hold.

Gillian closed her eyes, not for fear of injury, but so she might concentrate on ignoring the way her entire body betrayed her.

After all that had gone before, all that had happened between them in the past week, how could she still want him to hold her?

How could she ache to hear him murmur against the sensitive flesh of her neck, regardless of the words he spoke, simply to feel once more the shiver of delight he—he alone, she feared—sent dancing along her spine?

March stopped. Opening her eyes, she greeted the sight of the pool in all its splendor with a sigh of relief.

Worst of all, how could her own mind betray her, swamping her with emotions that carried the power to overcome her intellect?

Mindful of what their haste had cost her the last time she dismounted, she waited with a patience she did not feel for Rannulf to slip from the saddle and help her down. Once her feet touched the ground, she could have knelt and kissed the mossy soil in gratitude.

She placed the basket safely away from March's restless hooves and headed immediately for the pool.

Kneeling on the rocky bank, she slipped off her veil, pushed her loose sleeves above her wrists and scooped the cool water into her hands.

She let it trickle through her fingers, easing her heated blood, before raising her hands to her flushed cheeks.

"What are we looking for here?" Rannulf asked as he joined her. He paced along the rocks, his boots slipping on the wet moss, peering down at the flowers growing along the water's edge.

"You'll be looking at the bottom of the pool if you don't have a care," she warned. Feeling cooler now, more composed, she rose and made to move away from the stones just as Rannulf jumped from one large rock to another.

They met on the same slick ledge, slid into each other and, clutching hold of each other for support, instead pitched sideways into the water.

Chapter Nine

They landed with a huge splash, both of them dropping beneath the surface until they hit hard against the rock-strewn bottom.

Gillian's skirts tangled about her legs, and Rannulf lay half atop her besides, pinning her under the water and rendering her unable to move. She'd landed in the cold layer along the bottom, the chill shocking her motionless for a brief moment.

Panicking, she struggled to stand, then burst into the sunlight when Rannulf found his footing and hauled her upright and onto her feet.

Gasping for air, she leaned against his solid form, allowing him to support her until she caught her breath. As soon as she thought she could stand without his help, she tried to move away from him, but the bottom was so slick with muck and weeds where they'd landed that she slipped and would have gone under again if Rannulf hadn't caught her by the arms.

"Take your time," he cautioned. "Let me hold you until you're steady."

She gazed up at him through her wet lashes, then

stared at his eyes, his face, stark and handsome, slick with moisture that glistened in the sun.

Rannulf appeared equally transfixed by the sight of her, for his eyes trailed heat as they roamed her face, then down over her body in its sodden, clinging garments. "My lady," he whispered, his gaze fixed on her face once more. His brown eyes holding her captive, he bent his head and lowered his mouth to hers.

No glancing touch this, no forbidden brush of lips laden with guilt and sorrow. He traced his mouth over hers, his tongue darting out to lick away the water beaded on her lips, teasing at the sensitive corners of her mouth until, with a moan of surrender, she opened and let him in.

His taste was familiar, the sweetest subtlety, sustenance after loss and pain. Gillian accepted the caress and returned it full measure, letting him feel all she'd once felt for him....

Felt for him still, to her shame.

But shame held no sway over her now, with her love in her arms once again.

She dragged her hands over his chest and up to measure the width of his shoulders, broader than before, the feel of his leashed strength beneath her palms making desire smolder hotter still within her veins. Fingers trembling, she carried the caress higher, to frame his face, moaning when he deepened the kiss.

Rannulf tightened his hold, one hand slipping low to cup her bottom and raise her until her feet scarce touched the slippery ground, the other buried at her nape in the soaking mass of her hair. His heat branded her as he molded her to him, front to front, her aching mouth still captured by his lips.

He groaned low in his chest, a rumbling vibration that echoed within her own body before he eased his mouth from hers and lowered her until she could stand. "You taste sweeter than wine," he murmured, raising his hand to brush his knuckles lightly over her cheek. He stroked a finger along her throat, then used it to tilt her chin. "How I've missed you," he whispered before reclaiming her lips.

Even as she savored the warmth of his touch, a chill settled within her as his words sank into her consciousness.

He'd missed her? Missed what—this? She herself, or the passion they'd once shared?

Although the movement made her feel as if she were wrenching her heart from her breast, Gillian tore her mouth from his and took a step back. Despite the uncertain footing, she managed to reach the shore without further mishap. Her gown streaming water, she trudged onto the grassy bank of the pool and sank to her knees.

She heard Rannulf sloshing toward her, but concentrated on wringing out her sopping skirts until an icy droplet landed on her head. "Gillian, what's wrong?"

Her attention focused on the task with an intensity the well-worn garment didn't deserve, she ignored him until the drop became a steady stream of cold water pouring over her head.

"You bastard!" she gasped. Rolling out of the way, she struggled to her feet and looked at him. He lowered his tunic—which he'd removed and held over her as he wrung it out—and grinned unrepentantly. Her teeth chattered. "Haven't you done enough already?"

He cast aside the tunic and stalked after her as she retreated toward the trees. "Not nearly enough," he said low-voiced.

"Let me be!" she shrieked as he snatched her off her feet and back into his arms.

His lips felt warm against her chilled skin, brushing flame over her cheek, her chin, her eyelids before settling on her mouth. "Rannulf," she moaned, fighting the temptation to sink once more into the heated morass of his caress.

Sheer force of will kept her hands down at her sides, fighting the compulsion to touch him in return. But neither could she force herself to move away. He continued to kiss her, easing her down his body to stand on her own while he stroked his callused fingertips along the sensitive flesh of her throat, her nape, until her skin felt burnished with sensations too compelling to bear.

Finally the gentle assault gave way to his arms about her, holding her snug against the firm strength of his chest. She could feel his warmth through the thin linen of his shirt, hear the racing of his heart beneath her ear slow to its normal pace. When he finally laid his cheek atop her head and held her to him, Gillian lifted her arms and returned his embrace.

How long they stood thus before he spoke, she could not say, but between Rannulf's hold and the midday sun, she no longer felt cold.

"I didn't mean for this to happen," he murmured into her hair. "But I've no will to resist you, it appears." With a sigh, he slid his arms away and set her free. His expression solemn, he reached out and smoothed her hair back from her face. "I don't know how I ever thought I could."

"There was a time when it seemed you felt no need to." She caught his gaze and held it captive with her own. "Will you tell me why that changed?"

His eyes grew darker still, shadow-filled and cold. "I cannot."

There was a time he'd kept no secrets from her, or so she'd believed. "Cannot?" she asked, challenge in her voice, her stance. "Or will not?"

He looked away from the intensity of her questioning gaze. "Does it matter which?" He picked up his wet tunic and shook it out. "The outcome is the same either way," he said before drawing the rumpled garment over his head, hiding his face, his eyes from her completely.

When his head emerged from the neckline, his face bore no expression at all. "You've come to no harm?"

"Would you care if I had?" she couldn't resist asking. She bent to wring her sodden skirts once more, not even bothering to watch him further.

Why bother? 'Twas clear he'd reverted to the man she didn't recognize...the man who'd refused her hand.

Rannulf made no reply, simply settled his sword belt about his middle and went to untie March's reins from a tree.

How dare he toy with her, make a mockery—to her mind, 'twas what he was doing—of what they'd once shared? She'd have sworn he'd been as deeply affected as she but a brief time ago, though he exhibited little sign of those feelings now. Mayhap she could find some way to make him pay—or at the least, to make him suffer. 'Twould go some distance toward easing the hurts he'd caused her.

'Twas clear to her that one thing hadn't changed between them; it seemed he still wanted her physically, if for nothing else. Even if 'twas naught but lust on his part, what better way to make him suffer than to play upon his ardor, taunt him with that lust?

Then refuse to satisfy it.

Had she the strength to brave the fire of passion with Rannulf once again and emerge unscathed?

She'd never shied from a challenge, and she'd not begin now. Decisiveness lending her a peace she'd not felt since before Rannulf's arrival at l'Eau Clair, Gillian hid her triumphant smile and awaited his return.

He led the stallion to a small boulder she could use as a mounting block. "We've tarried here too long. We'll have to come back another time to search for the plants."

Gillian stepped up onto the rock and clambered onto March's back. She waited until he'd handed her the basket and was in the midst of swinging up into the saddle to ask, "Tarried, did we?" He landed in the saddle with an abrupt thump. She wriggled about until she sat nearly in his lap. "Is that what you call what we were doing?"

A sound suspiciously like a growl issued from deep in Rannulf's chest, all the answer he gave.

'Twas enough. She leaned back against his broad chest and permitted her smile to grow, now that he couldn't see it.

"Sit still, damn it," he snarled, voice dagger-sharp. He urged March into motion and remained silent as they wove through the ancient trees.

Gillian settled back to enjoy the ride. This plot of hers bore unforeseen rewards already, the pleasure of

Rannulf's lean, muscular body nudging against hers with every step March took a prize she intended to savor.

She bit back a laugh at her success when Rannulf set March to a fast trot up the road to the castle.

Mayhap he was eager to be rid of her?

If that was so, she planned to see that he was doomed to disappointment.

Rannulf urged March up the last of the path to l'Eau Clair at a fast clip, the stallion eager for a run for even so short a distance.

He, on the other hand, was simply eager for this hellish morn to be over.

Much of the trouble had been his own fault, 'twas true. His carelessness every time he spent any time in Gillian's presence seemed to tie him in knots, his behavior erratic and confusing—to them both, from the look of it. He could scarcely blame Gillian for wondering at his actions.

He didn't understand them himself.

In all the years he'd spent in Pembroke's service—as a squire, then later as essentially a noble spy—he'd carried out his duties swiftly, efficiently, with little difficulty. Oftentimes, especially in the past few years, he'd found himself in situations where the slightest mistake on his part could lead to death—for himself, and sometimes for others as well. But his training had been thorough and complete, and he did his job well.

Why, then, did barely a moment's time spent in Gillian's company render him a complete idiot without one whit of self-control?

If he didn't leave her alone, Talbot was bound to realize they'd something between them.

God help them both if her guardian ever discovered the truth.

As soon as they reached the stables, he dismounted and helped Gillian from the saddle. She accepted his assistance with a serene smile and murmured words of thanks completely at odds with the Gillian he'd known of late…the woman he'd faced by the pool.

Suspicions aroused, he excused himself to go change out of his wet clothing and left her to return to the keep on her own. Though he'd been taught better manners, he didn't trust this pleasant, amenable woman a bit. He'd be best served to get away from her as soon as possible—and stay away.

He'd complications enough to deal with for the nonce, without adding the ultimate complication of Gillian to his already overflowing agenda.

His step lighter already, Rannulf crossed the bailey and entered the keep, intent upon finally doing the work he'd been sent here to perform.

Spying on Nicholas Talbot.

But when Rannulf entered the hall, intent upon reaching his chamber to dry off, then going about his business, he arrived on the heels of a messenger from the gatehouse tower.

He used the chaos of servants preparing the room for the midday meal to make his way across the long chamber undetected.

"FitzClifford—just in time." At the sound of his overlord's voice, he halted near the door to the stairwell and turned to face the dais.

He should have known he wouldn't make it, he thought with a groan. He bowed. "Milord?"

Talbot descended from the dais and joined him, drawing him into the stairwell where it was relatively private. "Much is happening of a sudden," he said, his voice holding more excitement than Rannulf had ever heard him express. "While Sir Henry was patrolling the southern border he discovered signs that a sizable party camped there recently. We'll need to go out there, look over the area, as soon as possible." He nodded toward the departing messenger. "But that will have to wait, for I've received word that a large party of Welshmen are headed here. Sir Henry is still out guarding what he found, and Will has gone to watch over a work party repairing the damage at an outlying farm. I don't believe there's any connection between what Sir Henry discovered and the party coming this way, but it pays to be prepared for the worst."

"Aye, milord." Rannulf kept his tone even, but his impatience must have shown through, to judge by Talbot's sudden, sharp look. "What would you have me do?"

"I need you to go to the gatehouse tower, gauge what's happening there while I begin to muster our forces. I've just sent word to sound the alarm for the villagers to seek shelter here at once."

"Lady Gillian and I returned from the village not long ago, milord. I noticed nothing unusual outside the walls."

Talbot dragged a hand back through his hair. "Of course not—the message I received came from a sentry posted along the northern boundary. He likely rode in just before you did. We've plenty of time to set our defenses, if we get to it now," he said, his tone finally tinged with command.

"Aye, milord."

Rannulf took one step, then came to a halt when Talbot reached out and caught him by the arm. He surveyed Rannulf's garments, eyes narrowed. "Since you've supposedly just left my ward, I trust you have a good reason why you're soaking wet on a sunny day." For the first time since Rannulf had met his overlord, Talbot exuded menace.

'Twould be a mistake to underestimate the man, a fact he should have assumed all along.

"Aye, milord—an excellent reason, one I'll share with you at the first opportunity." Bowing once again, Rannulf left the hall to carry out Talbot's bidding.

L'Eau Clair's soldiers had been well trained. Preparations to defend against an attack were already under way when Rannulf crossed the bailey to the gate tower. Although he couldn't imagine a Welsh war party riding straight for the castle, or permitting themselves to be detected, Talbot was right to prepare for the worst.

He was curious to hear what Sir Henry had to report once he returned, as well.

Rannulf gazed down the road to the village from his vantage point on the wall walk near the gatehouse tower, the same spot where Gillian had awaited his party when they arrived. The position commanded an excellent view of the surrounding area, although not, he was relieved to see, of the pool in the forest.

All he needed was for one of Talbot's men to have seen him with Gillian the two times they'd visited the spot.

If that had happened, he'd likely be residing in the cellars now, under lock and key while he awaited some well deserved punishment, instead of helping to defend l'Eau Clair.

Safe for the moment, he reminded himself. If he'd half a brain, he'd see he stayed that way.

The Welsh arrived much sooner than Talbot had led him to believe they would. Rannulf heard them before he saw them, for they made no secret of their approach. The thunder of hooves on the hard-packed track heralded their arrival before they came into view.

Once he saw them, he knew they'd no need to bar the gates, for it appeared they rode well armed for defense while they traveled, not for war.

A massive wolfhound loped ahead of them, gamboling about like a frisky pup until a sharp command from a dark-haired woman near the front of the column brought the dog to a stop near the edge of the moat.

She looked familiar. Rannulf scanned the group spread out below him, then cursed roundly when he caught a clear look at their leader. By Christ's bones, could he ask for worse luck? he wondered as the man nudged his horse forward and hailed them.

"Why is this keep closed up tight?" he demanded. "Where is your lady?"

The guard posted near the gatehouse stairs to relay messages ran up to Rannulf. "You must let him in, milord," he gasped. "Lady Gillian'll be right furious when she learns we slammed the gate nigh in her cousin's face."

He'd the right of that, Rannulf knew, though he could not admit he knew anything about it.

There might be hell to pay for this insult, and Rannulf would rather not be on the receiving end of the transaction.

Too bad Talbot hadn't taken to the walls, instead of sending him. It would have prevented—or at least postponed—what could prove to be a delicate situation.

For him, at any rate.

Rannulf took a deep breath. His work here might be over almost before it had begun, should Lord Ian ap Dafydd take it into his head to tell Talbot *everything* he knew about Rannulf FitzClifford.

Chapter Ten

A woman's angry shriek carried across the bailey, followed by her raised voice echoing up the stairs. Rannulf didn't even bother to turn and look, for he knew it was Gillian. She'd be here soon enough.

She strode onto the walk, skirts flying, her eyes flashing emerald fire. "Open the gate at once!" She shouted additional orders down to the guards, then, ignoring Rannulf's presence, leaned into a crenel and gazed down at her kin.

"Go tell them to do it," Rannulf said to the guard at his side. "Then go to Talbot and tell him we needn't muster the troops just yet," he added before sending the man racing down the stairs.

"Ian," she called. "My apologies."

"Gillian, what is going on?" the woman below called. "Do you need help?"

Rannulf peered over the wall and shook his head when he saw how angry the woman looked. No surprise there; from what he knew of her, she was rarely in any other mood.

A ponderous creaking heralded the lowering of the drawbridge and the portcullis's slow climb. Straight-

ening, Rannulf moved to stand beside Gillian, careful
to avoid her fiery gaze. "Enter, and be welcome," he
shouted. Not waiting for a response, he took Gillian
by the arm and led her away from the guards near the
tower.

"You must talk to Ian at once," he said quickly.
"Make him understand...."

She sighed, but she nodded. "Yes, milord, I'll
speak to Ian and Catrin about keeping your secret—"
she gave him a searching glance "—whatever it is,
as soon as they're within." She stared at his hand,
still clutching her arm, until he released her. "But *you*
must promise *me* that no harm will come to them
while they're here."

"No harm? Who would harm the Dragon? For the
love of God, Gillian, the man is Llywelyn's assassin.
Mayhap you should show some concern for Talbot,"
he suggested dryly. "I doubt Lord Ian will be pleased
to learn you've a Norman—King John's man—as
your guardian. Have you considered how he'll react
to that?"

"Ian is my cousin, lest you forget. I'll thank you
to cease insulting him." He allowed her to pull free
of his hold. "He's also no fool. Nor am I," she added
with a pointed look. "I cannot wait to learn all the
reasons why we must hide you in our midst. You *do*
intend to explain it all to me eventually, I trust."

"Perhaps." Perhaps when hell froze over. Or if she
had him pinned in a corner with her sword while he
was tied up and unarmed. He glanced away so she
wouldn't notice the amusement—and heat—in his
eyes when his mind conjured that image. In that situation he'd give her anything she wanted, he thought.

By the rood, in *any* situation he'd give her whatever she wanted, he thought with a frown, for where Gillian was concerned it seemed he'd no will to refuse her anything.

What had brought about that strange expression on Rannulf's face? Gillian wondered. Humor and lust together, it appeared to her, followed by frustration. Or disgust? But whatever thoughts were passing through his mind mattered not a whit to her, especially now that Ian and Catrin had arrived. She could count on them for anything, she knew. If she could convince them to lend her their support, perhaps all her troubles might be resolved.

She glanced at Rannulf, patiently waiting, and felt her heartbeat falter. Nay, some problems would never disappear so easily.

She forced her pulse to steady. He'd drive her mad before long, she knew it. But she could not ignore him, no matter how hard she tried.

Almost every moment she'd spent in his company since he returned to l'Eau Clair, she felt as though they were carrying on conversations on several different levels at once—or speaking at cross purposes much of the time. 'Twas enough to confuse the most clear-minded person, a description she wouldn't apply to herself when she was anywhere near Rannulf.

As for her earlier plan to entice him, to make him long for her, to make him suffer…she must have been mad to consider such a foolish notion. Even if it worked, she'd likely suffer just as much as he, if not more. *She* had loved him once, after all. How could she bear to lose him again?

The hollow clatter of hooves on the drawbridge roused her to motion. ''I'll go down to welcome them,'' she said. She shook out her skirts and grimaced when her hands touched the cold, damp material; she'd forgotten what she—what they both, she added, peering quickly through her lashes at Rannulf—looked like after their unplanned swim. She shrugged. 'Twas too late to do aught about it now. "You stay out of sight until I've had a chance to speak privately with Ian and Catrin."

He nodded, then glanced over the rail of the walkway into the bailey and frowned. Following his gaze, she saw her guardian, garbed for battle in mail hauberk and leggings, on the stairs outside the keep, speaking with the guard who'd just left them. "You'd best get moving, before Talbot comes to greet them," he said. He bowed, then turned and headed away from her along the wall walk.

Casting a last, despairing glare at her dress—afraid to even consider how her hair looked—Gillian shrugged and hurried down to the bailey. Most of the time she took care with her appearance, but she'd very little vanity about it. Still, her cousins might be startled by her disheveled state, though they'd seen her dressed worse than this. Lord Nicholas, however, had not.

What he thought of how she looked mattered nothing to her. She only hoped he wouldn't ask how she'd ended up that way.

Especially if he'd noticed Rannulf's similar condition.

Ian had just helped Catrin from her mount when Gillian joined them. Catrin turned to enfold her in her arms at once, a stream of Welsh words flowing from her lips so quickly, 'twas all Gillian could do to follow half of them. "Slowly, else I won't know what you're saying." She leaned down a bit and gladly returned her cousin's warm embrace, more grateful than she could say for the wave of love and comfort that washed over her. Fighting back tears, she gave Catrin a last squeeze.

"You obviously need more practice," Catrin admonished, slowing her speech to a more understandable pace. "We must visit you more often. We cannot allow you to forget your heritage." She gave Gillian another squeeze, more gentle this time. "We were sorry to hear of your father's death. He was a good man," she murmured. "And following so close upon losing Lady Alys...."

Gillian nodded her appreciation, but did not try to speak, for she knew her voice would betray her sense of loss.

Once Catrin released her, Ian swung Gillian up into his arms and held her tight for a moment. "Are you all right?" he asked urgently as he set her on her feet. He bent close enough to whisper, "You're not being held here against your will, are you?"

"What?" Startled as much by his insistent tone as his words, she looked up and met eyes as green as her own—though she didn't believe hers ever held the questing drive that was so much a part of Ian's very being. "Of course not. What would make you think such a thing?"

Catrin stepped closer. "I cannot imagine," she said dryly. "Never before have the gates of l'Eau Clair been shut tight against us, and the guards are strangers to us, as well." She reached out and touched the tangled end of Gillian's braid. "And do you have any idea how you look?"

Gillian laughed. "Aye—like a madwoman, most likely." She raised her hand to her hair and shoved it back over her shoulder. "That I can explain later. But I've more important concerns for the moment." Catching sight of Lord Nicholas drawing near, she took Ian by the hand. "Rannulf FitzClifford is here, but Talbot doesn't know we know him. You must not let Talbot know that—"

Ian cut off her frantic whisper with a sharp nod. "'Tis all right, Gillian. You can tell us the rest later."

"Talbot?" Catrin asked. "Who might he be?" She peered past Ian at Lord Nicholas bearing down on them, his handsome face solemn, his dress, even when hurriedly garbed for battle, perfect as always.

Particularly when compared to her own, Gillian thought as she fought back a smile.

"Who is this pretty popinjay?" Catrin asked in Welsh. Gillian bent close to her cousin and jabbed at her side with her elbow, then straightened to drop a polite curtsy when her guardian halted before them.

"Lord Nicholas Talbot, may I introduce my cousins, Lady Catrin uerch Dafydd and her brother Lord Ian ap Dafydd? They've just heard of my father's death and have come to offer their sympathy and to see to my welfare."

Lord Nicholas bowed, the movement far more elaborate than Ian's terse bow in reply. His eyes lingered on Catrin, Gillian noted without surprise, for a moment longer than mere civility required. Catrin, petite and lovely, her dark hair streaming down her back in a glorious cascade, possessed a dainty beauty certain to appeal to any man with eyes to see.

Gillian couldn't help wondering, however, how he'd react once he'd become acquainted with Catrin's rather forceful personality.

"I'm pleased to welcome you to l'Eau Clair," Lord

Nicholas said. "And I'm certain Gillian will be glad of your company, though her well-being is now my concern."

"Is that so? 'Tis her family's duty—our right—to care for our own," Ian said, subtle menace threading through his silky voice, his hand moving to his sword. "What brings you to l'Eau Clair, milord, that you believe *you've* any say over my cousin's welfare?"

Lord Nicholas's welcoming expression faded, transforming to a look of...challenge? Gillian's instincts sharpened.

His lips curled into a smile that made her distinctly uneasy. "Didn't Gillian tell you? Her overlord, King John himself, made me guardian of your cousin and all she possesses."

Standing so close to Catrin, Gillian heard her cousin's indrawn breath at Lord Nicholas's provocation; she only hoped her guardian didn't notice. She didn't want him suspicious of anyone or anything associated with l'Eau Clair, although he could hardly suspect her family's concern for her. 'Twas bad enough he had some degree of power over her and her life—too much power, in her estimation.

"Come within the keep where we may all be comfortable," she suggested. "'Tis nearly time for dinner." Lord Nicholas and Ian each eyed her with a proprietary air; she wouldn't be surprised if they began to snap and snarl at any moment.

Just so had she seen two dogs act, when faced with one juicy bone between the two of them, she thought with disgust.

Did they think her a pawn to do battle over?

Outrage—and a lingering aura of helplessness she refused to acknowledge—stiffened her spine. She linked arms with Catrin and led her cousin around the two men and toward the keep, striking up a conversation about their journey. A glance over her shoulder showed Lord Nicholas and Ian walking in silence behind them.

Their bearing, however, spoke more loudly than words of the tension sparking between them.

"Lady Gillian," Lord Nicholas called. She halted, released Catrin's arm and turned to face him. "Have you seen FitzClifford since you returned from the village? I sent him out here when I heard of your cousins' approach."

"Aye, he was on the wall and ordered the gates opened." She gave him an innocent smile; she'd done enough to conceal Rannulf's intrigues for one day. "But he left as soon as he gave the order. I don't know where he went," she added with a shrug.

Her guardian frowned, but motioned for her to proceed. Gillian turned and focused her attention on Catrin, though she could barely concentrate on her cousin's words. The weight of too many concerns pressed upon her. Their unknown attackers, Lord Nicholas, Rannulf...and now Ian and Catrin arrived to add spice to her melee of cares and woes.

Never before had the thought of escape—of actually picking up her skirts and running until she'd left the walls of her home far behind—seemed so appealing as it did at that moment.

Catrin's fingers tightened about Gillian's arm and Gillian ceased her inconsequential chatter. Catrin paused at the top of the stairs, suspicion darkening her steady gray gaze. "What's wrong?" Catrin murmured, her words hidden from the others' notice by the creak of the great door into the keep as Ian opened it.

Gillian shook her head and gestured for them to go on to the table on the dais, already prepared for the midday meal. Servants swarmed about the room, carrying in dishes and pitchers of drink to set out on the trestle tables in the hall. "Would you care to retire for a bit, refresh yourselves before you eat?" she asked her cousins.

"Nay—later will be fine," Catrin said. She leaned close to Gillian and whispered, "You cannot expect us to wander away now."

What *had* she been thinking? Gillian wondered wryly. "Then please, sit and be comfortable," she suggested, leading them to the head of the room and waiting to see them take their places at the long, narrow table. She motioned for a servant to lay two more settings. "Help yourselves. I'll join you once I've arranged for your chambers to be prepared."

It suddenly occurred to her that her guardian stood behind the table arrayed for battle. Had he been about to leave when her cousins arrived? Or had he believed Ian's party a force come to attack l'Eau Clair?

Either way, she could not imagine her so-proper guardian would wish to dine while wearing mail.

"Lord Nicholas, I apologize for my thoughtlessness. Would you like to change before we begin?"

He shook his head sharply. "Nay—I'll be leaving soon. Proceed with the meal," he added, lowering himself to the chair at the center of the table.

"As you wish." She motioned for the two pages who would serve her guests to come forward with their basins of warm water and towels before turning to face the hall, where the rest of her household were pulling up benches to the tables arrayed there. "You needn't wait for my return," she told them, raising her voice to be heard over the din. "Go ahead and eat."

Ella met her as soon as she left the hall, and they quickly decided where to lodge the newcomers. Catrin could share her chamber—she'd done so before, and it would give them a chance to talk—but Gillian made certain that Ian had a room of his own.

She couldn't imagine asking either Rannulf or Lord Nicholas to share their quarters with Ian, or with each other. Three more independent and stubborn men she'd never met! Indeed, 'twould be a miracle if they could make it through this meal peacefully. Though she shouldn't be surprised by it, it seemed that Ian and Lord Nicholas together could prove a most volatile combination. Once Rannulf joined them…

Whether it would be dangerous or entertaining, she couldn't decide.

Mayhap 'twould be both.

After a swift stop in her chamber to change out of her still-damp clothes and cover her disheveled hair with a fresh veil, Gillian returned to the hall.

Hot on Rannulf's heels.

She could hardly ignore him, so she resigned herself to…to what? Would he be civil, or treat her with the coldly impersonal air she'd seldom seen? She had come to loathe it, though she knew she ought to welcome it.

Rannulf mounted the step up onto the dais, then paused and glanced over his shoulder at her as though he'd heard her behind him—unlikely, given the volume of sound filling the hall. His face solemn, his expression one of polite disinterest, he waited for her to reach him.

She focused on his face—and then upon the sight of him in a dark green tunic that hugged his lean form. It reminded her of the way his muscular chest had looked garbed in wet linen, had felt beneath her hands earlier this morn. Distracted, she didn't notice his hand, outstretched to assist her onto the platform, until he quirked a brow and held out his hand to her, palm up. "Milady."

She had no choice but to place her hand upon his and accept his escort. They approached the table and halted before it.

Rannulf released her with a slight bow.

Mindful of his earlier instructions that Talbot believe her cousins were strangers to him, Gillian dropped a curtsy in return and introduced Rannulf to Ian and Catrin.

'Twas a blessing Lord Nicholas's attention seemed centered on her, not on Ian and Catrin, for their reactions would most certainly have roused his suspicion. Ian's scowl appeared much too extreme for a simple introduction, though his response sounded civil enough. Catrin, however, gifted Rannulf with a welcoming smile, her eyes widened in appreciation, before she turned a teasing glance in Gillian's direction.

Wise to Catrin's scheme, nonetheless Gillian narrowed her eyes at her cousin in promised retribution.

"'Tis a pleasure to meet you, milord." Catrin held out her hand to Rannulf over the table.

He brought it to his lips. "The pleasure is mine, milady," he said smoothly, the provocative look he gave her when he straightened enough to tempt Gillian to take her boot to his backside.

Preferably while he stood perched atop the battlements.

Instead, the amenities over, she allowed him to lead her around the table to her seat.

"Join me, milord," Catrin offered. She slid over on the bench to make a place for him.

Deciding her cousin had much to answer for, Gillian resolved to ignore them both and concentrate her attention upon maintaining the flow of conversation between Ian and Lord Nicholas.

But it seemed her guardian had other plans.

"FitzClifford, if you're through slavering over Lady Catrin's hand, perhaps you'd care to join me so we might complete our earlier discussion." He pushed his chair back and stood, turning a strained smile upon the others at the table. "If you'll excuse us, ladies, milord?" His bow as terse as his tone, he headed off toward what had once been Lord Simon's private lair without so much as a backward glance to see if Rannulf followed.

His face expressionless, Rannulf waited until Talbot had passed halfway down the long hall before bowing to Gillian. "By your leave, milady." With a nod to Ian and Catrin, he left as well.

Catrin scarce waited until Rannulf had moved out of earshot before turning to Gillian, her lips curved into a satisfied smile. "This may turn out to be a far more interesting visit than I expected."

Her mind awhirl as she sought some meaning to Lord Nicholas's behavior, Gillian reluctantly dragged her attention away from Rannulf and swung on the bench to frown at her cousin. "I'm so gratified you'll be suitably entertained," she said dryly. "I've never been able to provide you with this level of intrigue before."

"Enough, both of you," Ian snapped. His gaze pensive, he stared out over the busy hall for a moment, then faced Gillian and reached for the platter of mutton. "All right, Gillian, now that your keeper's gone, tell me everything you know about Talbot." He stabbed a slice of meat and laid it on her trencher before serving himself.

Gillian nodded her thanks, picked up the pitcher of mead and filled Catrin's goblet. "I don't know what to say."

Ian pushed his cup toward her and gave her a smile that sent a shiver down her spine. What did he want of her? She set down the pitcher and shoved the empty cup back to him. "Ian?"

"If you cannot tell me about your new guardian, perhaps you can tell me what FitzClifford is doing here."

Chapter Eleven

Huw settled into the saddle and raised the wineskin to his lips, savoring the heady wine while his master fumed silently beside him. He enjoyed his noble lordship's frustration as much as the wine, and the sense of power he felt at that moment was even more intoxicating. He lowered the skin and glanced over at the man glowering at him. "You needn't worry. They haven't any idea that we're behind it, milord. No idea at all."

"So you say." Leather creaked as the other man shifted in his saddle, sending his showy stallion prancing dangerously on the steep slope. "How much longer must you keep this up before I can have her?" he growled. "I cannot wait forever, you know."

"You can scarcely ride into l'Eau Clair and take her, either. Especially since her ladyship refuses to allow you entrance."

"She said they'd sickness within," he growled, his eyes snapping with fury. "I vow 'twas a ruse, nothing more."

"Judging from the number of people going in and out of the place, you've got the right of it."

"Fractious bastard," Lord Steffan growled. Huw fought back a smile as his master slipped from the saddle when the stallion—sensing the anger emanating from the man atop his back—refused to settle down. Looping the reins about a tree, he stepped away from the beast.

Probably afraid he'd get pushed and tumble down the mountainside.

"Perhaps you'd better leave him home next time, milord," Huw suggested. "He doesn't seem too quiet. Wouldn't want them to catch us, would we?" he added with a nod toward the Normans poking around at the abandoned campsite below.

Lord Steffan's scowl worsened, twisting his face into a gross mockery of his usual pleasant mien. Huw shook his head. What was it about this woman that drove his master to such lengths to have her? Aye, she was a comely armful, but if 'twas a bedmate he sought, women were easy enough to come by.

Especially if you were a handsome lord gifted with property and influence, he thought, burying his bitterness deep before dismounting to join Lord Steffan.

Of course, the woman herself was not the only lure driving Lord Steffan to this madness. L'Eau Clair boasted a position of power in the Marches, and Lady Gillian had connections to men of prominence on both sides of the border.

Men whose loyalty and aid a middling Welsh lord could not hope to command otherwise.

They moved to the edge of the clearing and watched the troops from l'Eau Clair as they milled about in the valley below. "What are they waiting for?" Lord Steffan asked. "Can't they see they're too late?"

Huw moved away from the edge and shrugged. "Perhaps they think to find something that will tell them who was there." He spat on the ground. "As if I'd be so careless. All they'll see is what I wanted them to find—clues to lead them away from us."

Lord Steffan walked over to untie his horse. "That's all well and good, Huw, but we're not out here to toy with Gillian's men." He swung up into the saddle and adjusted his cloak. "I want her with me. If I cannot have her at l'Eau Clair, then bring her to me at Bryn Du. Once she's by my side, 'twill be easier to wrest control of l'Eau Clair from the Normans. I don't understand how you've allowed the fools to foil your efforts."

"I've set plans in motion, milord, but they'll take time before they come to fruition." Huw mounted his own horse, barely resisting the urge to reach out and nudge Lord Steffan's steed with his sword and send the foolish beast, and its even more foolish master, careering down the mountain.

But that would solve nothing, and lose him what little power he had, never mind all he stood to gain once he'd done as Lord Steffan demanded. "Just be patient a while longer," he said, the words spoken as much to reassure himself as the other man.

"You'd best bring my cousin within my grasp, Huw, and quickly, else I'll find someone who can," he threatened, his voice vibrating with rage. "I refuse to wait for Gillian and l'Eau Clair much longer."

Rannulf caught up with Talbot on the stairs, both maintaining their silence until they'd entered Talbot's lair and closed the door behind them.

Curious as to what Talbot had to say, Rannulf remained on his feet, his expression one of polite deference. Patience would serve him best, until he knew precisely what his overlord wanted of him.

Talbot tossed his sword belt onto the documents scattered across the table and dragged a hand through his hair. "Why aren't you wearing your mail?" he demanded. "Guests or not, we've little time to be doing the civil when we should be riding out to join Sir Henry, looking over what he found."

Rannulf nodded. "Aye. But since I didn't know if you'd want me to stay here or go with you, I chose the middle ground," he said with a glance down at his well-worn tunic. "It will take but a moment to don my mail, if you want me to accompany you. But I wasn't certain whether you'd rather I stayed here, kept an eye on your ward—and her guests."

"You're right," Talbot admitted with a sigh. He rustled through the parchments piled haphazardly at the head of the table until he found the one he sought. "Someone should remain here with Lady Gillian, make sure she doesn't decide to go off with her cousin—or that he doesn't try to use her to his own ends. Do you think he'd try to take l'Eau Clair through her?"

"I doubt it. He didn't bring many men, and he doesn't appear to have come here armed for war." Besides, the Dragon's methods were generally more direct, Rannulf thought, though 'twas wise of Talbot to have considered the possibility.

"There's something about Lord Ian I don't trust," Talbot said, a pensive expression on his face.

How far should he carry his ruse? Rannulf wondered. The Dragon's reputation was well-known along the Marcher border, even into the fastness of

England itself within some circles. If he feigned complete ignorance, it might appear as strange as if he knew too much.

But Talbot appeared little-schooled in much of the local political situation. Doubtless he'd not suspect Rannulf of concealing information, whichever approach he took.

Still, he'd not care to seem *too* uninformed. "Have you never heard of Llywelyn's Dragon, milord?" he asked, relaxing his stance enough to lean back against the heavy planks of the door even as he observed his overlord with a keen eye.

"Vaguely. He's rumored to be a ruthless enforcer of Llywelyn's will, is he not?" Talbot picked up the map he'd pulled from the pile and tilted it toward the light from the narrow window.

"That's one of the many legends attached to him. In fact, he is Llywelyn's kin. And Lady Gillian's as well. Lord Ian is the Dragon."

Talbot's attention focused on Rannulf with surprising speed, his violet eyes taking on a steely hue. "What!" He tossed aside the map and rounded the table. "What were you thinking of, remaining silent when we left him alone with Gillian?"

"Hold, milord," Rannulf said, slapping his palm on the door to keep Talbot from opening it. "He's hardly alone with her. His sister is right there with them, as are nearly the entire household. What harm do you think he could do to her in a hall full of people?" He lowered his hand when Talbot stepped back a pace. "The Dragon may be a legendary warrior, but I doubt even *he* is capable of that much," he added wryly.

Talbot turned toward the table and retrieved his

sword belt, focusing his attention upon buckling it. "You're right," he admitted. "Instead of taking you to task, I should be thanking you for preventing me from making a complete fool of myself." He glanced up at Rannulf and gave a rueful grin. "This guardian business is enough to drive a man mad. I find it far less horrifying than I feared back in London, but the task holds many surprises I never envisioned as well."

They'd tarried here long enough—especially since Rannulf had little desire to discuss Talbot's ward with him. "Shall I stay here to guard Lady Gillian, or would you rather do so?" he asked. He grinned. "'Twould provide you with the perfect opportunity to know Lady Catrin better."

"An aspiration to be avoided at all costs," Talbot said, his voice full of dread. "She's lovely, but I'd venture she's a waspish tongue." Talbot shook his head and reached for the door latch, tugging the portal open. "Perhaps I should worry more about Lady Catrin's influence upon my ward," he added with a rueful laugh. "Lady Gillian has proved compliant thus far, and I'd hate to see that change."

Rannulf choked back a laugh of his own at that untruth, turning it into a cough when Talbot looked at him curiously. "As you say, milord."

"Nay, I'll leave the dubious pleasure of Lady Catrin's company to you, FitzClifford. You stay here with the ladies. I'm dressed for fighting," he pointed out with a glance at his hauberk. "I'll go join Sir Henry." He glanced out the window. "And I'd best get to it."

The lucky bastard, Rannulf thought, but he kept that sentiment to himself. "Until later, then," he said, giving a brief bow as Talbot preceded him out the door.

Pulling the door closed behind him, he headed off down the corridor toward the hall, his footsteps lagging.

He couldn't decide which of them had gotten the better bargain.

By the time the meal ended and the women retired to the solar, leaving the men to go about their business, Gillian was ready to do violence to anyone who so much as glanced at her the wrong way. Exhausted by Ian's demand for information, confused by Rannulf's ever-vacillating ways, and hungry besides—for how could she eat under these circumstances?—she wanted nothing more than to escape to the peacefulness of the forest pool.

Alone this time. She could stare into the water streaming from the rock-strewn hillside to her heart's content, enjoy the sweet-scented flowers and clear her mind of all thoughts, all feelings.

But 'twas a beautiful dream, nothing more.

Instead she ushered Catrin into her solar, closed the door behind them with a decisive snap and turned the key in the lock.

"Am I to understand you have a death wish?" Gillian demanded as she tore the veiling from her hair and snatched her hairbrush from the table. She unwound her braid, nearly dry now, and began to draw the brush through the tangled strands with long, soothing strokes as she paced the confines of the room. She paused before the crackling fire and whirled to face her cousin. "Or do you simply enjoy flirting with danger?"

Catrin settled onto the bench with a sigh. "Danger? From whom—Talbot?" She made a rude noise. "Don't you think I named him properly when I called him a pretty popinjay?"

"He probably heard what you said," Gillian said, exasperated.

"He wouldn't have known what I said even if he did hear me. He's a pretty fool, nothing more."

"Looks can deceive, Catrin, as you well know."

She'd swear Catrin's face paled, though perhaps 'twas naught but the shifting afternoon light, for her cousin's voice resounded with its usual tartness when she spoke. "Aye, I know it well. But there's naught to Lord Nicholas but a pair of fine eyes in a handsome shell."

"Whether that is true or not doesn't concern me." Though her body nearly quivered with pent-up energy, in the aftermath of the day's events—and 'twas scarce past noon—she felt so shaken that 'twas all she could do to stand. She drew forward a stool and sank down upon it with a sigh. "Though I'd not dismiss my guardian so easily, not after today." She pulled her hair over her shoulder to spill into her lap and stroked the brush through several times, eyes downcast, while she marshaled her thoughts.

And her courage.

"Perhaps the danger comes from you," Catrin commented. Gillian glanced at her cousin's sharp gray eyes, questioning as they focused on Gillian's face. "There's little more dangerous than a jealous woman."

She met Catrin's patient look. "I meant Rannulf when I spoke of danger."

"Did you?" Catrin asked. "To whom—me? I only

flirted with him to annoy Ian. You know how he can be about Normans.'' She rose and came to stand beside Gillian, placing a hand upon her shoulder. ''And perhaps to tease you a bit, I admit, though 'twas cruel of me to do so.'' She bent and pressed her cheek to Gillian's for a moment. ''Forgive me, please,'' she murmured as she stood back. ''I didn't mean to cause you pain. But I didn't realize until 'twas too late that all is not well between you.''

Gillian gave a bitter laugh. ''You could tell that easily enough, I'd imagine.'' Tears welled in her eyes, tears she'd held back too often this week past.

Knowing Catrin would understand, she gave up the battle and let the tears fall.

Once started, she could not stop. A sob rose from deep within her, carrying all the pain and confusion swirling inside her.

Catrin knelt beside Gillian and enfolded her in her arms. ''Hush, dearling, hush. Tell me what's wrong, and I'll mend it, see that all is well.''

Gillian felt wrapped about with her cousin's love and care, and sobbed all the harder at the uncommon sensation. ''You cannot mend this,'' she whispered.

''Is it so bad, then?'' Catrin asked against the mass of Gillian's hair. ''Rannulf loves you, 'tis clear enough to see. He would never hurt you or do you harm. Come, tell me and I'll go speak with him.''

''There's naught you can do,'' Gillian told her, pulling away from her cousin. ''Whatever Rannulf felt for me is long gone.''

Catrin stood and smoothed her skirts. ''How can you say that? I saw for myself this very day how he looks at you.''

Gillian snuffed out the tiny flicker of hope kindled

in her heart by Catrin's words before it could take root and torment her more. "Don't confuse lust with love, Catrin," she said. "I made that mistake once." Rising, she poured a cup of mead from the ewer on the table and handed it to Catrin. Several deep breaths gave her the opportunity to calm herself, to ease her shaking hands and pounding heart. More composed, she filled a mug for herself and drank deeply of the sweet brew. "I don't intend to make it again."

Her cousin thumped down her drink untasted and took a step toward Gillian, her gaze fixed on Gillian's face. "What do you mean?"

Lying to Catrin would be next to impossible, 'twas clear, but she had to try, for if Catrin decided to take Rannulf to task, there'd be no stopping her.

And Catrin in a temper was more than she could bear to face at the moment.

Gillian placed her mug on the table, took up her hairbrush and resumed her seat on the stool. "I simply mean that I believed Rannulf loved me long ago, when I was too young and ignorant to know any better." She worked the brush through a tangle, making it appear her attention was focused upon the task, rather than the storm of anger she could see brewing on her cousin's face. "Now, with the passage of time, I see nothing but lust in his eyes when he looks at me." She paused, glanced up and held her gaze steady as she met the questions in Catrin's eyes. "'Tis nothing more than that. Watch him when next we meet—you'll see it for yourself."

The sound Catrin made in response was as insulting as a curse. "Do you believe I'm a fool?" she demanded. "I've already seen how he looks at you. Aye, there's lust in his eyes." Hands on her hips, she paced around the table, stopping before the hearth and whirling to face Gillian. "And why shouldn't there be? You're lovely, desirable—and he is a normal man, I assume. Jesu save us, I'd be more surprised if I *didn't* see lust in his eyes when he looks at you."

"There, you see—"

"I see far more than you wish me to, I warrant. What I noticed at dinner today was two fools too proud—too stupid, more like—to reveal what they feel for each other. Those feelings were clear enough to me, however."

"You're mistaken. You don't understand how it was…how it is between us." *And please don't make me explain,* Gillian pleaded silently. *How can I admit what a fool I was? The fool I still am, if truth be told?*

Something of her thoughts must have shone in her face, for Catrin's eyes narrowed and her expression grew more determined than before as she stalked around the table.

She halted in front of Gillian, hands still on her hips, and huffed out a breath. "Tell me you didn't do what I think you did," she said, low-voiced.

Gillian's pulse quickened, though she remained outwardly calm—no shaking, at least—as she adopted an arrogant pose. "I don't know what you mean." But she could not withstand the weight of Catrin's knowing stare; she lowered her gaze and rose, going to tend the fire so she could turn away and hide her cowardice.

It made no difference. "Don't think you can escape me so easily," Catrin said, following her and taking her by the arm. "You might as well face me, cousin, for I'll not stop until you give me the answers I seek."

Gillian stirred the fire with the poker, then dropped it to clatter against the hearthstones as she shrugged free of Catrin's hold and rose to face her. "What if I tell you 'tis no business of yours? Will you let me be? Or will you hammer away at me until I admit my sin to you?" Her heart pounding wildly in her ears, she choked back a sob and looked her cousin in the eyes. "Aye, Catrin, I did exactly what you suspect I did four years ago. Rannulf told me he loved me, wanted me for his wife. It was my heart's desire. So I gave myself to him, body and soul." At Catrin's gasp, she added, "And I've spent the time since— since he left me without another word—wishing I could repent my sin, but I cannot." A tear traced a warm path down her cheek. "Because, despite all that's happened since, I fear I'd do it again in an instant, should he but ask me to."

Chapter Twelve

Rannulf slipped from the dim hallway filled with late-afternoon shadows into his darkened chamber and slumped back against the door for a moment. Christ's bones, but he'd no stomach for doing this work here! he thought, straightening and unbuckling his sword belt.

Always before he'd enjoyed the thrill of ferreting out information, of being Pembroke's eyes and ears, traveling about where Pembroke could not go. It had been the perfect occupation for him after he'd abandoned all hope of a life with Gillian.

After he'd killed his father.

He gave a weary sigh. What had he left to lose at that point, after all? His life had been worthless once his father was gone, not that he'd ever been any kind of a father to him or Connor. But 'twas by his hand that Bertram FitzClifford had met his well-deserved death, a death Rannulf had had no right to mete out.

And afterward, his mother disappeared into the fastness of the convent—never to leave it, for all he knew. Her loss pained him deeply, as did that of his brother, Connor...his twin, the better part of him, with his quiet ways and lack of temper.

He'd naught but his own temper to blame for the break with Connor, to his shame, but he hadn't a clue how to go about mending the breach, assuming Connor could ever forgive him for all he'd said and done.

But more and more of late he'd felt he had to try. Before he'd left London for l'Eau Clair he'd sent a messenger to Connor at FitzClifford. Though he had no skill with words, he'd written from the depths of his soul, hoping Connor would understand.

Giving up Gillian had been a natural extension of it all, for how could a man who'd killed his own father—destroyed his family—expect the same joys a better man might have? Wife, family, love and hope? All gone now, and no one's fault but his own.

All he could do now was to make amends for his sins, if that were possible, before God saw fit to send him on his way to another version of hell.

"I was beginning to wonder if you'd found yourself a warm and willing wench and disappeared for the night," Ian said from the chair beside the cold hearth. Rannulf caught his breath in surprise, though he should have expected this visit. Ian would want to know why Rannulf was really here, what Pembroke was about.

They'd dealt together often enough over the past few years. Rannulf knew the Dragon as well as anyone knew him, save for Catrin and Gillian, perhaps. He *did* know that Ian would not care to remain in ignorance for long.

Flint struck steel with a snap, kindling a spark, then a candlewick. The growing flame illuminated Ian's face, lending a satiric cast to his features. "Or is my cousin still your heart's desire?'' he asked, his voice as cold as the emerald glow of his eyes.

It appeared Ian knew him as well, unfortunately. Read him too well. So far as Rannulf could recall, he'd never revealed his feelings for Gillian to her kinsman.

'Twas just as well he had not, for 'twas clear the idea found no favor with Ian.

He set down his sword on the bed, then turned to his uninvited guest. ''I wondered how long 'twould be before you sought me out,'' he said, his steady voice revealing nothing. He took a candle from the tall stand beside the bed and went to light it from the one Ian had kindled. ''I should have realized you wouldn't wait long.''

''I doubted you'd be in any hurry to tell me what you're doing here, with Gillian.''

''I'm not here for Gillian's sake.'' The truth, so far as it went.

''I'm pleased to hear you admit it.'' The chair creaked as Ian shifted in his seat. ''You don't belong anywhere near her, FitzClifford.''

''I'm here by Pembroke's command, for no other reason,'' he snarled. ''Do you think I'd inflict myself upon her otherwise?'' Hot tallow dripped on his hand; with a muttered curse he crossed to the stand and thrust the candle onto the pricket, then shook his hand to cool it. ''I know as well as you do that I'm not fit company for her.''

''See that you don't forget it,'' Ian snapped.

''I'm sure you'll remind me if I do,'' Rannulf replied, his tone as cold as Ian's. He took up the candle and lit the remaining tapers on the stand, filling the chamber with a warm glow at odds with the chilly atmosphere between him and Ian. Sinking down onto the bed, he set his head in his hands for a moment, closed his eyes and prayed for patience—with Ian, and with himself. After a moment he looked up at the other man. ''I'd have stayed away if I could,'' he said quietly. ''But Pembroke needs me here, for reasons that have nothing to do with her, as far as I know. I prayed I'd never have to see her again. This is pure hell for me, I assure you.''

Ian raised a drinking horn to his lips, watching Rannulf over the rim of his drink, his eyes measuring, weighing the truth of Rannulf's words. ''Do not hurt her more,'' he warned. ''Else I'll see to it you pay with your life.''

Rannulf nodded. ''I'd hand you the knife myself.''

He would, too, to save Gillian from harm. His life for hers. 'Twas an exchange he'd make gladly.

''You're here to watch Talbot, I assume?'' Ian asked.

''Aye.'' Rannulf rose and went to open the window shutters, breathing deeply of the cool, fresh air. ''He's become close to the king in a short time, and although he claims that John sent him here as punishment for some misdeed, Pembroke—and others—don't believe it. Despite the fact that the king has disposed of boon companions as easily and more permanently before, no one could discover that Talbot did anything amiss.''

''It may be naught but a ruse,'' Ian suggested. ''An excuse to send him here. Although Gillian told me she *did* send a message to the king after Lord Simon died, asking for his help.'' He paused, drummed his fingers on the arm of the chair. ''The timing *is* convenient, though.''

Rannulf thrust a hand through his hair and spun to face Ian. "You've seen Talbot. He's so precise, so perfect, I'm tempted to push him, see how far I can go before he breaks down and does something human," he said with disgust. "And when I find him watching Gillian…"

"He watches her the way any man would watch a beautiful woman," Ian told him. His wry tone caught Rannulf's attention as much as his words. "In fact, you'd best pray he never catches *you* watching her in an unguarded moment. Face it, FitzClifford. You're jealous."

"That's ridiculous." He turned back toward the window, as much to hide his flushed face as to let the slight breeze cool it. "I didn't see you looking at her that way."

Ian chuckled. "She's my kin, if you've forgotten. I'd no more feel lust for Gillian than I would for my own sister. Besides, in my mind she's still the same scrappy, smudge-faced brat in braes that she was before Simon let Lady Alys take her in hand to make a lady of her."

Rannulf's blood cooled. "She's still that, but there's so much more to her now."

"I know." Ian took another sip of his drink. "But you need not list her virtues, for I know them well. Besides," he added with a taunting grin, "I've no desire to sit here listening to the maundering of a love-struck fool. Tell me about Talbot instead."

Aye, 'twould be a relief to change the subject, for he found Ian's insistence upon bringing his feelings for Gillian, past and present, into the conversation an annoyance. It would be a relief to discuss Talbot with Ian, to hear his opinion of what Rannulf had discovered thus far. He drew a stool closer to Ian's chair, sat down and began to share what he'd learned.

His arms filled with a bundle of Lord Nicholas's shirts bound for the laundry, Richard made his way down the steep spiral stairs, his attention fixed yet again on the fine position he'd held in London, far away from this barbaric backwater. He'd been the personal manservant to a wealthy merchant awash with ambition to buy his way into the nobility. 'Twas a snug berth, and he'd believed a secure one as well, for his master had been so busy currying favor, he'd scarce a spare moment to notice what his servants had been up to in his absence.

How were they to know they'd a spy in their midst? Richard's booted feet pounded harder against the stone steps as his ire grew. And the traitor little more than the meanest churl in the place, emptying slops and scouring pots, watching and listening all the while, as it turned out, for juicy tidbits to feed the master.

The sly bastard! Evidently he'd kept closer watch than any of them had suspected; he'd known every detail of the scheme the upper servants had hatched to skim money from the household expenses. He'd even known about Richard's private arrangements to trade some of the master's fine clothes in exchange for little luxuries for himself.

The lot of them had been tossed out in the street with nothing but the clothes on their backs—and in Richard's case, the master had examined him from head to toe first, to be certain he'd stolen nothing more.

He'd been lucky to escape with his life—cold comfort when he'd had nowhere to go.

It had been a stroke of good fortune that brought him to Talbot's notice, or so he'd believed at the time. Of course, by then he'd been desperate for a roof over his head and a crust to eat. How was he to know that in a matter of months they'd fetch up here, in a crude wilderness filled with coarse, ill-clothed louts who believed they were noble?

And the mistress of this place… She bore little resemblance to any noblewoman he'd ever seen! Ladies did not carry swords, or dirty their hands by laboring alongside their servants. And any true lady would have recognized Richard for the superior servant he was, he thought bitterly, instead of ordering him about as though he were nothing more than a lowly scullion.

Still seething, Richard rounded the corner at the foot of the stairs and slammed headlong into the woman coming the other way. They collided with enough force to slam them both to the floor, their burdens scattering around them like leaves in the wind.

"You should watch where you're going, you great lout!" she gasped. Dark eyes flashing, she squirmed beneath him, her ample body cushioning him in all the right places and sending a lightning bolt of fire rushing straight to his loins.

"Have a care who you call a lout, wench." He tightened his arms about her and pressed himself against her belly.

Her eyes and body softened, and her hands slid down his back to press him more firmly against her. "I always did have a soft spot for a man who's ready for battle," she murmured, her voice a throaty purr. "Could be you're not so bad after all."

Lost to any thought but that of the woman beneath him, Richard ground his mouth against hers and thrust his tongue between her lips to duel with hers, his groan of pleasure rising to echo her breathy moans.

Mayhap this place wasn't so bad after all.

Gillian descended the stairs slowly, her mind still focused upon her conversation—or should she call it a confrontation?—with Catrin. Though she hadn't kept her cousin from learning something of her former relationship with Rannulf, at least she'd managed to escape without revealing everything. How could she share with her Welsh kin the words Rannulf had penned on the betrothal agreement—that he believed her Welsh blood tainted and unfit to join with his? Evidently she'd been good enough to dally with, but not to wed. If Catrin didn't strike him down for the insult, Ian surely would once he heard of it.

He'd not learn of it from her.

She nearly trod upon the couple writhing on the landing before their passionate moans broke through her preoccupation. Halting beside them, she grabbed the man by the hair and gave a sharp tug. "Get off her at once!" she demanded.

Richard, Talbot's manservant, rolled aside, revealing Marged, one of the new maids she'd brought in to help in the keep since Talbot's arrival. The woman lay sprawled on the stone floor, shirts and apples scattered everywhere, her headrail askew about her rosy face and her skirts rucked up above her knees.

Clearly neither of them had any sense of decency,

or of propriety, at any rate. "I will not tolerate such goings-on in my hall!"

Marged rose slowly to her feet without any offer of assistance from her erstwhile lover. Richard, his face twisted once again into his usual expression of distaste, merely lounged back against the plastered wall. "Beg pardon, milady," Marged said quietly, dropping a respectful curtsy. "It'll not happen again, I swear it."

It would happen again where she'd not catch them at it, more like, Gillian thought wryly. Still, as long as they indulged their passions elsewhere, beyond the common view and in their free time, there was little she could do to prevent them.

But she could make them pay for today's transgression. "If you wish to behave as animals, you shall be punished accordingly." She resisted the temptation to fist her hands upon her hips like the village alewife and instead straightened her spine and, recalling Lady Alys's training, assumed the pose of a proud dame pronouncing judgment. "Marged, you may feed and care for the swine and geese for the next few days."

"Yes, milady." Her voice resigned, her face sullen, the maid bobbed another curtsy and bent to gather the apples into her apron.

"And you, Richard, shall lend your assistance in the stables mucking out the stalls once your duties for your master are through each day."

"For how long, milady?" he asked. "My master's needs must come first, of course." She caught a glimpse of his hatred-filled glare before he hid it behind a mask of servility.

Did he think to bend her to his will? She'd show

him his error, wipe that smug expression from his eyes. "Until I tell you otherwise."

"As you wish, milady," he said evenly, his bow so deep as to be an insult.

"You may be sure Lord Nicholas shall hear of your misdeeds," she told him, her voice cold. She cast a haughty glance about her. "Clear away this clutter," she told them. "Then go about your business."

She stayed to make certain they did her bidding. "Remember what I said," she warned them once they'd finished. "I'll be watching you both."

Eager to escape them—eager to escape all the troubles she'd had to face of late—Gillian swept out of the stairwell and into the hall without another word.

"Arrogant bitch," Richard muttered after Lady Gillian left, then thought better of his comment. Insulting the mistress was no way to endear himself to the maid, and he did want the maid. He braced his shoulders against the wall and enjoyed the view as Marged stooped and bent to gather the apples that had rolled about the landing.

He smiled, remembering the feel of her welcoming body cushioning his, pressed beneath him. Aye, she was a tempting armful, and he'd no intention of allowing the Lady Gillian's dictates to interfere with his pleasure.

Marged straightened and sidled closer to him, her eyes alight with resentment. "Aye, she's a haughty dame now, but she won't be so high-and-mighty once—" She slapped a hand over her mouth, nearly dropping the apples gathered in her apron. Face pale, she looked away from him.

He grabbed her by the chin and made her face him. "Here now, none of that!" He bent and took her mouth fast and hard to get her attention. The feel of her got his attention, too, but he thrust aside the desire to push her up against the wall and finish what they'd started and growled, "What were you saying?"

A hunted look crossed her face, filled her eyes. "Nay, I must not," she whispered. "I did not mean to—"

He kissed her again and drew away gasping. She'd a talent for the sport, a skill he'd never before encountered. "Meet me in the stables after supper tonight." He glanced over his shoulder to make certain no one was about. "If the bitch wants me out there, I'll obey her in that." He snaked his arm around Marged's waist and pulled her close. "But the only work I plan to do is this." He ground his body hard against her belly, until her eyes drifted closed.

"Tonight," she murmured. Her eyes opened. "I've plenty to share with you tonight."

He let her slip away. Aye, tonight she'd give him everything he wanted of her, he thought, smiling. And once he'd had his fill of her, she'd be his to use as he wished.

His smile widening, he bent and snatched Lord Nicholas's shirts off the floor. This might require some planning, but Marged looked to be a resourceful wench. Mayhap together they might send Lady Gillian toppling from her lofty perch.

He'd taken enough orders over the years from those who thought themselves his betters.

He'd follow their dictates no more.

Chapter Thirteen

Gillian stared out over the sun-bright bailey, at the puddles shimmering amidst the churned-up sea of mud, and sighed. Two days of rain, an unremitting deluge, seemed to have transformed all within and without the keep into snarling, short-tempered idiots.

Herself included.

And now her cousins were preparing to leave. Though she hated to see them go, she could not deny she felt relieved.

She glanced at Catrin, who stood beside her at the head of the outside stairway leading from the keep to the bailey, and bit back another sigh. Catrin had been one of the worst instigators, though 'twas doubtful the rain had anything to do with her behavior. Her cousin had seemed determined to stir up everyone's tempers with her taunts and teasing. Rannulf had avoided Catrin—avoided them all at every opportunity, from what she could see—and Catrin had driven Ian into a silence even more profound than his usual close-mouthed manner. Only she and Talbot were on speaking terms with Catrin, she because she'd little choice, and Lord Nicholas… She glanced down to where he stood at the foot of the stairs, deep in conversation with Rannulf. 'Twas anyone's guess why her guardian continued to treat Catrin with a courtesy she'd done little to deserve.

She hadn't any idea what had prompted Catrin to such madness. Though Catrin's quick temper—and sharp tongue—were well-known, 'twas unusual for her to ignore Gillian's requests to cease.

Especially under the circumstances. Catrin knew how difficult it was for Gillian to manage with Rannulf here, while also trying to keep their secrets from Lord Nicholas. Yet her cousin had maintained a steady verbal assault upon them all, leaving Gillian feeling more drained and overwrought than before her cousins' arrival.

She glanced at Catrin from the corner of her eye, and saw how attentively Catrin followed Lord Nicholas's every move.

Why hadn't she noticed before now the spark in Catrin's eyes whenever she looked at him? Although Gillian had never seen Catrin thus, she would have sworn 'twas passion or desire that lent that smoky glow to her cousin's eyes.

Could Catrin be interested in Lord Nicholas?

Gillian struggled to suppress a grin at the recognition of an all-too-human trait in her iron-willed cousin. Catrin claimed to have no use for men. How, then, did Catrin dare to trust Rannulf, Gillian wondered, when she—who loved him still, God help her—could not bring herself to do so?

Because Catrin didn't know everything she did about Rannulf. She didn't know him the way Gillian did.

Or did Catrin know Rannulf better than she? Catrin

viewed him through eyes untainted by the past, and free of the glow—or was it the tarnish?—lost love lent to the eyes of the lover.

'Twas enough to drive her mad! She thrust those thoughts into the back of her mind and returned her attention to the scene playing out before her.

If Catrin found Talbot attractive, it might explain why she'd sniped and gibed at him constantly since she'd arrived, many of her comments to him scarcely civil.

Her discourtesy caught his attention, however. Mayhap that had been Catrin's goal all along, whether she realized it or not.

Gillian turned her thoughts to her guardian's behavior, observing him and her cousin all the while. Lord Nicholas had maintained a surprisingly good humor though Catrin beset him at every turn.

Her cousin was beautiful, and mayhap Talbot found Catrin's fiery manner more appealing than appalling. She saw that he glanced at Catrin near as often as she did at him, though they were both quite skilled at disguising their interest.

Rannulf and Lord Nicholas headed across the bailey toward the gatehouse, picking their way through the muck, talking all the while. Catrin started down the stairs and whistled for Idris, her massive wolfhound, to join her.

The dog raced toward them from the stables, running fast and surefooted through the mud and splashing anyone unfortunate enough to be in his path. Before he reached them, a startled maidservant gave a terrified shriek and slipped, falling flat on her back in a filthy puddle.

"Catrin, make him stop!" Gillian shouted as Idris

began to dash about the bailey again. Mud flew everywhere as he barked and gamboled from person to person. "Idris, enough!" The beast ignored her.

Catrin gave a delighted laugh as the dog crashed into Talbot's servant, Richard, as he walked out of the stables. A spray of dirty water flew up in his face; he tripped and fell, upsetting the basket he'd been carrying—filled with filth from the stables—and spilling its foul contents over him from head to toe.

Gillian hurried down the stairs after Catrin and grabbed her by the arm. "Stop him now, Catrin—please." Not waiting to see if her cousin obeyed her, Gillian hoisted her skirts up above the muck and gingerly began to make her way across the bailey toward the dog.

Idris ignored Richard and romped over to the gatehouse, where a number of Talbot's and Rannulf's men had gathered with Ian's troops. Intent upon preventing another mishap, Gillian shifted direction midway across the sea of mud, nearly losing a boot in the process, and tried to place herself in the dog's path to distract him.

"I swear, Catrin, if he knocks me over, I'll have his hide for a carpet," she threatened, provoking a wave of laughter from the crowd. Undaunted, Idris continued to play. "I'll place him right before the fire in the hall, where I can tread upon him often." She tugged her foot free of the sucking mud yet again. "Starting today, I believe."

"If you insist," Catrin said, exasperation tingeing her voice. She gave a sharp whistle and the dog ran to join her, sides heaving and tongue hanging out.

Gillian turned her back on Catrin and her hound of Satan and concentrated on keeping her footing as she made her way to the stone-flagged area in front of the gate.

Lord Nicholas started toward her. "Wait, milady—let me come and get you."

"Nay, I'm nearly there," she said, lengthening her stride with care. "There's no need for you to play the gallant, milord, lest we both end up in the muck." She'd rather take her chances on her own, than be at fault should she cause them to fall. Lord Nicholas's costly clothes would never survive such a dunking.

She thought for a moment that he'd come after her anyway, but he gave a shrug and awaited her at the edge of the paving stones, hands outstretched to assist her.

"Thank you, milord." She took his hand gratefully, for without his support, she knew she'd have landed face first at his feet. She'd scarce set her mud-encrusted boots on the cobbles and stepped away from him when a great cry rose from the men gathered nearby.

Glancing over her shoulder, she jumped aside just as Idris shot past her and leapt onto Talbot, sending man and dog to the ground.

Dirty clothes were the least of Lord Nicholas's worries at the moment, for Idris, usually a gentle beast, stood atop Talbot's chest and held him pinned to the ground, his massive jaws spread wide at her guardian's throat.

Bending, Gillian clutched the dog's studded collar in both hands and tugged, but to no avail. Idris likely weighed more than she, and she was no match for him in strength. "Rannulf, come help me," she gasped.

But Idris would have none of it, growling deep in

his throat as soon as Rannulf reached for his collar.
Hands held out at his sides, Rannulf backed away and
shook his head.

Gillian ceased tugging and looked behind her for
her cousin. Catrin remained standing at the foot of the
stairs, arms folded at her waist, one corner of her
mouth quirked up in amusement.

A wave of anger washed through Gillian, heating
her blood and her temper. She'd had more than
enough trouble from Catrin, and she'd not stand for
any more. "Catrin!" she shrieked, letting go of the
dog and stepping carefully around her guardian's motionless form. She started toward her. "Haven't you
caused enough problems already?"

Both her feet slid out from under her; she let out a
screech as a pair of strong arms wrapped about her
waist from behind.

Rannulf jumped forward in time to catch Gillian,
swinging her up and into his arms, heedless of her
filthy boots flailing against his legs. Grinning at the
temper in her eyes—and at the sight of his overlord
still lying prone beneath the wolfhound, if truth be
told—he pivoted and set her on her feet on the cobbles.

As soon as he released her, she tried to slip past
him to go after her cousin again, but he caught her
about the waist and slung her over his shoulder. "Stay
put," he warned her. He pressed one hand flat upon
her backside, the fact of so many watchful eyes all
around them reason enough to resist the temptation to
stroke those delectable curves.

If he should be foolish enough to try.

"Put me down," she muttered in his ear. "And
take your hand from my…"

He chuckled, low enough so the others wouldn't hear. "You never used to be so proper."

"That was before I met you." She reached up and behind her, trying to grab his hair, but he raised an eyebrow and caught her hand. She tried to tug free. "I've learned any number of things since then, not all of them good."

At least she hadn't claimed all of it was bad.

He noticed movement on the landing; Ian started down the stairs from the keep and strode toward his sister. He caught Catrin from behind, pinned her arms to her sides and let out a shrill whistle.

Idris ignored the summons.

Talbot gave a muffled cough and the dog growled. "Could someone get him off me?" he wheezed. Rannulf stepped closer; the dog's teeth pressed harder against Talbot's throat.

"Call him," Ian ordered, his voice like ice.

Lady Catrin frowned, but did as she was bidden. As soon as her whistle cut through the air, Idris stepped off Talbot's chest and abandoned his victim without a backward glance as he ambled to his mistress's side and sat down beside her.

Rannulf set Gillian gently on her feet and sent her a saucy smile in response to her furious glare. He couldn't help himself—her eyes sparkled with temper, color rode high on her cheeks, and she looked so beautiful in the sunlight, 'twas beyond his will to resist.

Talbot stood and made a useless attempt to brush the mud from his ruined clothes. The look he turned Lady Catrin's way now had nothing of the courtier in it.

Evidently his overlord was as capable of foolishness over a woman as any man, Rannulf thought, for who but a fool would take as much abuse from a woman as Talbot had from Lady Catrin and not choose to ignore her completely?

Though from the look of it, that was about to change.

Ian leaned down and spoke to his sister, his words inaudible but his anger clear enough. She shook her head sharply, but allowed him to swing her into his arms. He carried her across the bailey as though the slick mud did not exist and lowered her to her feet before Talbot.

Fury shone from the Dragon's eyes, but his face wore its usual unruffled expression and his voice was calm. "My apologies, milord, for my sister's ill manners." He clapped his hand over her mouth to muffle her angry shriek and continued, "I hope you won't bar us from visiting Gillian because of it."

Lady Catrin's eyes fairly shot sparks, but Ian kept her under control, and Talbot ignored her attempted outburst.

Talbot squared his shoulders and nodded. "Of course not, milord. You are welcome here at any time." He bowed politely to Lady Catrin. "And I hope you'll be in a better mood when next you visit us, milady." Her glare intensified. "But I trust you'll choose to leave yon beast elsewhere," he said with a nod toward Idris, seated calmly by the waiting horses. "I wish you a safe journey."

"Thank you," Ian said. "Send FitzClifford to me if you have further problems with raids, and I'll see what I can do to help."

Rannulf bowed in acknowledgment, although he

was surprised that Ian had gone so far as to mention him specifically. 'Twas unlike him.

Perhaps his sister's actions had rattled his composure. Rannulf glanced at her as she said goodbye to Gillian, both of them looking uncomfortable, their words stilted. He'd never met a woman as unpredictable as Lady Catrin; he couldn't imagine what Talbot had seen in her. She could be good-hearted and kind one moment, as changeable as a spoiled child the next.

But she *was* lovely.

Perhaps to a man like Nicholas Talbot that was all that mattered.

Ian hoisted Lady Catrin onto her waiting horse, swung onto his own mount, waved and led his party out through the open gate. Rannulf felt an immediate rise in the tension that had pressed upon him since his arrival at l'Eau Clair...since he'd first learned from Talbot that they'd be traveling there, in fact. Ian was not his friend, but they were allies of a sort.

Talbot gave a gusty sigh and turned to Gillian. "Will you accept my help now, milady?" He eyed his filthy clothes, his smile rueful. "I'll not offer to carry you back across, but I can lend you my support." He held out his arm. "Unless you'd rather Rannulf carted you over like a sack of grain." He glanced from Gillian to Rannulf, his gaze curious, measuring. "'Tis less elegant, but more effective, I'd imagine."

What did he mean by that look?

When neither of them made a move to do as he'd suggested, it seemed to Rannulf that his curious gaze intensified. "Come, FitzClifford, surely you've manners enough to help a lady."

Rannulf looked at Talbot again—really looked at him, past the fine clothes and polished air—and realized that the expression in his overlord's eyes, the man peering out at him, didn't match that elegant shell at all.

Talbot's arm dropped to his side just as Gillian reached for it, and he shook his head. "Nay, Lady Gillian, I'll only get you as dirty as I am. Go with FitzClifford."

Gillian's face matched Catrin's for stubbornness. "I need no help getting across my own bailey, milord, though I thank you for the offer. I'm used to fending for myself." She dropped a swift curtsy, turned on her heel and left before either man could do aught but stare after her.

In two long strides Rannulf caught up to her, grasped her about the middle and tossed her over his shoulder. "Is this necessary?" she asked, sounding short of breath. He shifted her into his arms in a tangle of loosened hair and trailing fabric. She tore off her veil and shoved her hair from her face, revealing her eyes glowing hot with anger. "Or is this simply some crude male ritual to show me who really holds power over me?"

He ran lightly up the stairs to the keep and swept through the doorway—out of Talbot's view—before setting her on her feet in the hall with a flourishing bow. Her guardian wasn't the only man here with manners. "It's been a pleasure, milady."

"I fear I cannot say the same," she muttered. Before his curious gaze she seemed to grow weary, her shoulders hunched, the glow in her eyes replaced with a tired resignation.

Conscious of the occasional servant passing

through the hall, he moved a step closer to Gillian. "What is it?" he asked, teasing bravado replaced with sincere concern for her. "What's wrong?"

She shook her head and looked past him, but her eyes appeared unfocused, unseeing. "Go on, you've done as your master ordered." She waved him away. "'Tis nothing," she said when he wouldn't leave. "I'm just tired, nothing more."

The circles beneath her eyes attested to the truth of her words, but the shadows lurking within her eyes revealed a weariness of the spirit as well as the body. Never had he seen Gillian appear so disheartened.

"Come to the pool with me," he offered impulsively. "'Tis quiet there, and no one can bother you. I'll leave you alone, if you wish. I could guard you while you rest."

A glimmer of eagerness shone on her face, but she shook her head. "I've too much to do."

"You've always too much to do—'tis part of the problem." He reached for her hand, then released it when boots thumped against the stairs outside.

"Besides, what would Lord Nicholas think if he discovered we rode out there again? I know he learned nothing of the raiders the other day, and it's been quiet of late. But still, if we leave he's bound to be suspicious, and you don't want—" She broke off as raised voices sounded on the other side of the door. Before they could move away, the footsteps faded as the speakers went back down the stairs.

Despite her protests, he could see she was tempted to agree. Coming to a decision, he took a deep breath, clasped her hand firmly in his and drew her across the hall and into the shadow-filled area at the far end beyond the dais. He paused only to snatch an unlit candle from a stand near the table and tuck it into his belt.

"Rannulf!" she whispered frantically. "What are you doing? That must have been Talbot on the stairs. He'll be back at any moment—what if he sees us?"

"Don't worry." Glancing around to make certain they were alone, he led her into a seldom-used narrow corridor, lifted the edge of a long, faded wall hanging and stepped behind it, pulling her in after him. The musty fabric settled back into place behind them, enclosing them in a dark cocoon.

"If this is some trick to get me alone, I'll—"

He covered her mouth with his hand. "Hush," he whispered. "Give me a moment, and you'll understand the reason I brought you here." Leaning closer to her ear, he added, "Not that I don't enjoy being alone with you."

She growled against his fingers. Chuckling quietly, he reluctantly let his hand slip away.

Rannulf held his free hand out in front of them until his questing fingers encountered the smooth wooden edge of a window seat.

"What is this?" Gillian asked as she reached past him and ran her hand along the outline of the embrasure.

"There used to be a window here, but 'twas walled up before the castle was completed." He felt beneath the carved end of the seat until his fingers encountered the mechanism hidden there. A firm push against the lever unlatched the bench; Rannulf lifted it up and eased it back to rest against the wall behind it. "I believe your father feared if this embrasure was open and in use, its secrets would be too easily discovered."

Letting go of her hand, he removed flint and steel from the pouch on his belt and fumbled to kindle the wick. Once it caught fire, he held up the light and gestured toward the dark opening in the embrasure. He climbed over the edge into the chestlike frame of the seat and stood on the top step of the stairs inside. "Shall we go, milady?" he asked as he held out his hand to assist Gillian.

She paused in the act of placing her hand in his, her palm poised just above his, then snatched it away. "Should I trust you?"

He drew in a deep breath. "In this, you may."

The flickering light cast long shadows in the close space, highlighting her uncertain expression. "This leads outside, I take it?"

"Aye. 'Tis a passageway to the pool."

"I never knew this was here. How did *you* learn of it?"

He glanced away for a moment, then met her questioning gaze. "From your father. The last time I came to l'Eau Clair, he shared its secrets with me."

Chapter Fourteen

Rannulf's words sent a wave of betrayal through Gillian, thrusting into her heart like a knife.

How could her father have told Rannulf, but not his own daughter? He could have told her any time in the past few years, or barring that, before he died. His death had not been sudden; he could have let her know....

If he'd wanted to.

The fact that he'd revealed the existence of this passageway to Rannulf—and who knew what else? a sad voice in her mind asked—exposed her father's plans to her as clearly as if he'd blazoned them on the curtain wall for all to see. He'd believed Rannulf FitzClifford would wed her, be the son he'd never had, protect and defend what he'd labored so long to establish—the powerful Marcher keep of l'Eau Clair.

What else had her father concealed from her?

What else did Rannulf know about her home, her family, that she did not?

An insidious little voice in her mind taunted her. What if the words Rannulf had penned on the betrothal contract were true?

Her heartbeat skipped at the implications of that thought, at the complications that might tear her plans for a future, for children of her own, into shreds, though she knew in her heart that what Rannulf had claimed was naught but a foul lie.

"We cannot stay here all day," Rannulf whispered. He reached out and took her hand, leaving her little choice but to go with him. "Come on."

Despite the pain weighing her down, she couldn't suppress an overwhelming curiosity about the passageway. As a child she and her playmates—her father's pages, mostly—had explored l'Eau Clair from towers to cellar vaults, yet never had they discovered anything like this.

She gathered up her skirts in one hand, tightened her grasp on Rannulf's warm, callused palm and climbed over the front of the seat onto steep wooden stairs.

"Let me go down first," he said once she'd balanced herself on the first tread. "It's little more than a ladder, and there's nothing to hold on to."

Leaning her back against the inside of the "chest," Gillian watched as he swiftly descended the ladder, the candle flame steady, his steps sure.

How she missed her boyish garb, especially in situations such as this! Her women's clothing, with its long, trailing sleeves and skirts, seemed designed to trip her up or pin her down. Although wearing proper attire made her more aware that she was a woman, at times she longed for the freedom of movement she'd once had.

In Rannulf's presence, she'd be glad of anything that helped her *forget* she was a woman, for he reminded her of that fact far too often—and too easily.

He moved a few paces down the narrow corridor, his light revealing a short, fat candle stub on a pricket in the wall. A swipe of his hand cleared away its shroud of cobwebs before he lit the wick. A shudder slithered down her back as she considered what might dwell there.

She hoped the passage wasn't very long, although she knew it had to be, to come out near the pool. No matter—she'd simply walk as fast as possible. Rannulf could lead or follow, she didn't care which, as long as they made the journey quickly.

He dripped hot wax onto a tiny ledge near the stairs and stuck his candle in it. "Here, let me help you." He reached up, clasped her about the waist and eased her down to the floor.

His strength still amazed her, though he would have to be strong, to fight while garbed from head to toe in mail, to wield a sword for hours on end. Though she'd a modest skill at swordplay, she hadn't the endurance to fight for long.

More amazing still was the thrill that raced through her when he lifted her so easily or showed his strength in other ways. He had the ability to snap her in two, yet he could also be gentle, tender, kind.

In spite of the walls that stood between them, she knew he would never physically harm her.

She realized she stood staring into his eyes, her hands still grasping his shoulders. Lowering her hands, she broke the spell that held them both.

"Ready?" he asked.

At her nod, he took her hand once again and placed it in the crook of his elbow, picked up his candle and led her through the passageway.

She scarce noticed their surroundings. Rannulf

must have realized how uncomfortable she felt in the narrow darkness, for he distracted her with a humorous tale of leprechauns and fairies. He kept his sword at the ready, brandishing it before them to remove any cobwebs in their path.

The candle flickered in a draft, and the muffled sound of running water caught her attention just as he tried to convince her that the passageway was inhabited by the elfin creatures.

"I don't believe a word of it," she told him, laughing still at the antics he'd described.

"Hush, you'll scare them away." He leaned close to whisper, "They're really very shy, you know."

The noise grew louder and muted light glowed up ahead. The pathway rose steeply, to emerge into a shallow cave edged with tumbled boulders. Rannulf extinguished the candle and set it near the end of the passageway.

Gillian moved past him to the mouth of the cave, gasping at the beauty surrounding them. Sunlight streamed through the falling water, bathing them in soft light and a fine mist. Swaths of green showed through—the plants growing down the rock-strewn hillside, no doubt—and the air bore the scent of rich soil and sweet flowers.

It smelled of life.

She spun to face Rannulf. "How lovely! But can we get out of here without getting wet?"

"You mean you don't want to end up in the pool like we did the last time we were here?" He grinned, his dark eyes warm, inviting her to join in his amusement.

"'Twould make our skulking through the tunnel all for naught, for I'm sure we'd have to explain ourselves this time.'' Pushing up her sleeve, she stuck her hand into the shimmering stream of water and scooped some toward her mouth.

Cool and sweet, it tasted heavenly. She cupped her hand for more, less careful this time, and it trickled over her chin and dripped onto the bodice of her bliaut. A shiver raced over her but, ignoring the cold wet spots it made on the light brown linen, she filled her palm with more and held it out to Rannulf. ''Have some—it's wonderful.''

He cradled her hand in his and raised it to his mouth. His gaze held hers captive as he drank, magnifying the sensation of his warm lips against her cool skin. Dragging his tongue over the well of her palm, he finished the water. ''Delicious,'' he murmured, then trailed his tongue to her wrist to place a lingering kiss there.

She could not breathe or think, nor could she snatch her hand away as she knew she should. It seemed her heart ceased beating in her chest as they remained frozen in place, in time.

His eyes made such promises as they stood there—of pleasure, certainly, but so much more. How could she mistake the emotion shining from his eyes for anything but love?

Tears spilled down her cheeks, jarring her heart into beating again. ''Why?'' she asked, the word filled with both hope and pain.

Given his cryptic behavior since he'd returned to l'Eau Clair, she didn't expect an answer. Her heart nearly stopped again when he opened his mouth to speak.

''Because—'' He folded her hand between both of his and pressed it against his chest. His pulse thundered beneath her fingers, and she'd have sworn his entire body shook. ''—I am not worthy of your love, your respect. You deserve a better man than me in your life.'' Raising her hand to his lips, he pressed a gentle kiss into her palm and closed her fingers over it. ''If I stay out of your life, perhaps you might find that man.''

What could she say to change his mind? she wondered.

All she knew was that he was wrong—about so many things.

Before she could find the words to tell him so, he stepped back, directly into the stream of water.

He gasped, but let the water pour over his head for a moment. ''Little in our lives ever goes as planned, does it?'' He moved out of the waterfall and shook his head, sending droplets flying. ''Come on.'' He took her by the hand and led her to a narrow opening among the boulders strewn in the mouth of the cave. Gillian had no difficulty fitting through the crevice, but Rannulf had to do some wriggling—and to remove his sword from its belt—to make it out of the cavern. ''I must have been thinner when your father showed me the way,'' he said once they emerged into the sunlight. He hooked the scabbard back onto the belt and buckled it around his waist. ''You should have seen him squirm out of there.'' Taking her hand in his, he scanned the rock-strewn hillside.

That must have been quite a sight, for her father had been a tall, burly man, much heavier about the middle than Rannulf.

Rannulf stopped outside the cave and scanned the area. ''I know there's been no trouble nearby, but I

still should look around, make certain no one is lurking about, before you go down there.''

Although she appeared impatient to go down to the
pool, Gillian nodded.

''Wait inside the cave until I return,'' he told her.
''If anything happens, don't come out to help me. Go
back to l'Eau Clair through the passage at once. You
can send reinforcements from there.''

She did as he bid her and reentered the cavern,
though he couldn't be sure she'd obey his dictate
should he come under attack. He'd have to trust that
she'd remember her early training and do the most
logical thing—what he'd ordered her to do.

He scouted the area surrounding the pool quickly.
He found nothing unusual or suspicious as he passed
through the trees; more at ease, he climbed the slope
to rejoin Gillian. He'd brought her here to escape the
tensions back at the keep, not to lead her into further
difficulty.

'''Tis safe,'' he told her. She crawled back out between the boulders, pausing to straighten her clothing
and tuck the hem of her gown into her woven belt.

Rannulf paused to look back over his shoulder at
Gillian as she followed him. Her face alight with
wonder, she gazed down at the pool below, a faint
smile brightening her face. She'd smiled so seldom
since he'd returned to l'Eau Clair—his fault, at least
in part. He hoped he could help her find some happiness, if only by bringing her here.

At least 'twas more peaceful than l'Eau Clair had
been the past few days.

They both remained silent, giving Rannulf the opportunity to take himself to task. The cool water atop
his head could not have come at a more opportune

moment, just as he'd been about to commit the ultimate folly of unburdening himself to Gillian. His
heart constantly made a fool of him; all he had to do
was gaze into the crystal purity of Gillian's eyes and
all sense of self-preservation flew straight out of his
head.

Exposing himself—his true self—to her could
serve no purpose, save make her loathe him more,
perhaps. Since she already knew the foul untruths
he'd penned on the betrothal agreement, she knew
him to be without conscience, without any scruples
at all.

How else could he have taken the gift of her vir-
ginity—in this very place, he reminded himself—and
then refused her the protection of his name?

Not that there was much pride or honor left to the
FitzClifford name, at least not in the eyes of anyone
who knew his family well.

A man who tormented and beat his wife and sons,
who was cruel just for sport, and a son who'd killed
his father and torn his family apart. *There* was a leg-
acy worth sharing with his bride, he thought, disgusted by the notion.

Yet he'd had the gall to question her bloodlines, to
insult her mother, a woman long dead. Even if what
he'd said was true, he was in no position to cast as-
persions on anyone else's family.

But Lord Simon's offer of Gillian's hand had come
hard on the heels of his father's death, catching him
in the darkest depth of his guilt and pain. He'd lashed
out at Lord Simon's offer of happiness. Once he'd
refused, how could he later take back his words, accept an offer that was never tendered again?

The silence stretched like a cord between them as

they worked their way to the bottom of the hill, the tension growing until he could not bear it a moment longer. He released Gillian's hand immediately, turned his back on her and walked around to the opposite side of the pool. Perching on a rock near the water's edge, he picked up a shiny stone and held it clenched tight in his fist as he stared down into the greenish depths of the water.

"Rannulf?"

He looked up from his contemplation of nothing and peered over his shoulder. She stood right beside him, though he hadn't heard her approach. She sat next to him and placed her hand on his shoulder. "There's much you need to say, I think. Whether it will help you to tell me, I don't know, but I'm willing to listen if you wish."

He could not meet her sympathetic gaze. By the rood, he'd rather she hated him than pitied him! He turned away and tossed the rock he held into the bushes far across the pond.

How could he tell her? How could he admit his sins, his cowardice…and the fact that he'd lay down his life for her gladly, should it be necessary?

How could he tell her without also admitting that he'd already sacrificed everything he'd ever wanted when he gave up any chance of a life with her?

But what else had he left to lose?

"You have no idea how bad it is, Gillian." He drew in a deep breath and shook his head. "I don't even know if I can tell you.…" Closing his eyes, he wished himself anywhere but here.

That childish trick had never worked before, as he well knew, and it wasn't likely to start now. If it had to be done, 'twas best to do it quickly, without tormenting either of them any longer.

Gillian leaned over his shoulder and brushed a kiss on his cheek. She eased closer to him, pressed herself against his back and wrapped her arms around his waist, leaned her cheek on his shoulder. "You can tell me, you know." She gave a weak laugh and swiped her cheek against his shoulder—to blot away her tears? "It cannot be any worse than what I've imagined since I found the betrothal contract among my father's papers."

He reached down to his waist to clasp her hands beneath his own. "You must know that I didn't mean those lies I wrote, that much I can tell you freely. I only wish your father was still alive, so I might apologize to him for what I said. He was a good man who always treated me far better than I deserved. I could have found some better way to refuse your hand than that." He tightened his fingers about hers. "I know the words can never be enough, but I offer them to you, Gillian. I am more sorry than I can say that I wrote what I did."

"Is that true, or are you only sorry I know what you wrote?" she murmured, her voice muffled against his shoulder.

"The correspondence was between Lord Simon and me. I didn't know you would ever see the contract."

She drew in a deep breath and straightened, easing her weight from his back, but not releasing him completely. "When I didn't hear from you again, I assumed you'd gotten what you wanted, and had no further use for me."

Her words struck his heart like a blow from a dagger's blade—biting, deadly. "That's not true," he said quietly.

"What else was I to believe? You left here afterward, and I never heard from you again."

He closed his eyes against the pain he'd caused, and because he would hurt her more, before this discussion was over. "You believed what I wanted you to."

She pulled away from him slightly, so he no longer felt her sweet warmth along his back. "I never knew about the agreement until recently—only a short time before you arrived, in fact. But I believed you lost to me long ago, Rannulf." Grabbing him by the shoulder, she forced him to turn and face her. "How do you think I felt, after I gave myself to you in love and joy, and heard nothing from you ever again?" Tears streamed unhindered down her cheeks, winding the pain wrapped around his heart tighter.

"At first I told myself something had happened to you—you'd been wounded, or sent somewhere so far away there was no way to send word to me." She seized the front of his tunic in both hands and held tight. "After a time, I believed you must be dead, for you'd not ignore me for so long otherwise." Her eyes held him pinned in place as securely as her hands. "But then I realized my godfather would have sent word to me if that were so."

He had nothing to say in his defense, so he let her hold him there. She deserved the chance to tell him how he'd hurt her.

"What if we'd made a child together that day?" she asked, her voice ragged. "Did that possibility ever once cross your mind?"

He reached up and cupped her face in his hands.

"You don't know how much I wished we had," he said, smoothing his thumbs over the softness of her skin. He closed his eyes for a moment, afraid for her to see the hope, the yearning that lingered still. When he looked at her again, he let all he felt, joy and sorrow both, shine from his eyes. "If we'd made a child—" he shook his head, uncertain how to express himself "—your father would probably have forced me to marry you."

"Forced?" Gillian released her grip on his tunic and pushed against his chest. "No one could force me to wed a man I didn't want, whether I carried his child or not! I have no use for a reluctant groom."

How could he make her understand? He took her hands in his and held them tightly. "Reluctant? Only because I felt I wasn't worthy of you. I wasn't then, and I'm not now. But if we'd made a child, your father might have forced the issue, insisted we wed— if *he* could accept what I'd done."

"'What you'd done'? I don't understand. What did you do that was so terrible?"

"I cannot tell you like this, when you comfort me," he said. His heart heavy with the loss, he released her hands and stood. "In truth, your father would never have forgiven me enough for what I did to give you into my keeping, nor should he have. He'd never have offered me your hand at all had he known that I killed my father—" He met her stunned gaze and forced himself to hold it with his own. "And that I'd do so again, if I had to."

Chapter Fifteen

Shock tumbled through her, brought her to her feet. "I don't believe you!" she cried. "How dare you concoct so horrible an excuse? If you don't want me, then say so." When he backed away from her, she swung her skirts out of her way and stalked after him. "You need not go to such lengths to turn me away. Even your insults to my mother were not so bad as this...this fabrication."

His bitter laugh sent a chill of unease skittering along her spine. "'Tis no lie, Gillian. I *did* kill my father. 'Tis not widely known, but it is the truth. Lord William knows of it. Send word to him if you don't believe me."

Her mind reeling, she seized upon the first thought that came to her notice. "Then why did he never say anything about it? If not to me, then to my father?" she demanded. "My godfather must have known that my father wished us to marry. Surely he'd have shared that important bit of news with him—if he believed it mattered."

"I don't know why he didn't say anything to Lord

Simon, but it certainly does matter, Gillian. I am a murderer.''

He sank down on a large, flat rock, his face weary and strained. When he looked up and met her pleading gaze, she could see nothing but honesty in his eyes.

Perhaps it *was* the truth, as he understood it, at any rate.

''Couldn't you be wrong?'' she asked, hoping—nay, pleading—for him to admit 'twas a mistake.

''I lay injured beside him as his life's blood drained away, my dagger thrust into his chest, my hand clenched about the hilt.'' His movements slow, tired, he shook his head. ''There's no mistake, Gillian. My father is dead, and by my own hand.'' He held his hand out to her, then let it fall into his lap. ''Now do you see why we could not wed?''

She sat down beside him, her gaze fixed on his face, his eyes—so full of sorrow, of pain. Her heart ached for him, yearned to absorb some of his pain and give him ease. ''You must have had a good reason, an important one,'' she said softly. She believed that with every fiber of her being. The Rannulf FitzClifford she'd known four years ago, the man she'd grown to love, could not have committed such a deed without one.

Rannulf ignored the hand she settled on his arm, but she left it there anyway, determined to offer him what comfort she could whether he wanted it or not. ''What reason could possibly make patricide acceptable?'' he asked despairingly. Reaching down, he squeezed her hand before moving it to rest in her lap. ''You cannot rationalize it, Gillian, nor make it go away by finding some justification for what I did. It simply is, it happened, and nothing we can do now will change that." He glanced away from her, out over the water. "Believe me, if there were a way out of this coil, I'd have found it by now."

Despite his protests to the contrary, she knew he was wrong. His torment was plain to see, written large upon his face, glowing from deep within his dark eyes.

She'd have sworn, however that what weighed the most heavily upon him was not so much the sin of his deed as it was guilt for what he'd done.

Or for something associated with it.

"If it was as you say, without reason or excuse, I doubt you'd be free. You'd have been executed for the crime. Pembroke would not permit you to live if you'd slain your father in cold blood!" She caught his chin in her hand and tugged until he faced her. "Make me understand, Rannulf," she pleaded. "This is important to me as well, for I refuse to sit idly by while you brand yourself a murderer."

Though he didn't try to pull free of her hold, he remained silent.

Before her eyes Rannulf's expression changed— sharpened to the face of a warrior. "Aye, you're right that there's more," he snarled. His hold firm but gentle, he slid her hand away from his chin and held it fast within his. "But you're wrong that we can explain it all away." He leaned closer, until his lips moved beside her cheek and she could scarcely see his eyes. "If there were an explanation to be found, no matter how weak, I would accept it." Tipping her chin with his free hand, he pressed his mouth to hers, his kiss both promise and demand. He brushed his mouth over hers again, then whispered, "Rather than ever give you up."

Did he love her still? The words echoed through her mind, drowning all else he'd said in a sea of hope.

He released her and stood. He would have turned away, would have abandoned her there with her emotions naked and raw. Every time they came close to talking about the past—and their present—one of them put a stop to it before they could ever come to a resolution, a *conclusion,* to anything.

She was tired of confusion, of half-spoken words, of half-truths that led them deeper into the morass that was her relationship with Rannulf.

She'd not stand for it a moment longer!

Gillian rose and grabbed Rannulf by the hand to pull him back to her, wrapping him in her arms and raising her hand to press her palm against his cheek. *"Can* you give me up so easily?" she asked softly, brushing her lips over his mouth, ignoring his resistance to her touch. "Is your guilt stronger than your love?"

"Gillian, stop!"

"Why?" she demanded. She framed his face with both hands, forcing him to meet her eyes, lending him her strength, her determination. "Tell me why, damn you! Tell me everything. Did you mean to kill him?"

"No!" He drew in a deep breath and let it out slowly, stopped trying to avoid her searching gaze, brought his hands up to cover hers and drew them down to rest, still joined, upon his chest. "But I wanted him dead," he added more quietly. "More than you can imagine. So many times I thought of killing him that once the deed was done, I could scarce believe 'twas true."

She flattened her palms against his chest, felt the fast, steady thrum of his heart beneath her fingers as she considered what that might mean. "What had he done to make you hate him so?"

He sighed and slid his hands to her shoulders. "He was the cruelest bastard who ever lived."

Frustration mounting, she drew him down to sit beside her on the boulder. "This serves nothing!" she cried. "How can you expect this wound to heal when you keep it walled up inside you to fester? It has already tainted your entire life. Will you allow it to continuing growing until you've nothing left?"

"I have nothing left."

"You have me," she said, the words a solemn vow.

His eyes burning with some inner fire, he snatched her hands up in his and interlaced their fingers, his grip firm. "So be it," he said, his voice barely above a gravelly whisper. "What kind of man abuses his sons' trust—beats them simply for the sport of it? A warrior who refuses to permit his son to learn a warrior's ways, then mocks and belittles him till he is afraid to meet anyone's eyes, instead skulking from shadow to shadow, from room to room, like a frightened animal, like a ghost of the child he used to be?"

Within the nest of their fingers, his hands shook. Gillian couldn't tell if 'twas Rannulf's reaction, or her own. "My mother could not protect us—she couldn't protect herself. So many times he hurt her, and we could do nothing to stop him." She trembled inside at the images his words conjured up, although she doubted what she pictured could be anywhere close to the terrible reality of it.

"No one could stop him. I was more fortunate than

Connor, my younger brother—my twin. When I was seven, Lord William came to my father and offered to take me with him, train me to be a knight. My father let me go.'' He gave a shaky laugh. '''Twas the only thing he ever did that surprised me. I believed he'd refuse simply to torment me, for he had to have known how badly I wanted to leave. Anything I ever wanted, he took away for his own amusement. I missed my mother and brother, 'tis true, but I thanked God every day for allowing me to escape.''

And buried himself with guilt because his mother and Connor had to stay.

''Lord William saved my life by his offer, for as I grew older, grew in size and strength, eventually my father and I would have come to blows. I doubt I'd have had the patience to hold off until I had the skill to best him, for even at seven my hatred of him smoldered within me till I thought I'd burst with it. When he'd go after Mother or Connor...'' He glanced away, but not before she saw the shame in his eyes, in his face.

She loosened one hand from his hold and stroked his cheek. '''Tis not your fault they couldn't leave.''

He pressed his lips to her palm, his expression under control once more. ''What kind of monster punishes his wife for not bearing him more children when he already has two healthy sons? Or mocks her for her foreign blood even as he enjoys the benefits reaped from the holdings she brought to him in another land?'' His gaze never leaving hers, he shook his head, even as a flush rose to his face. ''Perhaps I'm more like him than I realized.''

She knew what he referred to, but she couldn't believe his intent had been to hurt her. ''Nay, I refuse to accept that. You had no way of knowing I would ever see what you wrote.''

He kissed her fingers again. ''Your father saw it, as I knew he would. He didn't deserve my carelessness, my cruelty. I was wrong to insult your mother as I did.'' He made a sound of disgust. ''I violated a dead woman's memory—not just any woman, which would be bad enough—but the woman who gave *you* life. 'Twas the act of a coward. There are times I wish I could remove every drop of my father's blood from my veins.''

''You are not your father. And I know you're not a coward. How can you slander yourself so?'' Raising her hand, she stroked it through his hair, smoothing the unruly locks back from his brow. ''You did it for your mother and Connor, didn't you? He threatened them again, and this time, you fought back.''

The color drained from his face. Though he faced her still, his attention seemed focused inward. ''I'd come to FitzClifford to see them—my father wasn't supposed to be there. I wanted to tell them about you, that I hoped we'd be wed soon,'' he added, the corner of his mouth quirking up in remembrance. ''It was not long after we'd made love, and I was so eager to make you mine.''

Rannulf turned his attention from the scene in his mind to the woman seated beside him. He couldn't believe she was here with him still, despite what he'd told her.

That she apparently believed in him he counted nothing less than a miracle.

Could she be right? That he'd had valid reasons to fight back, that in spite of his yearning over the years to destroy his father, it had been an accident?

Or was her support nothing but the wishful thinking of the woman who loved him?

She ran her fingers through his hair again, her touch soothing him, healing him in ways he could scarcely begin to understand. A sense of calm settled over him, allowing him back into the past once more.

"Aye, I was protecting them. It was my fault as much as anyone's that he became enraged. In my eagerness to share my happiness with my mother, as soon as I entered the hall for the evening meal I blurted out that I'd found my bride. My father walked in right behind me and heard every word. It sent him into a tirade such as I'd never seen. And I'd forgotten, in my years away from FitzClifford, how angry he got over naught, how easily something could set him off.

"I bore his sneering comments about me—and even about you, though it galled me to hear his insults—with more patience than I knew I had." He captured Gillian's hand in his and pressed a kiss to the back of it. "But then he turned his attention to Connor, ranting and screaming. Connor sat there at the table and suffered the abuse in silence—he's not a fighter," he added, the memory of his own words to his twin in the aftermath of their father's death slicing through him like the keenest blade. "The bastard finally lashed out with his eating knife and raked it across my brother's left cheek." He closed his eyes for a moment, as much to shut out the look of horror in Gillian's eyes as to witness again his brother's bloodied face. "'Twas a wonder he didn't lose his eye."

"Did he go after you next?" she asked, her voice soft, calm—precisely what he needed to continue.

"Nay. For the first time in my memory, Mother went after him."

Gillian drew in a sharp breath. "Did he harm her?"

He shook his head. "I think he was so startled by seeing her fight back that he stood there and let her come at him. Neither Connor or I had moved, Connor because of his injury, and I—" he gave her hand a squeeze "—I didn't know what to do. Never before had I been in the position to do anything against him. But when she grasped him by the surcoat and began to scream at him, I could see that his surprise had disappeared. He hit her across the face, then raised his hands to wrap them around her throat, but I pulled her free of him and slid my knife from its sheath. I could not allow him to harm them any more."

Tears streamed unhindered from Gillian's eyes. "You saved their lives," she said. "You must realize 'tis true."

"Aye. But perhaps if I'd turned away instead of fighting back, talking back, he'd still be alive."

"But would any of you have survived?" She released his hands to grasp his shoulders, her face alight with determination. "He'd have killed you all before he was through, Rannulf, if not that day, then some other. He'd terrorized you all for so long. Why would he stop?"

"I've wondered that myself, as I've wondered about so many things tied to that day. What if I'd kept my mouth shut—would he have left them alone, would we have muddled through my visit without an outburst from him? I don't know."

"There would have been another time, perhaps the next time you were there—or mayhap once you'd left—when he might have still done them harm. You cannot believe that he only behaved thus when you were there." She slid her hands up to his neck, moved her fingers up over his shoulders, stroked them over the tense cords of his neck in a soothing caress. "They were lucky. If it had happened some other time, you wouldn't have been there to save them."

"I've told myself that before," he admitted. "Though it hasn't brought me a moment's ease, for it seemed naught but the excuse of a guilty man eager to find a way around the truth to his own benefit."

"You're wrong," she whispered. "Let it go, Rannulf. You've shared your burden with me. Let that sharing ease your mind, give you peace."

"It's not that easy," he told her, afraid to hope, to look beyond the past to a future that might include her after all. "There's so much you still don't know."

Gillian watched Rannulf's face, saw the honesty, the integrity, he wore like a mantle around him, saw the shadows still lurking within his dark eyes and knew what she must do. "This is enough for now," she said, her voice so soft he leaned close to hear her. But she could speak no louder; it took all her strength to ask the question she must. "All I need to know for now is, do you love me still?"

He brought his hands up to cup her face. "I've always loved you, Gillian—and I always will."

Chapter Sixteen

Gillian and Rannulf slipped back into l'Eau Clair without being seen, and with Talbot, to all appearances, none the wiser that they'd begun to draw closer together.

Talbot kept Rannulf busy for the next few days as they explored the environs of l'Eau Clair with a thoroughness Rannulf found exhausting. They rode from one end of the demesne to the other, leaving Rannulf to fall into his lonely bed each night and dream of Gillian.

To dream of the next time they could be together.

'Twas just as well he had scant opportunity to see her, else he'd surely have given himself away. Her taste, the memory of her body pressed to his haunted him until he thought he'd go mad for want of her.

Three days after he showed Gillian the passageway to the pool, he led her through the corridor again.

They made the journey in silence, though their bodies, their eyes, told of their passion, their yearning to be together. Hands linked, they sat by the edge of the pool.

Rannulf slipped both hands beneath the weight of

her hair, feathered his mouth in a gentle caress across her aching lips and stole his way deeper into her heart.

He loved her still.

Despite all that had come between them, she'd hoped against hope that it might be true, but she hadn't believed it would ever come to be. Tears slipped down her cheeks, balm to an aching heart that had never hoped to feel such joy again.

The tenderness of his touch, the racing of his pulse beneath her hand, spurred her passion, filled her entire being with a lightness and pleasure beyond her ability to express.

She'd not allow that lack to deter her, however. They had four lost years to reclaim, and she'd not waste a moment more.

She leaned into the warm strength of his chest, but 'twas not enough to satisfy the yearning to hold him tight, to press as close as possible to him.

She perched on his lap and wrapped her arms about him. He groaned and shifted her to settle more firmly on his thighs.

His mouth opened over hers and his tongue slipped out to tease along her lips, tracing over them, then darting inside to dally with hers. Sighing her pleasure, she returned the caress, taunting him as he teased her.

She smiled against his mouth. Here was a battle they both might win.

He smoothed his hand over her belly and down her legs, outlining them with the flat of his palm, then dragging the hem of her gown up on the return journey. The warm breeze caressed her skin, sent a shimmer of sensation over her already responsive flesh, adding heat to the fire smoldering inside her.

His warm, rough palm retraced its path over her

bare thigh. The feeling traveled from her leg straight to her heart, sending a shower of sensations flowing through her body.

They spread a fiery heat through her veins, lent a boldness to her touch that the maiden she'd been at their past encounter would never have dared indulge. But she'd changed in that time—changed since he'd returned to l'Eau Clair—enough to obey what her heart bade her do, to satisfy the dictates of her soul.

She wanted Rannulf, needed the sharing, the sense of belonging, that only he could give her.

If that meant she took a chance, trusted him not to hurt her again, then that was a gamble she had to take. Loving Rannulf was worth the risk.

She tugged loose the ties at the neckline of his shirt, pushing aside the well-worn linen and skimming her fingertips over his wildly throbbing pulse.

"Gillian," he moaned into her hair. His mouth opened against her skin and he raked his teeth lightly over her throat, sending her own heartbeat pounding. He captured her mouth again, his tongue tracing her lips before plunging deep to explore further.

He stroked her so gently—with hands and tongue, with the soft sigh of his breath over her skin—that she found herself moving deeper still into his embrace in search of those subtle caresses. Wherever he touched her she ached for more, till her entire body seemed suspended in the throes of a yearning so great, 'twas a wonder she didn't lose all sense of reality.

Instead it honed her senses, made her more aware of the warm male scent of his skin—of sandalwood and man—surrounding her, of the rasp of whiskers beneath her questing fingers when she outlined the strong line of his jaw, his aura of power enveloping her with the knowledge that this man would protect her, lend her his strength.

"I've missed you more than you'll ever know," he murmured against her throat. His lips skimmed over her sensitive skin and she bit back a moan. "Not just this, but you." His voice vibrating against her flesh sent a corresponding shiver of reaction through her, making her want to purr, to wrap herself tighter still around him.

She must have made the sound, for he gave a weak chuckle and clasped her more firmly in his arms even as she cuddled closer. "Though we've been fools—" he met her gaze, his eyes alight with more than mere passion "—our bodies know they're meant to be together."

"So it seems for the moment," she whispered, her voice trembling with reaction to his touch, the look in his eyes, the honesty in his voice.

But would that feeling remain once they'd sated their passion?

Rannulf scooped her off his lap and stood, holding her snug in his arms as he scanned their surroundings. Lips curved into a faint smile, he carried her away from the rocky shore toward a small grassy area near the foot of the path from the cave. Trees and bushes screened them from the trail through the forest, but here the grass grew all the way to the water's edge.

He set her on her feet. "A moment," he said, stepping away to pull his tunic over his head. He laid it on the ground and bent to smooth the wool over the springy grass. "For you, milady." He straightened and held out his hand to her.

She placed her hand in his, surprised—and pleased—by the faint tremor of his palm when they

touched. He raised her fingers to his lips for a lingering kiss, his gaze holding hers, promising her untold
delights. Before he could release her she turned her
hand and slipped her fingertips along the seam of his
mouth, his indrawn breath setting her blood ablaze
with longing.

He guided her down onto the tunic with him and
eased her to sit between his outstretched legs, her
back to him.

"I want to savor every moment, every bit of you,"
he murmured. He lifted the band holding her veil in
place and, with a tug of his fingers, sent the slippery
material sliding over her shoulder to pool in her lap.
"Four long years I've dreamed of this moment,
though I never allowed myself to believe we'd be
together again."

She could feel both his hands moving in her hair
as he loosened the plaits, then burrowed his fingers
deep within the unbound waves and spread them to
cover her like a cloak. "Your hair is like the finest
silk, smooth and cool against my skin." He raised a
lock of her hair to his lips, let it sift through his fingers till he held the ends grasped within his hand.
"Feel it, Gillian," he whispered as he stroked the
feathery curl over her cheek and down her chin to the
sensitive flesh of her throat. "So many nights I drifted
off to sleep with the memory of your hair draped over
me lingering in my mind, the image so vivid it felt
real, until I knew I'd not rest. Dreams of you—" he
smoothed it away from her face and nuzzled her
cheek "—not just of the time we made love, but of
all the times we spent together, have haunted me,
waking and asleep, nigh every day we've been
apart."

His words weighed heavy on her heart, the press of them cracking through the armor enshrouding the tender, precious feelings she'd once had for him... setting her love for him free once more.

With that freedom came all the pain she refused to hide any longer.

"If you felt that way about me, how could you turn from me, push me away?" she cried. Shrugging off his grasp on her shoulders, she spun to face him, rose on her knees and tossed her hair out of her way. Sympathy, understanding—the emotions she'd felt when he revealed the details of his father's death, of his own shame—abandoned her, swamped beneath her own sense of loss.

Her own clear-burning anger.

"Did you trust me—my love for you—so little that you'd prefer to suffer in silence, to abandon all we had together and condemn us both to a life of loneliness?" She caught his face in her hands and forced him to meet her eyes. "Our love was strong enough to withstand *anything,* Rannulf, if you'd only have given it the chance."

Face pale, he brought his hands up to cover hers and closed his eyes. "I was a coward," he admitted, his voice awash with pain. "Afraid to risk what we had, too weak to put it to the test." He opened his eyes, their brown depths pleading.

Pleading for what?

"I believed 'twas better to distance myself from you, rather than give you the opportunity to decide you wanted nothing more to do with me. I thought to protect you, as well as myself. I thought 'twould make losing you easier to bear." He tightened his grip on her hands. "But I was wrong, my love, so very wrong."

"Aye, you were," she said. "You should have trusted me. You should have believed in us," she added, sadness for all that might have been filling her voice, her entire being. Her eyes welled with tears, but she refused to let them fall.

All the tears she'd shed in the past four years had done nothing to change anything in their past. Only she—nay, *they*—had the power to alter their future.

Starting now.

"Are you strong enough to believe now, to believe in us?" she asked. Though she spoke the words softly, calmly, she knew her eyes told a different tale. *Nothing* in her life had ever been so important. Had he understanding enough to notice?

Still holding her hands cupped within his, he brought them to his lips, gifting each with a kiss so gentle, 'twas enough to break her heart. "I trust you, Gillian." He kissed her fingers again. "I believe that together, we've strength enough to face any trial." His touch firm, sure, he smoothed his palms over her shoulders, entangling his fingers in her hair. "I love you," he murmured, lowering his mouth to hers.

Gillian twined her arms about Rannulf in return as she gave him back his kiss—his vow—full measure. He eased her down to sit on the tunic, his outstretched legs around her, their muscular strength adding to the sense of security, of sanctuary, that he wrapped about them like a cloak to keep the outside world at bay.

No other people, no other place existed but this— the two of them in their own private Eden, their love the only emotion that mattered here.

Rannulf felt as though his heart might burst with

the sheer joy of holding his love within his arms again—and with the knowledge that she wished to be there. His recent encounters with Gillian had been bittersweet, filled as much with confusion as with longing.

Gillian tugged aside the neckline of his shirt and slipped her hand inside, her fingers cool as they stroked over his neck and shoulders once again, sending a shudder of delight throughout him. This was longing, lust, trust…and so much more.

'Twas love.

He gave himself up to rediscovering that wonderful emotion with Gillian. Drawing back from her, he smiled at the expression on her face—yearning and determination mixed together into a fiery brew that was pure Gillian. Gazing at her beloved face, he realized anew that his love for her, having once been lost, was more precious to him now than he could ever have imagined.

He would never let her go, he vowed. Whatever their future might hold, she was his.

Her eyes popped open, the green depths soft and cloudy with dreams, from the look of it. Dreams that included him, he hoped, his smile widening in pleasure when he saw no hint of hurt or pain lurking there.

"Come back," she purred, pulling him closer. "If you think to leave me—" She glanced down at his lap, at his body's enthusiastic, unmistakable response to her, and her kiss-reddened lips curved into a knowing grin. "If you think to leave *us* in this state yet again, I tell you now I'll not allow it."

"Will you not?" he asked, moving toward her, guiding her to lie beneath him on the tunic. He propped himself on his elbows and wriggled his hips to settle into the welcoming cradle of her thighs. "What do you suggest we do about this…" Reaching down, he tugged at her twisted skirts to loosen them from about her legs and sank more snugly against her. "This 'state'?"

He felt her hands at his waist, then the sun's warmth upon his bare back as she shoved his shirt up. "You could take this off, for a start," she said.

Giving a swift tug on the neckline, he pulled the shirt over his head and cast it aside. She smoothed her palms over his waist and around to his chest, their warmth rivaling the sun for heat. Despite that warmth, he shuddered as her touch sensitized his flesh, made him ache to take her now, with no further preparation than this.

He stared down into the emerald beauty of Gillian's eyes and knew he'd best do something to slow the pace, else he'd never last long enough to give her the pleasure, the sharing, she deserved.

Where he found the strength to roll off her and sit at her side, he didn't know. Gillian reached for him and settled her hands upon his chest, confusion clouding her gaze. "I meant what I said," she told him. "You'll not escape me so easily."

"I've no desire to escape you." He glanced away from her, lest she be frightened by the nigh uncontrollable yearning he knew he couldn't disguise. "'Tis just that I want you so much—" Holding out his hand, he showed her how it shook. "I doubt I was this nervous, this eager, the first time we made love," he said with a rueful laugh. "But it's been so long for us both, and I want to make it last, to give you pleasure."

The heat in her eyes cooled, the look of yearning

faded from her face. "It's been four years for me, but I doubt 'tis been so long since you last took your pleasure," she said, lowering her hands to rest in her lap and not meeting his eyes.

Although he felt a flush rising to his cheeks, a chill settled onto his flesh where she'd touched him. "Do you think I would seek what we once had with another?" he asked with a calm that belied the fire, the sense of outrage, kindled by her assumption.

"Why wouldn't you, especially since you chose to break off all contact with me?"

The hurt he heard in her voice was nothing compared to what he saw in her eyes when he made her look at him. "I didn't want anyone else," he told her quietly. Holding her gaze with his, he willed her to understand. "Nor did I wish to taint what we'd shared, to cheapen it for a moment of mindless release." He reached out, brushed a fiery lock of hair behind her ear and settled his fingers against the delicate flesh of her throat. "Since I met you, Gillian, the only woman I've ever wanted is you."

"I cannot believe that is true," she said, her tear-bright eyes a stark contrast to her scornful tone. "I was little more than a child when first we met, and more lad than lady. I doubt you found anything appealing about me at all." She tried to shrug away from his touch, but he refused to permit it, instead clasping her arm with his free hand to hold her steady.

"But it is true," he assured her. "I could see from our first meeting that you'd strength and courage, more heart than most anyone I'd ever known. Everything I've learned of you since has served to bolster that opinion. Then there's your beauty...." He smiled and traced a finger along the firm line of her jaw.

"There was a lovely young lady hiding beneath those lad's clothes and that coating of dust. How could I resist her? And the woman you've become takes my breath away." His breathing unsteady, he leaned forward and gently kissed her lips. "You are all I could ever want, and more than I deserve. 'Tis my good fortune that you've not seen much of the world beyond l'Eau Clair, for otherwise you'd never deign to so much as notice me."

Tears streamed down her cheeks, striking him like a sword through the belly. She opened her mouth to speak, but her breath caught on a sob. Shaking her head, she tried once again to slip from his hold.

"Nay, my love. I never meant to make you cry." He snatched up his shirt from the ground and dried her face, but more tears fell to replace those he'd wiped away. "I never should have brought you here again, nor allowed things to go this far," he said, more to himself than to her. "If only I'd the strength to leave you alone," he muttered.

"What makes you believe you're the only one involved in this, in deciding what is said and done?" Gillian asked, her words startling him as much as her abrupt change of mood. "I'm no weakling without a mind of her own, as you well know," she pointed out. Grabbing the shirt from him, she swiped it over her tears and tossed it aside. "Must we go back and forth, blaming ourselves for things beyond our control? Dredge up the past and allow it to taint our future?" As he watched her, she pulled herself together, straightened her spine, tossed back her hair, assumed the bearing of the strong, commanding woman he knew her to be. "Assuming we ever get beyond all this and *have* a future."

"You are an amazing woman, Gillian."

"Do you want us to have a life together?" she demanded.

"'Tis my dearest wish," he said.

She moved closer to him, wrapped her arms about him. "Then what are we waiting for?"

Chapter Seventeen

It took Gillian nearly every bit of will she had within her to be so bold, to force the past behind them—where it belonged—and forge ahead. She'd do whatever she must to drag Rannulf with her into the future, into *their* future, the one they'd create between them. She knew he'd not shared with her everything that weighed heavily upon him, but 'twould do neither of them any good to delve further into the past, not now.

Onward, then, she ordered herself. There'd be time aplenty later to sort out all their cares and worries, to decide together how they'd resolve their troubles.

For now there was just Rannulf and Gillian, two lovers who'd not shared their love, their passion, in far too long.

Willing her hands not to tremble, she reached out and stroked her fingertips over the smooth muscled flesh of Rannulf's shoulders, tracing a path from freckle to freckle along his collarbone till her hands met in the center of his chest. The heat of his skin ignited a matching warmth inside her, bringing a flush to her face and making her lips tingle with the urge to follow her fingers' journey.

Her clothing felt too tight, too heavy for the sunny day, but she couldn't force herself to stop what she was doing long enough to loosen her laces and remove it. Rannulf enjoyed her touch, she could see, for his eyes had grown darker, heavy-lidded, and the smile on his lips spoke of pleasure. She didn't dare risk breaking the spell she wove by ceasing her caresses.

But why should she stop? Passion was a game for two to play, and while she'd be perfectly happy to give Rannulf all the pleasure she could, mayhap he'd be willing to return the favor.

She was attempting to be bold, after all.

All she had to do was ask.

Twining her fingers in the reddish curls covering his chest, she bent and brushed her lips over his— and avoided meeting his eyes to keep hold of her courage. "I find I'm growing overwarm," she whispered by his ear. "Would you help me with my gown?"

He moved back enough to see her face, his gaze as he scanned her face a caress she felt from head to toe. "'Twould be my pleasure." His eyes held hers captive while he loosened the ties of her bliaut, his fingers' slow movement at her sides, her throat, heaping fuel upon the already smoldering burn of desire pulsing through her veins.

The bonds of sight disappeared when he helped her to her feet and tugged her bliaut over her head, then did the same with her undertunic, but he did not permit her to feel the lack, binding her to him with words instead. "Your skin is softer than silk, more delicate than a dream. I cannot wait to see how it glows in the sun, to feel it beneath my lips."

Leaving her clad only in her shift, hose and shoes, he knelt at her feet and caught her gaze with his once more as he unbuckled her shoes and slipped them off. "Your hair—" He shook his head, and a flush of color rose to his cheeks. "I've dreamed of your hair draped over us both as we seek our pleasure. The mere sight of your unbound hair is all it takes to fill my mind with images of us together, cloaked in nothing else."

The pictures he painted in her mind, coupled with the touch of his fingers as they crept up her legs and untied her garters, nearly caused her knees to give way. But she focused instead upon his beloved face, on the thought of where this all would lead, and resolved to savor every moment of it.

He slipped off her hose, then rose to his feet and took her by the hand and led her to the grassy edge of the pool. She followed along, uncertain what he intended, but willing to wait and find out.

"The taste of water on your skin has haunted me," he told her, "ever since we fell in." He eased her down onto the soft grass and sat beside her. "But I doubt any explanation would satisfy Talbot should we return in the same condition again," he added with a chuckle. "Not to mention the fact that then he'd know we'd left the castle." He shook his head. "We cannot have that, so this will have to do." She watched as he trailed his hand through the water, then brought his fingers to rest on the bare skin above the neckline of her shift.

The water and his fingers painted a cool path over her overheated flesh. She closed her eyes at the sensation, then gasped at the feel of his tongue, hot and moist, following the droplets' course down her chest and into the cleft between her breasts. "Delicious," he murmured, the brush of his lips, the vibration of his voice, winding tight the tension building within her. He nudged aside the strap of her shift until it fell down her arm, then captured more water in his hand and let it trickle from her shoulder down to her breast. "I want more."

She did, too. She wanted to share this with him. She'd no desire to sit quietly, to be a passive recipient of his caresses. Somehow she found strength enough to break through the cloud of passion engulfing her, to reach beside her and dip her hand into the pool. "My turn," she said, holding his gaze captive with hers as she painted a trail of water over his shoulder and down his chest.

She watched, fascinated, as he drew a hissing breath through his teeth and shuddered. "Finish it," he muttered when she continued to stare at him. He reached for her even as she bent close to follow the water's path over tight muscles and soft hair, ending at the flat coppery nipple in its nest of curls. He wove his fingers into her hair and held her to him for a moment, then pulled away. "'Tis heaven, my love, but if you do much more, I swear I'll be through before we've started," he told her with a shaky laugh.

Not yet willing to stop, she traced her fingers over the same route she'd taken with her tongue. "Are you sure?"

Rannulf grabbed her hand, brought it to his mouth and nipped at her fingertip. A bolt of molten heat streaked its way to her core. "Aye."

Her sense of disappointment vanished when he scooped her into his arms and brought her back to their scattered clothing, settling her among the garments and following her down onto them. "We'll not stop again, I promise you." His hands shook as he smoothed her hair back and rested his hands palm-down upon her aching breasts. "Not until I've made you mine once more."

His hands were never still, stroking her, teasing her as his mouth teased hers, making her shudder with need. Gillian wanted to make him burn as well—he could hardly push her away when he was busy himself, and she took full advantage of every opportunity. She loosened the drawstring at his waist and had his braes halfway to his knees before he tried to stop her roving hands, and by then 'twas too late—his only response when she closed her hand about his manhood was a groan of pleasure.

"You like that?" she asked, smiling when he reared up over her and tugged at her shift until it lay pooled at her feet.

"What do you think?" he asked, his voice rough.

She chuckled, then could do naught but gasp at the wave of yearning crashing over her when he stroked his fingers from her breasts to the juncture of her thighs, then captured her nipple in his mouth and cupped her with his hand. "Rannulf!" Eyes open wide, she stared down at him, at the muscled perfection of his body highlighted by the sun.

He raised his head from her breast and rose on his knees to kiss her lips with a tender thoroughness at odds with his hand's continued bold caresses. "What is it, my love?" he asked when they paused for breath.

"Now," she gasped. "I want you *now*."

He kissed her again, wrapped her in his arms and rolled until she lay atop him. Before she could give voice to her confusion, he reached up and gathered her wildly disordered hair in both hands and arranged it over her back and shoulders, smiling when it settled about them both. "You see? 'Tis just as I said."

But it seemed a strange way to make love. Still, once she stared down at him, spread out beneath her like a banquet of delights, she could see some definite advantages to this position. And she wanted him so badly, she'd not refuse him much of anything at this point.

Rannulf helped her shift to take him into her body; once she did, she could do naught but *feel*—his strength beneath her, surrounding her as his hands on her hips helped her to move atop him; the rasp of his chest hair against her already sensitized nipples; the brush of her hair sliding over them and adding another caress to the multitude of sensations overwhelming her.

But what she felt most was *love*—Rannulf's touch, the way he gazed into her eyes, the words he whispered to her, all cried out that he loved her.

She hoped her love for him shone out as brightly.

All too soon 'twas too much to bear. Never taking her eyes from his, she gasped her pleasure, then cried out again as he followed her into fulfillment.

She collapsed on him, her arms unable to support her any longer. He nudged aside a swath of her hair and kissed her cheek, nuzzled his way to her lips. His touch gentle, he gathered up her hair and moved it away from her face. "I love you," he whispered.

"And I love you," she replied, smiling at the way his eyes shone with happiness.

In the end, nothing else mattered.

* * *

So much time had passed since they left the keep.
Once they'd recovered from their lovemaking, they
had to scramble into their clothes and hurry through
the passageway to make it back in time for the midday meal. Gillian's hair beneath her veil was a tangled
mess despite Rannulf's best efforts to help her comb
it. He just hoped she didn't run into anyone on her
way to her chamber.

What Ella would have to say when she caught sight
of her mistress, he didn't want to consider.

After he judged she'd had time enough to reach her
room, he cast a quick look into the hall, where servants were busily setting up for dinner, before slipping away along the corridor and up the spiral stairs.

Marged stepped out of the shadows lining the back
hallway and stared after the Norman. What had the
two of them been up to? She gave a crude laugh.
'Twas clear enough to *her* what they'd been doing.
Lady Gillian—her high-and-mighty mistress—looked
as though she'd been dragged backward through a
hedgerow.

Although milady would not be out swilling the pigs
in penance for *her* sins, she'd wager.

She gave a satisfied smile. She could scarce wait
until her master heard this bit of news. Mayhap
'twould cure him of his yearning for the lady, though
knowing him, 'twas just as likely he'd desire her all
the more.

What Richard would make of all this she dared not
guess. His dislike of Lady Gillian grew by the day—
nay, with every shovelful of dung he tossed onto the
midden—till now he wore his hatred gathered around
him like a mantle.

He was lucky no one else but her had noticed his hatred for the lady; if they ever did, mucking out the stables would seem good work indeed compared to what he'd find himself doing.

If he survived at all.

Richard's master had been too busy to take much notice of him of late—and 'twas her good fortune as well. She and Richard found chances aplenty to sneak off to the loft, or to places like this hallway, for a quick coupling.

He was a lusty man, 'twas true, but 'twas all to the good. She'd seldom found a man her equal when it came to satisfying her hunger. She grinned. Or one as skilled, if truth be told. Richard had proved a most gratifying lover.

'Twas why she was here now, waiting for him, but he must have been delayed by some task. It wasn't like him to refuse himself a chance for pleasure.

The sound of voices coming from the hall had been rising steadily; a glance out into the large chamber showed the benches filling fast. She twitched her bodice up to a more modest position and tucked her hair back under her kerchief before slipping into the hall. Taking a brace of pitchers from a harried manservant, she headed for the table on the dais as though she belonged there.

She gave a satisfied smile. Aye, she'd serve the mistress herself this day, observe Lady Gillian and Lord Rannulf, see what she could learn.

The sooner she gathered enough information for the master, the quicker he could take possession of l'Eau Clair.

And the sooner she'd be paid. Her heart beat faster

in anticipation. Who knew how Lord Steffan would reward her?

Perhaps there'd even be a position here for Richard as well.

'Twas all she could do to hide her excitement. Before much longer Lady Gillian would have a new master, and Marged's life would be much richer than she'd ever dreamed possible.

Rannulf had no sooner closed the door of his chamber behind him and begun to undress before someone pounded on the portal. Wrestling his tunic back into place, he crossed to the door and jerked it open. "What is it?" he snarled, noticing too late that Talbot stood before him.

"Rough morning?" Not waiting for an invitation, Lord Nicholas slipped past him and walked into the room, going to stand by the half-open window shutters.

Rannulf swept his hand through his hair, smoothing back the tangled curls and searching his equally disordered brain for a reply. When none rose to the fore, he simply shut the door and turned to face the other man. "Something like that."

Talbot nudged aside a shutter and stood silhouetted against the bright sky beyond. "'Twould be interesting to know where you've been since we broke our fast. So far as I could discover, you were not within these walls, yet no one saw you leave or return."

On the attack? He shouldn't be surprised, for he and Gillian had been hard-pressed to conceal their passion for each other. He'd been careful to do everything his overlord asked of him, to leave no task unfinished, before he sought Gillian's company.

Rannulf's pulse picked up its pace at his overlord's words, calmly spoken though they'd been. But he refused to be baited. Talbot knew nothing of his tryst with Gillian. If he did, he'd not be standing there so unruffled. If he could only see Talbot's face, he'd have a better idea where he stood.

Best keep his mouth shut. No sense falling into any trap of Talbot's making. He should have realized—or perhaps accepted was more accurate—that there was more to his overlord than he'd thought. He knew better than most that hardly anyone showed their true face to the world.

He'd not make that mistake again.

Whether Talbot proved sharper than he'd believed or no, this was likely naught but an attempt to lure him into revealing himself—assuming, of course, that Talbot believed he had anything *to* reveal.

It could also be that Talbot suspected nothing, and that guilt—over any number of things—was turning him into an apprehensive fool.

Best to wait and see what Talbot had to say.

"I was about the place the entire morn, milord," he said. He gestured toward a seat before the empty hearth in the hope that he could move Talbot from in front of the window, but Talbot shook his head and remained where he was. "Busy with the work you set me to. It seems I never crossed paths with whoever sought me, 'tis all."

"Then Gillian must have been with you, for she's been missing all morning as well," Talbot said, his tone harsher now, challenging. He sauntered away from the window and moved toward the fireplace, ignoring the chair Rannulf had offered and instead leaning back against the mantle, arms folded across his chest.

Rannulf could see him clearly now, and what he saw did not reassure him in the slightest. Talbot's strange violet eyes looked hard, assessing, and his expression, his stance, all spoke of a confrontational attitude he'd not displayed before.

Should he speak the truth, at least so far as that Gillian *had* been with him? Would that satisfy Talbot's curiosity—for that had to be all it was—or would it be better to attempt to mislead him?

"I'd no idea 'twas so difficult to tell if Gillian was with you." Talbot laughed, the rough sound jarring against Rannulf's overstretched nerves. "I'd think you'd have noticed. God knows, she's a hard woman to ignore."

"Aye, she was with me for part of the morning."

Talbot's nod held approval, but his questioning gaze as it swept over Rannulf once more seemed to see too much, delve too deeply. "Perhaps I should have awaited Gillian's return rather than yours," he mused, stepping away from the hearth and circling Rannulf. "A woman's appearance might reveal more than a man's."

"Reveal what, milord?" Rannulf asked, though he knew full well what Talbot meant. Damn the man! Were the morning's activities writ upon him somehow, or did Talbot simply have a suspicious mind?

"Does her garb appear as disheveled as yours, I wonder?" Talbot reached out and plucked something from the back of Rannulf's tunic. "Although under the circumstances I'd think 'twould be hay adorning you, not this." He held out a small clump of grass. "I can't think of anyplace here where you'd have picked this up without someone noticing what you were about.''

"Are you accusing me of something, milord?" Rannulf asked. "If you are, do so and be done with it, for I've no patience to stand here while you—"

"While I do a guardian's duty?" Talbot snapped, his voice cold as ice now. "Aye, and an overlord's as well." Gone was every hint of the courtier. In his place stood a warrior who would brook no rebellion. "By Christ's bones, you wasted no time going after my ward!"

Rannulf's hand went to his waist to grab for his dagger—not so much to draw it as to clutch its comforting weight—but he'd removed his belt before Talbot's arrival. 'Twas just as well, for if Talbot continued along this vein, he might be tempted to a foolhardy reaction.

Lord knew, after the range of emotions he'd already experienced today, his temper had nigh reached its limits.

"What is it you accuse me of, milord?" he asked, forcing calm into his voice, his demeanor.

"I can see I'll get no answers from you," Talbot snarled. He stalked to the door and wrenched it open. "Mayhap I can convince my ward to tell me what I wish to know." His glare a challenge, he flung the door wide and started down the corridor.

Chapter Eighteen

"Talbot, wait!" Rannulf shouted. He ran out of the chamber, snatching up his sword belt along the way, and hastened after Talbot.

His overlord strode along the corridor, determination on his face and in his step—and Rannulf hard on his heels. "Milord," Rannulf called again, grasping the other man by the arm to stop him.

"Hands off, FitzClifford," Talbot said. He jerked his arm free. "You had your chance. Now I'd rather see Gillian, hear what she has to say about what you two were doing this morning." Not bothering to see if Rannulf followed him, he headed for the stairs, stopping on the first riser. "I warn you now," he said, looking Rannulf straight in the eye. "If you've caused Gillian the slightest harm, I'll see you suffer for it."

His temper flaring anew at the suggestion that he'd harm Gillian, Rannulf followed Talbot up the spiral stair, silent and uncertain what he should do. Other than telling Talbot that he'd attacked Gillian, he couldn't think of any other response but to admit the truth. Since that truth involved Gillian as well, he didn't feel it was solely his decision to make.

Whether Talbot would listen to anything he said at this point was unlikely, though he could try. 'Twould spare Gillian an unpleasant scene, at any rate. "Lord Nicholas," he called, but the other man ignored him completely.

He still held his belts in his hand, so he buckled them both about his waist. Perhaps he could block him from entering Gillian's chamber if he hurried.

As soon as they reached the landing they saw Ella bustling toward them from Gillian's room, her arms filled with clothing.

"Are those Gillian's?" Talbot asked.

Ella stopped. "Aye, milord."

Talbot placed a hand on her shoulder and turned her back the way she'd come. "Follow me."

"I'm to take these to the laundry, milady said," she protested. "She told me to do it right away." She shifted the bundle and gathered it more tightly to her chest. "If you'll wait but a moment, milord, I'll be back to do whatever you need me for."

"I need you right here," he said, herding her along the corridor to Gillian's door.

Ella cast a curious look at them both. "She was dressing, milord. I doubt she's had time to finish."

Brushing her aside, Talbot pounded on the door. "Gillian, are you decently covered?"

"Milord!" Ella protested. She tossed her burden on the floor and, moving faster than Rannulf would have believed possible, slipped between Talbot and the door. Her hands on her hips and bright color riding high upon her wrinkled cheeks, she made a surprisingly effective obstacle. "You cannot go barging into milady's chamber."

Rannulf folded his arms across his chest and looked

on with satisfaction. He'd not need to do anything after all—for the moment, anyway. He couldn't imagine Talbot would attempt to remove the old woman by force, and he doubted Ella would cease guarding her charge any other way.

His satisfaction was short-lived, however, for the door flew open and Gillian stood framed in the opening, clad only in her shift, sword at the ready. "Ella, what's wrong?" she asked, grabbing the maid by the arm and pulling her into the room.

Gillian looked past Ella, spied Lord Nicholas and Rannulf in the corridor and felt her pulse speed up even more. She shrieked and ducked behind the door until only her head showed. "What are you doing here?" she gasped. "Go away till I've finished dressing."

The expression on Talbot's face looked fierce enough to stop her heart altogether. What did he want?

And why did he have Rannulf with him?

Talbot picked up a tunic from the pile in front of her door and tossed it toward her. "You'd better cover yourself, milady, for we're coming in now."

"I think not," she said, already swinging the door shut.

He stopped her by the simple act of stepping into the opening. "Come on, FitzClifford," he called over his shoulder. "Get in here."

Clutching her undertunic to her chest, she backed into the room. "Can you not wait until I'm decently garbed?" she asked sharply.

Talbot's implacable expression hardened further. "Nay—I've questions for you, and I'll have the answers now." He took up a position by the door and motioned Rannulf farther into the room. "Don't be shy, FitzClifford," he said, something in his voice sending a chill down her spine.

Rannulf entered the chamber and crossed to stand between her and her guardian. Grateful, she stepped behind him and used his body to screen herself from Lord Nicholas.

"Milord, there's no need to do this," Rannulf said quietly. "If you'll leave here, permit Lady Gillian her privacy, I'll tell you whatever you wish to know."

What was Rannulf talking about? she wondered. What did her guardian want to know? To judge by his expression, she'd not like the answer.

"Nay, we'll not drag this out any longer." Lord Nicholas reached over and shut the door, the soft click of the latch sounding loud in the silent chamber.

And she'd not remain here with this crowd while scarce dressed, either. Still using Rannulf as a shield, she turned her back to Lord Nicholas and shook out her tunic, then wriggled it over her head.

The fabric tangled about her, trussing her arms to her body like a Christmas goose. "Damnation!" she muttered, squirming to free herself.

Rannulf turned to face her, reaching for the material bunched at her shoulders. "Here, let me help."

Unwilling to have his hands upon her now, with this audience, she stepped away, nearly falling over in the process. "Turn around," she ordered. Heat rose to her cheeks as she peered past him and caught Lord Nicholas gaping at her. "Both of you," she added. He frowned, but complied, as did Rannulf after sending her a look she didn't know how to interpret.

Ella, who'd stood motionless just inside the room till now, hurried to help her. "Let me do it, my lamb," she said. "Don't know what this world's coming to, with noblemen—" she glanced up from untangling the tunic to glare at Rannulf and Lord Nicholas "—barging into a lady's chamber when she's not decently covered." A final tug and the material settled around Gillian as it ought. "And look at you, your hair's not covered...."

"Enough," Lord Nicholas snarled. "Go sit somewhere out of the way, Ella. You may stay and guard your 'lamb,' but you'll not speak unless I tell you to."

"Yes, milord," she said, meekly dropping a curtsy while sending him a scathing look.

'Twas all Gillian could do to refrain from echoing Ella's attitude. She'd been sorely pressed of late, from the moment she rose and had to face Catrin—nay, since Rannulf and Nicholas arrived at l'Eau Clair—until she opened her door a few moments ago to this invasion. She was tired, hungry, and her mind—and body—still reeled from everything she and Rannulf had said and done.

She'd no patience to deal with this.

She could make her displeasure known, however, though she'd not reveal her embarrassment. If they'd not leave so she could dress and do something about her hair, she'd simply behave as if their presence didn't trouble her in the least.

If she could manage to preserve that bit of fiction long enough to endure whatever Lord Nicholas had in mind.

Gathering her unruly curls together and drawing them over one shoulder, she took up her brush and went to sit on the bench before the cold hearth. "If you're through ordering my personal servant about, and if you're determined to remain here infringing upon my privacy, you might as well be comfortable, my lords.'' Pointing with her brush, she indicated a chair and stool on the other side of the fireplace. "Though I think you'd be better served to go down to the hall and eat your dinner. Mayhap a hearty meal will help to improve your temper, Lord Nicholas,'' she added with an insincere smile. "You should take Lord Rannulf with you, of course.''

Talbot glared at her and paced to the window without speaking. Did he realize, she wondered, how much she wanted to leap up and rap him smartly with the brush?

She used Lord Nicholas's distraction to cast Rannulf a questioning look. He raised his eyebrows in reply—a useless show of innocence if ever she'd seen one—and sauntered over to sit on the stool across from her. He'd scarce said a word since they'd arrived, though she'd venture from his expression, and his continued silence, that he knew full well why his overlord had come to force his way into *her* chamber.

Not that his knowledge would do her any good since he didn't seem inclined to share it. Men! she fumed. They complicated her life nigh beyond bearing.

Though to be honest, he'd had no chance to say much of anything, and was probably wise not to try, given his overlord's present mood.

She glanced at Rannulf again, unable to resist the temptation, and was rewarded when a flush mounted his cheeks and he sent her a fleeting grin.

Some men—*one* man—was worth the bother, she thought with an answering smile as memories of that morn overtook her.

Lord Nicholas chose that moment to pound his fist on the table by the window, breaking the spell and startling her.

"By Christ's bones, I've had enough of this place!" he growled. He crossed the room and halted between her and Rannulf. "Conversations stop whenever I come near, servants go behind my back carrying mysterious messages…" He paused and looked first at Rannulf, then fixed his accusing stare on her. "My ward and my vassal creep away together more than once, so gossip would have it."

Rannulf stood and faced his overlord, his stance relaxed, his eyes reflecting his calm demeanor. "Aye, milord, you're right about that. We did steal away to be together this morning."

About to protest, to say *something,* Gillian held her tongue when she caught the swift, cautionary glance he sent her way. Her mind spun, though, as she wondered what he was about.

She'd have to trust him in this, as she had resolved to do in so many things.

Apparently Rannulf's admission satisfied some of Lord Nicholas's displeasure, for he dropped into the chair with a sigh.

However, the frown he sent their way once he sat up and raked his hand back through his tidy blond hair sent a different message. "I ought to lock you up at once for your effrontery, FitzClifford," he snarled. "I may do so yet, unless you give me some damned good reasons why I should not. Gillian is a *lady,* nobly born and gently reared. How *dare* you impose upon her delicate nature by—"

Gillian's burst of laughter cut through his stern lecture. "I beg your pardon, milord, but 'tis too ridiculous," she said, unable to keep the laughter from her voice. "You don't know me at all, if you believe a single thing you just said is true."

Now confusion added itself to the stew of emotions writ upon her guardian's face. "What do you mean?" he asked warily.

"She means her upbringing was a trifle unusual," Rannulf added, his eyes alight with amusement—or mischief, perhaps, she couldn't tell for sure which.

"Indeed? And how would you know that?" Her guardian rose from the chair as he asked the question. "I want answers, and I'll have them now—from one of you or the other." His frown grew. "I'm beginning to suspect either of you will do."

Gillian started to rise, but Rannulf stepped toward her, placed his hand on her shoulder and eased her back down onto the bench. "I'll do it," he told her quietly. He moved behind her to face Lord Nicholas, his hand still resting on her shoulder—lending his support, his strength to her, or so she'd assume, for she found his touch a comfort. "If I'd answered his questions before, we'd not have come to chase you down."

"I wouldn't count on that," Lord Nicholas drawled. "My mind was already chock-full of mysteries before I ran you to ground, FitzClifford. All you've done since then—" his sweeping look encompassed them both "—is to raise even more." He shook his head and gave a wry laugh. "I believed l'Eau Clair would be a boring place after the king's court. How could I have been so wrong?"

Rannulf squeezed her shoulder, then released her. Though she missed his touch at once, 'twas just as well he'd done so. Who knew what Lord Nicholas might make of a continued show of unity?

Rannulf glanced down at Gillian, seated in front of him on the bench and pondered how much he should reveal—to Talbot and Gillian both. He'd not told her all his secrets, nor had he decided if and when he should. But he'd rather not say much of anything, about either Gillian or himself. Still, the man would clearly not be put off any longer.

"I'd heard of Lady Gillian before we came here, milord," Rannulf said. The other man's expression grew more piercing at that revelation, but Rannulf ignored his show of interest. "You may be aware that the earl of Pembroke is her godfather." At Talbot's nod, he added, "I fostered with Pembroke, earned my spurs in his service. I heard her mentioned a time or two over the years. Believe me when I say her upbringing was different than most women's.... Or ask Gillian yourself," he added, for it seemed foolish for him to tell Talbot, not to mention risky. Just how much might he have "heard" about her, after all? Nay, let Gillian decide how much her guardian should know.

"The details don't really matter," Talbot said with a dismissing wave of his hand. "But why didn't you see fit to tell me this when I wondered if—" Looking uncomfortable, he cast a fleeting glance at Gillian. Rannulf suppressed a smile at the memory of Talbot's initial conjectures about his unknown ward; they weighed upon his mind now that he'd met her, no doubt. Did he worry that Rannulf might tell Gillian about those trivial assumptions?

As for Talbot's assumption that how Gillian was raised had no bearing... Rannulf shook his head at

Talbot's shortsightedness. Sooner or later, her guardian might have cause to regret his lack of knowledge about his ward.

By the rood, hadn't he noticed that she'd had a sword in her hand when she opened her door?

"It matters little now, but 'twould have eased my mind to know more of the situation," Talbot said.

"There was little I could tell you, milord, that would have helped you in any way." A true statement, and yet not the whole truth. "I know my duty to you. I'd not hide information that might bring harm to you."

"That's gratifying to know," Talbot muttered. "But what you've said thus far does nothing to give me the answers I seek." He eased back in the chair. "Tell me instead about this morning. Where were you both, that no one could find you?"

"There's a place in the herb gardens that's very sheltered, a bolt-hole of sorts." True as well, although he doubted Gillian was privy to that secret, either. He glanced down at her, then met his overlord's measuring gaze. "Truth to tell, milord, I heard voices—the search party, perhaps?—but I ignored them, being too—" he reached down, smoothed his hand over Gillian's wildly curling hair and settled it upon her shoulder once again, clasping it in a cautionary grip "—too pleasantly occupied to wish interruption."

Gillian tensed beneath his grasp, but remained seated and silent. *That's my love,* he thought, pleased by her trust.

Talbot looked far from calm, however. Had he gone too far, he wondered?

Half rising from his seat, Talbot growled, "You'd better not have taken—"

"Gillian remains as she was before, milord." His face already flushed from this conversation, Rannulf felt it heat more at Talbot's inference, his free hand clenching into a fist at his side.

"Enough, both of you," Gillian cried. "I'll not be discussed as though I'm not here." He could feel her tension beneath his fingers, but he refused to release his gentle hold upon her, for he found the connection between them helped calm him—and he hoped it helped her as well. "Lord Nicholas, I realize your questions arise from your concern for me, but you must believe that Rannulf has not harmed me in any way." She reached up and gave Rannulf's hand a squeeze, then rose gracefully to her feet. "I'm grateful for your concern, but there's no need for it."

Talbot stood and laid a hand upon Gillian's arm, stopping her when she would have walked past him. "You're wrong, milady, there's every need. King John himself set me to look after you, and I'll not violate that trust. Stay away from my vassal—from any of my men. They're not fit company for you." Though he spoke to Gillian, he sent Rannulf a look that promised more questions, retribution...Lord knew what else. "Obviously I haven't kept him busy enough before now, but 'tis time for that to change," he said firmly. "I'll see that he stays away from you."

Rannulf held his eyes and his expression to a calm he didn't feel—something he'd had plenty of practice doing his entire life.

If he could face down Bertram FitzClifford, then Nicholas Talbot didn't seem such a challenge. Unlike his father, his overlord had the dubious virtue of being a decent man, at least in his concern for Gillian's well-being.

How could he fault him for that?

The thud of running feet heralded a pounding outside the door. "Milady!" a man shouted.

"Enter," Gillian called. She broke free of Talbot's hold and hastened to the door just as Will flung it open.

"Good, you're here, milords," Will said breathlessly. "There's been another attack—if we hurry, mayhap this time we'll catch 'em. This time, the messenger had a horse and got to us quicker."

"Let's go," Talbot urged, leading the way out onto the landing, Rannulf, Will and Gillian right behind him. They raced down the stairwell, the sounds of chaos rising from the hall.

When they reached the foot of the stairs, Talbot waved Will on ahead, then halted for a moment and caught Gillian by the arm. "You, milady, are to stay within the keep," he ordered. "I mean it—no matter what happens, you will remain here. If we meet with delay or misfortune, you must be ready to defend l'Eau Clair. Promise me you'll obey me in this."

She nodded. "Aye, milord, you have my word."

"Thank you." He released her and turned to leave, then spun on his heel. "FitzClifford, you go impose some order on those fools in the hall, then bring them to meet us in the bailey."

"Aye, milord." At least Talbot still trusted him to do his duty.

Gillian remained on the landing once Talbot went out through the hall and left them alone. "Promise me you'll be careful," she murmured, moving to stand so close to him their chests were nearly touching.

But he would not leave Gillian without saying

goodbye, not even for so brief a journey as this. He scanned the area, but everyone's attention seemed focused elsewhere. "You've given me reason aplenty to do so," he whispered. He leaned down and brushed his lips over hers, savored her taste when she deepened the caress, regretfully lowered his hands to his sides before he succumbed to the temptation to crush her against him. "You'll do as Talbot asked?"

"I will." One last kiss, fleeting and sweet, and she stepped away from him. "We've both work to do," she added, heading toward the hall.

He swept his gaze over her, chuckling when the sight of her garb broke through his distraction. She never had finished dressing—or undressing—and her hair hung all about her in a wild disarray that sent a surge of heat rushing through his veins. Catching her about the waist, he swung her back to the foot of the stairs. "While I find your attire very appealing, love, first you'd better go put on some clothes."

She glanced down at her rumpled undertunic, gave a cry of dismay, and swiftly mounted the first few steps. Pausing, she leaned down and whispered, "Have a care, my love," then scampered up the stairs.

Her words hastened him on his way, his heart, despite the fact that he was going into battle, feeling lighter than it had in years.

It seemed that Gillian loved him still.

With that knowledge embedded in his heart, there was nothing he couldn't do.

Chapter Nineteen

Gillian peered out her window and watched the men ride away. Even from this distance, she could see that Rannulf and Lord Nicholas appeared involved in a heated discussion. What she wouldn't give to hear what they were saying!

What she wouldn't give to, just once, have a chance to go along, to help defend her home.

Would she ever grow accustomed to the sense of uselessness that assailed her whenever a threat to l'Eau Clair arose?

And how did ladies—delicate, *noble* ladies—learn to accept the fact that in the greater scheme of things, they'd no power?

While she might chafe at the restrictions placed upon her by her sex, she could not regret the ''unusual'' upbringing that had taught her to wield a sword, to think for herself, to want those rights a man took for granted.

Not that any of those things made a whit of difference, now that Lord Nicholas Talbot had come along to protect her.

Given the chance, he'd protect her from every

threat. Even from her own base desires, could he but know it.

As if she'd allow him, or any man, to dictate what she could do, who she gave herself to!

Since she doubted he'd accept her decisions, she'd simply have to make certain he didn't find out.

Stay away from Rannulf?

Impossible! That was one order she had no intention of obeying.

Talbot scarce waited until they were in the saddle before resuming his interrogation of Rannulf, and his patience clearly had worn thin after his earlier attempts had proved useless—although now he seemed less interested in discovering exactly what Rannulf and Gillian had been doing this morning, or where they'd been, than he was in tossing threats Rannulf's way.

Threats that didn't intimidate Rannulf in the least.

Gillian was his, now and forever, and he'd no intention of allowing Talbot—or anyone—to keep them apart.

It had been a blessing when the path became too narrow to ride abreast, but as soon as the trail widened, Talbot dropped back and seemed ready to pick up his tirade where he'd left off. They had more important concerns for the moment, however, and Talbot had harped on the topic enough. "I understand you, milord, I assure you," Rannulf told him before he could start in again. "Wouldn't we be better served to focus our attention on what we're about to face? We're nearly there."

"Aye, you're right." Talbot's mouth curled in a rueful smile, a vast change from his previous cold anger. ''Damn women anyway,'' he said. ''They cause me nothing but trouble. I used to believe I had trouble with women because nigh every beautiful woman tempted me, but I tell you, FitzClifford, Lady Gillian proves me wrong. I know she's lovely—you surely must find her so, else I cannot understand why you'd have risked my wrath to do whatever you two were doing earlier.'' He shrugged. ''But I tell you, she doesn't attract me in the least. I enjoy her company, but that's all.'' His bewilderment was clear.

''She's not like other women,'' Rannulf agreed. *One of the things he found most appealing about her.*

''Perhaps that's it,'' Talbot mused. He scanned the area they rode through, though there was little enough to see but the heavy forest surrounding the path.

The trail widened to a road, and they rode fast and hard through the thickly wooded hills, their troops somehow staying with them in the rough terrain, until they could smell, then see, a faint cloud of smoke winding through the trees. Talbot reined in and waited for everyone to catch up to them before he spoke. ''FitzClifford, you take the men of l'Eau Clair and attack from here once you hear my signal. I'll lead the others around to the far side of the holding. We'll hammer them between us,'' he said, low-voiced and urgent.

Rannulf nodded and gathered his men about him. Leaving a couple of youths with the horses, they crept through the thickening smoke and waited near the edge of the tree line.

The sounds of combat came through the murk, distorted and misleading. He couldn't distinguish much of what he heard, only the occasional clash of steel or pain-filled cry. Battle tension sent a fire through him, readying his muscles for work and sharpening his senses. For the first time in weeks he felt he could think clearly, free of the burden of emotion. 'Twas hard to wait for Talbot's signal when he wanted to rush out into the clearing and do what he could to help.

Will hunkered down next to Rannulf, his grin wide in a face alight with anticipation. "Seems like old times, don't it, milord?"

"Aye," Rannulf whispered back. "But this time, the enemy is real, not part of some childish game."

"And I don't have Gillian here to guard my back," Will added with a quiet laugh.

"Thank God." At least Gillian was safe within the walls of l'Eau Clair.

Talbot's signal sounded, piercing through the air. His war cry on his lips, sword in hand, Rannulf surged up and raced into the clearing, Gillian's men at his side.

As always, battle filled Rannulf with a cool, clean appreciation for life, an exhilaration that carried him through swordplay and dirty, punishing hand-to-hand combat with naught but a few scrapes and bruises. The addition of their men to the few who'd been sent to guard the holding carried the day. Dead men—raiders, mostly—littered the open space between the barn and outbuildings. Sword in hand, Rannulf stood catching his breath, wondering if any attackers were left alive, when several horses broke clear of the trees and raced past them, the riders masked behind plain armor and closed helms.

A few of their men gave chase on foot, but they couldn't catch up to the horses. "Will, take three men, get your mounts and go after them," Rannulf ordered, though he didn't hold much hope of capturing them.

Talbot crossed the clearing with angry strides. "Get anyone?" he growled.

Rannulf shook his head. "By Christ, when we find out who is doing this, I vow I'll spit the bastards and roast them over their own hearth!"

"Aye." Talbot sheathed his sword and peered through the smoke. "But in the meantime, we've flames aplenty to snuff out."

Fires continued to burn around them, mostly small, smoldering blazes that hadn't done much damage as yet, but couldn't be left unattended. They turned their attention to battling the fires before they spread from house to barn, fields to forest, while waiting for Will and the others to return.

Rannulf took out his frustrations by beating at the creeping flames with a blanket and helping to dig a ditch around the one barn that had somehow escaped the attackers' torches unscathed. He didn't mind turning his hands to such mindless work, for it gave him ample opportunity to ponder anew the situation.

How could they continue to be attacked, over and over, yet never catch the culprit? They needed more men, to guard the outlying areas more closely, to catch the attackers in the act and perhaps capture someone who could give name or face to the person behind this harassment.

For that was what it amounted to, he realized. Property had been damaged, and a few people killed or injured—but Gillian had not been harmed, nor had the more valuable of her properties been destroyed.

Obviously the person behind all this didn't want to

inflict too much damage on l'Eau Clair because they wanted the place intact.

And its mistress with it?

Mind racing with possibilities—when he wasn't mentally kicking himself in the backside for his stupidity—Rannulf gazed about him and saw that, thanks to the number of men they'd brought with them, the fires had been extinguished but for a few ruined outbuildings that still smoldered fitfully.

He discovered his overlord leaning on a shovel on the far side of the most damaged barn. "Milord, are we nearly through here?"

Talbot nodded. "We'll leave a heavy guard, of course, and send some men from the keep to begin repairs. Will has been gone so long, I doubt there's any sense in us waiting for him here. If he'd anything urgent to report, he'd have come back by now. If he needs help—" He shook his head. "We're nowhere close to give it, but we cannot linger here. 'Twill be dark soon. We'd best take our dead and injured and head home." He turned to one of his men. "Wait here and tell Will to meet us at the castle when he returns," he ordered, handing over the shovel and heading toward the forest where they'd left the horses.

"I've some ideas about the situation, milord, and some suggestions," Rannulf told him as they mounted up.

Talbot gave a weary nod. "Good. We need to take a different approach. Perhaps you've seen something I haven't." He climbed into the saddle. "Meet me in my chamber once we've had a chance to clean up."

Rannulf mounted his stallion and nodded, though Talbot had scarce lingered long enough to notice. There'd be no nagging chat on the journey back to the keep, he decided with relief. His overlord could badger as well as any shrew! Setting spur to March, he fell into line with the others, alert for any further signs of their assailants.

By the time the men returned near dusk, tired, hungry and incredibly filthy from their exertions, Gillian had had ample time to restore her usual neat appearance and to prepare for the wounded.

Plenty of time to think.

Although they'd lost several men in the attack, fortunately none of the injured had been badly hurt—an unexpected blessing. She gave a silent prayer of thanks as she herded men toward the laundry to wash and pointed out the food readied for them in the hall.

She couldn't help but look Rannulf over from head to toe, to assure herself he'd come through the battle unscathed. Though she'd always worried about him, actually watching him ride off to fight raised her concern for him to new heights.

Especially now that they'd begun to come to an understanding between them.

Her guardian stopped beside her. She could only stare to see the impeccable Lord Nicholas so filthy, even worse than after Idris's attack.

He surprised her further when he laughed. "Aye, I'm a sight." He laughed harder as she drew back her hand when he reached for it. "Fear not, I'll not sully your perfection with my dirt," he added, although she'd have sworn the amusement faded from his eyes at the words. "Twice in a week—'tis a new record for me." He sobered. "FitzClifford and I will eat in your father's private room," he told her, surprising her by referring to the chamber as her father's, not

his. "Send Sir Henry to us as well, for we've things
to discuss and plans to make. His counsel would be
welcome."

"What of me, milord?" she asked. "May I join
you?"

His reluctance obvious, he glanced past her for a
moment, appearing deep in thought.

"'Tis my home, milord, and my people being
harmed." She could not avoid sounding as though she
were making an impassioned plea—she was, and she
didn't care if he knew it. "I would know what you
believe is going on." Head held high, hands clutched
tight in the fabric of her bliaut, she awaited his decision.

He focused his eyes on her, his gaze measuring.
She felt as though he were looking at her for the first
time, *seeing* her in a way he hadn't before. "Join us,"
he said at last, his voice abrupt. Giving her a brief
bow, he hurried off toward the laundry.

Huw reined in his stallion and waited for the others—the few who had escaped with him—to catch up
before they traveled on to their camp. They'd lost
more men than he could afford this time, playing Lord
Steffan's foolish game of cat and mouse. The man
did enjoy taunting his opponent, although in this version of the game, Huw couldn't say for certain
whether his master saw Lady Gillian as the enemy or
the prize.

Whatever she was, he wished Lord Steffan would
act, do something *real*. An attack with form and substance, not these niggling little jabs at Lady Gillian
and her Norman warden.

But the addition of the Normans into the game—

once Lord Steffan recovered from his rage—had evidently lent new spice to the challenge.

Mayhap he needed to remind Lord Steffan that l'Eau Clair *was* the prize. The longer the Normans had to become entrenched there, the harder it would be to shake them loose from the place. They'd have been better served to strike the castle itself when Talbot first arrived and his party likely still in disarray—and before Lady Gillian had a chance to grow used to her guardian, become loyal to him.

But how long Lord Steffan planned to drag this out, Huw couldn't begin to guess. Hopefully they'd act soon—'twas damned uncomfortable making camp near Lord Steffan's mountaintop cottage, not to mention a hardship on the·men and horses to traverse the narrow, winding trail that led to it.

And the longer they remained there, the greater the chance the Normans would find their hideaway.

'Twas by the grace of God alone that they'd lost their pursuers this time. He watched the others as they rode up—the best of his men, and now naught but the bare backbone of a decent troop—the horses foam-flecked and blown, the men battle-weary. "Take a moment to rest," he told them. "We'll be safe enough here."

"'Twere a close one today," Cai remarked. He dismounted and accepted the flask of ale Huw held out to him with a nod of thanks. "Didn't think we'd get out this time."

"Left too many behind," Pedr added, taking his turn with the ale before passing it along to Gwilym, who nodded his agreement before draining the last of the brew.

"His lordship'll be right peeved." Pedr snatched a

clump of grass from the edge of the trail and wiped down his horse before turning to Huw. "Do ye think we should go back?"

"Where else would we go?" Huw said by way of answer. "You know he'll stomp and rage, then send us off to do his bidding yet again."

He hoped. Though Huw would never admit it to them, Lord Steffan's rages had been growing worse by the day—another reason he'd rather attack l'Eau Clair and be done with it. Or forget about gaining possession of the place and return to Bryn Du, Lord Steffan's manor.

The allure of taunting Lady Gillian had begun to pall, another truth he'd no intention of revealing to anyone.

Especially to his master.

By Christ, he grew maudlin standing here! Time to go, to seek food, rest and the courage he seemed to have misplaced somewhere along their headlong trek through the forest. A swift glance at his men showed that they and their mounts had recovered enough to start the final stage of the journey—the path up the mountainside.

"Come on," he growled. "Lord Steffan'll be wondering what's become of us."

"So long as you're the one to tell him what happened, Huw," Pedr said. Huw had to look away from the fear in his face. "You don't think he'll blame us, do ye?"

"Of course he will," Cai said mournfully as they led their mounts up the steep trail. "Don't he always?"

Night was closing in by the time they reached the summit and the end of the path, and they'd scarce have known where to go if it hadn't been for the thin bands of light glowing through the shuttered windows of Lord Steffan's cottage and the paltry fires where the meager remnants of their company gathered to fight off the darkness.

The guard at the top greeted them, his grim voice no doubt a herald of the reception awaiting them once their master deigned to appear.

Huw handed over the reins to the boy who cared for the horses and, girding himself as if for battle, approached the cottage and knocked on the door.

Steffan lounged back on the massive bed that took up much of the one-room cottage—little more than a hovel, by his estimation, but comfortable enough despite the lack of space. "Enter," he shouted before bringing his goblet of wine to his lips.

Huw came in and shut the door, but hung back in the shadows rather than striding forward as he was wont to do. "My lord," he said, sketching a bow just short of insulting in its brevity.

Steffan took the time to enjoy the rich red wine, allowing its warmth to flow through him as he savored the thought of Gillian sharing this bed with him. Ah, but that would be pure bliss. He chuckled. Nay, there would be little of purity once he brought his cousin here, save for her initial innocence, of course.

What a pleasure it would be to relieve her of that impediment!

Then she'd be his well and true, bound to him by blood and holy wedlock—a piquant combination he intended to enjoy to the fullest.

The fact that she would bring him a Marcher castle

and ties to one of the most powerful men in England as dower made the situation sheer perfection, in his eyes.

"How went your day, Huw?" he asked. "The raid on the farm proved a success, I trust?" He drained the goblet and reached for the pitcher to refill it.

"I fear it was not, milord," Huw replied evenly.

"Was it not? How is it that you're here, then?" He finished pouring the wine and turned his attention to Huw. The other man still lingered near the door, too far away to see well in the uncertain light. "Come closer, so I might see you while you tell me what went wrong." He ground out the last words as a host of possibilities, none of them acceptable, raced round in his brain.

His step sure, unhurried, Huw moved to stand by the foot of the bed, well lit from the tall rack of candles beside it. Soot dulled the gleam of his armor, and blood—someone else's, no doubt, since Huw appeared unharmed—stained his plain tabard in several places. He wore his usual intractable expression, a look that taunted Steffan every time he saw it—a look he'd never been able to decipher.

"You appear quite well for a man come to admit failure," Steffan said, proud of his even tone, of the fact that he'd not hurled the goblet across the narrow room.

Yet.

"I didn't say that we'd failed, milord." Huw relaxed his stance, folded his arms across his chest and leaned against one of the bedposts. "I said the attack wasn't a success." He leaned forward. "Talbot must have guards posted that we didn't know about. We'd scarce begun to fire the buildings before the Normans came out of the forest and stopped us. They came in force. 'Twas only by sheer luck alone that four of us managed to escape, and even then, they hounded us through the woods for the better part of the afternoon before we lost them.''

"You should have been more careful!" Steffan said, his voice shaking with rage. "Incompetent fools."

"I'd like to see you do better," Huw shot back. "'Tis no surprise to me that they're catching up with us—they're not about to let us keep after them forever without finding some way to fight us off. The rough terrain, and the Normans' ignorance of it, could only help us for a short time, milord. They're warriors, more experienced than Lady Gillian's men by far. I knew that soon they'd be on our tails."

Drawing a deep breath, Steffan sought to calm his thundering heart, the thoughts that threatened to overwhelm him. "What have you heard from your spy inside the keep?"

"I've had no chance to speak with her recently, but I'll find a way to do so soon. She's joined forces with one of the Norman servants, swears he's keeping her supplied with information, as well as what she's discovered herself." He snorted. "Keeps her supplied with *something,* I have no doubt," he added with a crude gesture.

"The success of my venture rests in the hands of some slut?" He fought back the sense of failure looming over him.

"Whores hear everything," Huw pointed out. "She'll find us a way. Perhaps we'll be able to attack l'Eau Clair, take Lady Gillian out, once I hear what she has to report."

"'Take her out'? I wish to remain there with her once I've taken control of the castle."

Huw's shout of laughter whipped Steffan's ire to new heights. "Milord, you cannot believe we'll ever take l'Eau Clair in fair battle? I haven't enough men."

"I care not whether the battle be fair or craven," Steffan growled. "Just ensure we win it! Send to Bryn Du for more men, or scour the alehouses of Chester to find them. I refuse to cry defeat after waiting this long for victory."

"But milord, I doubt—"

Steffan closed his eyes, the image of Gillian, strong and beautiful, heartening him. The power they'd have!

And the challenge of making her his... He sucked in a breath as the thought alone sent fire surging through his body.

Soon, he promised himself. *Very* soon. "I don't care how you manage it, but I *will* have Gillian as my bride. See to it!"

Chapter Twenty

After pausing in the corridor to speak with Ella, Gillian followed Rannulf into the room where her father had kept his private papers. 'Twas much like her solar, though not as bright and spacious, with much of the space taken up by the long, narrow table that dominated the center of the chamber. Late-afternoon light streamed through the single window, lending a brief, warm glow in its wake.

Her father had spent a great deal of time here in the last few months of his life—getting his affairs in order, she'd believed, although, given the events since his death, she doubted he'd done much in that regard after all.

But the room belonged to Lord Nicholas now, to do with as he wished during his tenure here. He'd changed little about the place from what she could see, merely scattering a few of his possessions around the room. But seated as he was in the heavily carved chair that had been her father's pride, studying the parchment spread out before him on the table, he appeared comfortable here, as if he'd made this chamber his by his presence alone.

As she took a seat at the opposite end of the table, she realized she'd never discussed with her guardian how long his guardianship might last.

With that thought came the awareness that she'd never taken the time to discuss much of anything with Lord Nicholas, including his opinion on the subject of her marriage.

Surely he didn't believe she'd remain unwed forever! He'd the right to forbid her marriage, however—and it certainly would be profitable for him to do so, for the reins of l'Eau Clair were firmly in his hands. Whether *he* needed those resources, she couldn't say, any more than she knew his circumstances. Was he wed?

Or might he think to ensure l'Eau Clair would remain in his control by marrying her himself?

'Twas past time to learn more about her guardian. She bit back a groan. The only man she was interested in learning more about was Rannulf FitzClifford.

Sir Henry thrust the door open wide and entered the room. "My apologies, milord. I got caught up in questioning Will and the others to see if they noticed anything about the attackers that we might find useful."

Lord Nicholas glanced up from the parchment, his gaze sharp. "And did they?"

"Nay, milord, not a thing." Sir Henry pulled up a bench and settled onto it with a sigh. "'Tis enough to drive a man mad, this uncertainty! We've had our problems with raiders and the like over the years, especially when Lord Simon first came out here and started building the keep. But the Welsh have pretty much left us alone since Lord Simon wed your mother, milady, not wishing to run the risk of angering the prince."

"The prince?" Lord Nicholas asked. "What prince might that be?"

"Prince Llywelyn of Wales," Gillian told him. It didn't matter if he knew—she was surprised he hadn't known, since 'twas no secret.

"Are you kin to him, too?"

She nodded. "'Tis how I'm related to Ian and Catrin. We're all cousins of some sort, not closely related. I've never met Llywelyn. Ian and Catrin are my only Welsh relatives I know."

"Saying it won't make it true, milady," Sir Henry said tartly.

She caught his meaning and frowned. "Steffan hardly counts."

"But Lord Steffan *is* related to you, as he's so fond of reminding you." Sir Henry chuckled, tempting her to reach over the table to poke him.

She resisted the impulse, contenting herself instead by picking up one of the small, wrinkled apples from the basket in the center of the table and hefting it in her hand, her smile a promise of retribution. "I'd just as soon you didn't remind *me* he even exists, the posturing fool."

"Another cousin? I assume I'll not be called upon to welcome him to l'Eau Clair?" her guardian asked.

She shook her head. "Not while I've any choice in the matter. Besides, he's already come to express his condolences." She took a bite of the apple and chewed before adding, "I refused to let him in—told him we'd vile sickness here and I wanted to protect him."

"I doubt he believed you," Sir Henry pointed out.

"What does it matter, so long as it sent him away?" she protested.

"Aye, sent him away angry." Sir Henry leaned toward her. "I doubt he's so easily dismissed, when he decides he wants something. And you know what he wants as well as I do. I've told you before, milady, he's not to be trusted." He turned to Lord Nicholas. "And he's the devil's own temper, milord."

"He never came back," her guardian said. "Perhaps he finally realized Gillian didn't want him here."

Sir Henry gave an inelegant snort. "He's too afraid to come back now that you're here, milord, 'tis all. Hell, he probably saw you on the road and nigh fell off that showy beast he likes to prance around on. He came the same day you arrived."

"How do you know he didn't return?" Rannulf asked.

"You'd have known it if he'd been here," Sir Henry said. "You'd be hard-pressed to ignore him. He dresses finer than any other Welshman I've ever seen—no offense meant, milady."

"None taken. Besides, you're right, he's very difficult to ignore."

"Besides that, he's arrogant, and mouthy with it."

Lord Nicholas frowned. "Then we shall hope he decides to stay away," he said. He put aside the parchment. "We've food and wine aplenty if you want some. Help yourselves." He indicated the platter set out on the table before reaching for the pitcher of mead.

Gillian hid a smile of pleasure at the thought that he didn't expect her to serve them. Perhaps he'd begun to see her as more than a simpering woman.

Or perhaps he thought it inappropriate to ask a noble lady to do so.

Let it alone, she ordered herself. *What does the reason matter, as long as the result is satisfactory?*

Once they'd served themselves, Lord Nicholas sat for a moment sipping his drink, then slouched back in his chair, the cup clasped loosely in his hands. "Rannulf, you told me earlier you'd some thoughts about this situation."

Rannulf finished slicing cheese from the wedge and, to Gillian's surprise, laid it on her trencher. "Aye, milord, I do."

"After all we've been through of late, you ought to call me Nicholas—you two as well," he said with a smile toward her and Sir Henry.

"As you wish, Nicholas," Rannulf murmured. Gillian couldn't decipher the expression in his eyes, but she thought he seemed pleased.

She gave her guardian—Nicholas—a nod of agreement. Perhaps his kind look was a sign he'd begun to grow comfortable with them. It was the perfect opportunity to know him better, she reminded herself.

Sir Henry looked uncomfortable. "I'd rather not, if you don't mind, milord. It's not my way."

He'd always called her father "Lord Simon," she recalled.

"That's fine," Nicholas told him. Straightening, he drained the cup, put it aside and leaned his elbows on the table, gazing hopefully at Rannulf.

"Even with the addition of your men and the ones I brought here to Gillian's troops, we haven't enough to guard such extensive lands and maintain an effective force within the keep as well. We're too spread out, and the raiders have continued to take advantage of that fact, hitting us where we're not prepared to defend." Rannulf popped a morsel of bread into his mouth and chewed. "Though today turned out well, I thought."

"'Tis true we haven't troops enough to safeguard the entire demesne, but we cannot conjure up more from nothing," Nicholas pointed out. "And I refuse to strip the castle bare of fighters, for I've no doubt that is the prize the raiders seek."

"The keep and Lady Gillian," Sir Henry said.

She shook her head. "I can see the sense in what you're saying, but it still seems beyond my ken— here—" she motioned to her stomach "—in my gut, for want of a better word, that anyone should see me as a valuable pawn."

Nicholas laughed. "Gillian, they'd want you for that reason alone, sight unseen, even if you were a haggard crone or little more than a babe in arms— simply for what you would bring them."

"Depending upon their inclination, they might actually prefer a woman very young or old," Rannulf pointed out with a wry smile. "'Twould be that much easier to be rid of you—having first gained all your worldly goods, of course—before moving on to the next victim."

Nicholas laughed again. "Do you truly believe that once a man has seen her, he'd wish to be rid of her?" He shook his head. "Nay, he's more apt to believe himself twice blessed."

Rannulf sent her a teasing look. "At least until he gets to know her."

'Twas pure reaction that had her pitch her half-eaten apple across the table at him, that and the banked heat she'd noticed in his eyes.

Still, she regretted it as soon as the fruit left her hand.

Rannulf caught it. A faint smile on his lips, he brought the apple to his mouth and took a bite, the fire in his eyes as he ate it kindling a like blaze deep within her. Unable to bear its intensity for long, especially since they'd an audience, she glanced away.

To find Sir Henry scowling at her.

Face flushed, she glanced at her guardian, uncertain what to expect of him. Nicholas glanced from her to Rannulf, his expression amused, pensive—but essentially unreadable.

Cheeks still awash with heat, she slumped a little in her chair, then forced herself to straighten as soon as she felt the carved chair back press against her spine. Lady Gillian de l'Eau Clair wouldn't cower in her seat.

She also shouldn't pitch food at others, she scolded herself.

She folded her hands on the table in front of her lest she succumb to further temptation. "Thank you, milords. I do understand what you meant. 'Tis sufficient, I think."

Rannulf's face sobered as he returned to the subject at hand. "I know how we can increase our numbers, at least for long enough to run our attackers to ground and vanquish them. I've sent word to my brother Connor, ordering him to send me a complement of FitzClifford's finest fighters. It's been quiet around my keep for some time now, so they should get by without a problem until my men return. And I'm certain Lord Ian will lend some of his people if Gillian asks it of him. Before he left, he mentioned something about doing so."

"We should have accepted his offer," Nicholas remarked. "Although he didn't bring all that large a party with him. Still, he might have sent some of them back once he arrived home.'' He served himself bread from the platter before him, pausing with his knife poised over the mutton. ''I wouldn't have asked while he was here,'' he admitted. He shook his head and resumed slicing the meat. ''Foolish pride has ever been one of my consuming flaws.''

''I'm willing to ride to Gwal Draig and ask for his help,'' Rannulf offered. '''Tis far too late to catch up to them, but I should arrive at his holding swiftly if I travel alone. I could lead the men back, assuming he is able to send any.''

''He will,'' Gillian told them. ''Ian hasn't a large manor, or many men under his command, but his people are well trained, and I know he'll help us.''

''Good. Rannulf, you'll leave—'' Nicholas glanced over his shoulder at the open window and the fading daylight. ''You'd best wait until first light. How large a guard should you take with you, I wonder?''

''I'll make better time if I go alone—''

''No,'' Talbot said firmly. ''What if you're attacked?''

''That could happen as easily if I've others with me.'' Rannulf toyed with his eating knife. ''I'll take Will—he's a good man in a fight, and he knows the area better than I. Is that acceptable?''

The three men fell into a discussion of the details, but Gillian had no desire to be drawn into it. She'd willingly admit that any of them knew better than she what they needed, and what Ian might be able to spare.

Instead she took advantage of the opportunity to observe Rannulf unhindered. The man she'd seen since they entered this chamber a short time before was one she knew well—far better, in fact, than the moody stranger who'd arrived here with Nicholas. This was the Rannulf she'd grown to love—a handsome man, strong, physically appealing to all her senses—but also a fun-loving tease, a skilled and intelligent warrior.

'Twas *her* Rannulf.

The happiness she felt at the fact welled inside her, was almost more than she could bear.

So she savored it, immersed herself in the sight and sound of him.

Having lost it all once, she vowed she'd never take Rannulf's presence, his love, for granted again.

If only they could stop the raiders and end the attacks upon her lands, her people, her joy would be complete.

By the time the men finished their plans, 'twas full dark, and Gillian could barely keep her eyes open. The day had been so full, spilling over with tension, with emotion. It would take time, and all her resources, to understand everything that had happened recently.

And it wasn't over yet.

She nodded her thanks when Nicholas held the door open for her. "I'll bid you all good-night, for I hear my bed calling me," she said with a faint laugh as she passed through the doorway into the corridor. "I'll see you in the morning before Rannulf leaves."

Surprised to hear her voice wobble on the last words, she dropped a swift curtsy, eyes lowered, and made her escape before she did something foolish.

Such as cry.

Or beg Rannulf not to put himself into danger on her behalf.

* * *

Rannulf spoke with Nicholas and Sir Henry awhile
longer after Gillian left them, one part of his mind
focusing on their discussion—and the fact that Nicholas seemed to have become more reasonable, more
approachable—the remainder of his thoughts distracted by visions of Gillian.

Gillian naked beneath him by the pool, tossing an
apple at him, trying not to cry when she left them.

Though 'twas naught but conjecture on his part, he
wondered if the tears he'd seen pooling in her beautiful eyes had been for him. Was she sorry to see him
go? God knew, he'd no desire to leave her, either, but
he could not stay, allow her to remain in danger, when
it was in his power to help her.

Besides that, he needed to talk to Ian, tell him all
he'd learned in the time since the Dragon had left
l'Eau Clair.

He sought his chamber, but found the room cold
and unwelcoming despite the fire in the hearth and
the candles scattered about the room to chase away
the shadows of night. He'd find any place cold now,
if Gillian wasn't there.

He drank deeply of the sweet spiced mead left
warming for him by the hearth. The heady brew sent
a wave of yearning through his veins, a boldness that
would not be denied.

Setting the cup aside, he bent and tugged off his
boots. He unbuckled his sword belt, but left his other
belt, with its sheathed dagger, about his waist. He
might be a fool in love, but he was not such an idiot
as to wander any keep completely unarmed.

As he turned to leave, he noticed a bowl of apples
on the table by the hearth. Grinning, he slipped one

into the pouch on his belt and, carrying his boots, headed off for a night of adventure with his love.

If she'd let him into her room.

He'd not ask, he decided as he crept through the torch-lit hall and up the stairs. Mayhap he'd be lucky and she'd be asleep. His blood burned hotter at the thought of creeping into her chamber—into her bed— and waking her.

He met no one—a blessing, for he had no explanation save the truth for wandering the hall with his boots in his hand.

And he knew that Nicholas, for one, would find his reasons no excuse.

Deep shadows shrouded her doorway, and the hallway stood silent and empty. He tucked his boots under one arm and carefully raised the latch and eased the door open wide to slip into the chamber.

The room stood in near-darkness, only the banked coals in the hearth lending their faint glow to hold back the gloom of night. He halted as an unwelcome thought assailed him. Did Ella sleep here, too? He hadn't any idea, and he couldn't see to tell. Explaining himself to her might be as perilous as meeting up with Nicholas.

'Twas too late to worry about that now, for he'd set himself upon this course, and he meant to follow it through until he reached his goal. If he met Ella lurking in the shadows by the bed, he'd deal with her then.

Gillian was worth any risk, as he well knew.

He made it to the bed unhindered and set his boots on the floor near the foot of it. The hangings were partly drawn on the side of the bed nearest him, cloaking Gillian from him.

And him from her, he thought with a silent chuckle.

Careful not to rattle the curtain rings, he eased open the drapery and rested one knee on the bed. Leaning forward, he reached for where he thought Gillian to be. Instead of encountering a warm woman, he felt cold steel pressed against his throat.

He remained motionless and silent, certain she'd not harm him, but unwilling to risk a mishap in the darkness.

"Sneaking about in the dark, milord?" she asked, her voice a silky caress. "What have you come to steal, I wonder?" She lowered the blade, drawing the flat of it along his neck, then rose up beside him to press the heat of her lips where the knife had rested.

He buried one hand in her disheveled hair to clasp her nape and closed the other over hers on the hilt of the knife and lowered it to rest on the mattress. "Need I steal what I want, or will I find it freely offered?" he asked. Tightening his grip on her hand, he brought it, blade and all, up to pull her closer to him.

Her fingers opened and she let the knife fall, turning her hand in his grasp and twining their fingers together. "You may take whatever you want, milord," she whispered. Raising their joined hands to her lips, she nipped at his knuckles, sending a bolt of fire streaking down his spine to pool in his loins. "I hoped you'd come to me tonight." Her tongue darted out to soothe the spot, then trailed over his fingers before she drew his fingertip into the warm wet cavern of her mouth.

She chuckled when he moaned in reaction, then did it again. 'Twas too much, yet not enough—he wanted that mouth, her tongue, elsewhere with a yearning he didn't try to resist.

He drew her back against the bolsters mounded at the head of the bed and captured her mouth with his. Despite the urge to seize her, strip off her silky shift and bury himself within the welcoming warmth of her body, he felt he'd rushed her before. He'd not do so this time, for he wanted to savor her, make memories to heat his blood while they were apart.

More than that, he wanted to show her how much he valued her, how much she meant to him.

Shifting the pillows, he propped them behind him and drew Gillian around to rest against his chest. "Do you realize, this is the first time we've been together in a bed?" he asked.

"Aye, 'tis wonderful," she said, wriggling against him as she sought a more comfortable position. "But 'tis so dark in here."

He laughed. "You just want to stare at my body," he teased. "Shall I tell you what effect your staring had on me this afternoon?"

She sat up, her hair slithering over his throat and making his breath hiss out through his teeth. "I'd like it even better if you'd show me," she said boldly. "If you don't mind if I light the candles."

He caught her by her shift before she could climb down off the mattress, tugging her back to him and pressing a kiss to her shoulder. Her shiver of reaction heightened his desire to not only feel her response, but to see it as well. "You wait here—I'll be right back."

He scrambled off the bed and groped along the table beside the bed until he found the flint and steel. His hands shook, but he managed to kindle a spark and light the single candle there.

Since Gillian wanted light, he would give it to her.

Taking the candle in hand, he roamed the room, lighting every candle he found until the chamber seemed filled with a golden glow. 'Twas chilly even to his overheated senses, so he stirred the fire into life, adding small pieces of wood until the flames caught hold.

He couldn't allow her to become cold, he thought with a grin.

"What's put that smile on your face?" she asked, reaching out to draw him down beside her on the bolsters. While he'd been busy lighting candles, she'd folded the coverlet at the foot of the bed and pushed the sheets down, out of their way. She lounged back against the pillows, her shift a tantalizing veil over her body, her hair strewn about her a fiery temptation.

"Nothing of importance." He'd make this night a memory neither of them would forget, he vowed, reaching out to stroke his finger over her eyebrows, down her nose, finally reaching her lips.

It scarce seemed possible they could be softer than her skin, yet they felt delicate as rose petals. Her tongue darted out to brush his fingertip, then just as quickly disappeared. He traced the outline of her mouth, watching her eyes grow dark, unfocused.

The expression in her eyes made him recall the apple he'd brought. Still holding her gaze with his, he unbuckled the belt, fumbled the fruit from the pouch and set the belt on the floor beside the bed.

"Where did your knife go?" he asked.

Her eyes widened and she sat up straight. "What do you need it for?"

What an idiot he was, to frighten her! "Nothing harmful, I assure you," he said, reaching out to stroke her shoulder and ease her onto the pillows. He held the apple out to her on his outstretched palm. "I need it for this."

Her expression brightened, and a teasing light appeared in her eyes. "I believe I'm supposed to offer this to *you*." She took it from him and held it out to him, her smile enticing. "Can I tempt *you*, milord?"

"You already do," he told her. "But I would tempt you, milady." He reached beneath the pile of pillows and found the knife. At her questioning look, he added, "Right where I keep mine."

He took the apple and cut a slice from it. After carefully returning her blade to its resting place, he brought the apple to Gillian's lips.

When she opened her mouth to take a bite, however, he edged the fruit away, instead dragging it over her lips and painting them with the tart, sticky juice. The tip of her tongue slipped out to taste it just as he bent and licked at her mouth. He would not allow her to hurry him, but lapped away every trace, then captured her lower lip with his teeth and nibbled at it.

Her moan filled his mouth. Still toying with her lip, he raised the piece of apple to the corner of her mouth and trailed it over her chin, down her throat and, nudging aside her shift, down to circle her nipple.

He had no word for the sound that Gillian made, but that it signified pleasure he had no doubt. 'Twas nothing short of a miracle that he hadn't melted into a puddle beside her; he hadn't realized that by teasing her, he'd well nigh drive himself mad with longing.

And he'd yet to follow the apple's path. Smiling, he drew a deep breath and set off on the journey.

Chapter Twenty-One

Gillian gasped as Rannulf slowly, tortuously followed the apple's path down her body. The anticipation of his touch alone sent heat pulsing through her to center deep within her. The reality of his tongue blazing its way over her sensitive flesh made her nigh mindless with need.

She ached for his possession, but it seemed he was in no hurry to bring their lovemaking to fruition.

Indeed, he seemed intent upon making it last a *very* long time.

She'd not complain about that, but she didn't know if she'd strength enough to endure this blissful torment.

He paused at her throat, raking his teeth over her skin, nibbling at the place where her blood pulsed just below the skin until she thought she'd swoon. "Does that please you?" he murmured, the vibration of his voice adding to the sensation.

She nodded weakly—all she could manage—and slid deeper into the pillows. He slipped his hand beneath her back and arched her to meet his questing mouth. His tongue traced over her chest, leaving dampness in its wake. He followed that course with his callused fingertip, spreading the moisture, then blew gently on the spot, sending a chill that wasn't cold at all skimming over her skin.

"Rannulf, 'tis too much—" she whispered.

He halted the words with a finger over her lips. "Hush, love, 'tis only the beginning." He reached for her hand and twined his fingers with hers, his free hand lifting her breast to his mouth.

He lapped away every trace of juice, his flexing grip on her hand somehow intensifying the feel of his tongue on her breast. Finally he left her nipple wet and aching and rose on his knees to brush his lips across her own. "You taste so sweet," he said. His voice shook—did he feel as she did, ache the way he'd made her ache?

She hoped so.

From someplace inside her she found the strength to return his kiss, to try to make him lie back against the pillows so she could torment him as he'd done to her. "Not yet, love," he told her, resisting her efforts and edging down her body once again.

Before she could argue with him, he closed his teeth carefully about her nipple and sent every thought flying from her mind. Waves of pleasure flowed through her, leaving her limp and throbbing with need.

She clutched him to her, burying her fingers in his hair, the feel of the soft curls brushing against her another caress. "Rannulf, please," she cried. Her hand still gripped in his while he suckled her breast, he smoothed his free hand over her—breast, belly, the sensitive flesh of her inner thighs—pushing her shift down her body and off her legs before answering her unspoken prayer and moving to caress her aching women's flesh.

Her senses shattered beneath his touch. He rose up and muffled her cries with his mouth; his kiss, and his hand still stroking her, eased her into awareness so subtly it seemed but another part of the pleasure he'd given her.

He brushed kisses over her cheeks, her brow, then her lips again, until her body quieted and she could think again. "Thank you," she murmured.

He smiled. "'Twas my pleasure, love."

"I doubt that," she said, casting a look over his still-clothed body. Her cheeks heated at the realization that she'd been so involved in her own pleasure, she'd scarce spared a thought for his. "'Tis your turn now," she said, the words a promise.

She only hoped she could bring him as much joy as he had given her.

Her fingers shook, but she fumbled open the neck of his shirt. "Off with your clothes," she commanded.

"As you wish, milady," he replied, his mouth quirked into a winsome smile, his eyes dark with appreciation as he caressed her with his gaze.

"Stop," she said. Perhaps if she covered herself... She reached for her discarded shift.

He snatched it away from her and pitched it across the room. "It gives me pleasure to watch you, love. Your skin is so beautiful, and your body..." Kneeling before her, he skimmed his hands over her from shoulders to knees. "Your body is made for mine." He eased away from her. "I'll behave, as long as you let me look my fill."

Since she intended to do the same, she could hardly

argue the point with him, so she focused her attention on him—a distraction, indeed.

He lay back on the pillows, his arms at his sides, and gifted her with another of his teasing smiles. He seemed as willing as she to have her pleasure him.

She helped him tug his shirt and tunic together over his head. His chest gleamed in the candlelight, limned in the warm glow. His arms bore the strength of years of a warrior's training, sleek and strong. She curled her hand about his upper arm, the flex of muscles beneath her fingers sending a wash of heat through her. "You're so much stronger than I." She traced her finger over the bulging muscles and down to the tender skin of his wrist.

He sat up, leaned toward her. "I will never use that strength against you, my love," he said, the urgency in his voice startling her until she realized the source of it.

She caught his hand in hers and raised it to her lips. "I know," she assured him. "I would never expect that of you, Rannulf. I trust you, body and soul, and I always will."

She pushed him down onto the pillows and, holding his gaze, spoke words she'd never thought to say, save that he needed to hear them. "Your strength excites me." Her touch light, she outlined his shoulders, chest, stopping at the waistband of his braes. "You make me feel delicate, cherished—not weak, but not as outwardly strong as you.

"There's something about feeling your size and strength surrounding me... I cannot describe it, but knowing that you could overwhelm me if you wished—yet knowing you will not—it sets fire to my blood." Fingers unsteady, she toyed with the knotted

drawstring. "You overwhelm me in other ways, with
your tenderness, your kind heart—" She untied the
knot, grasped his braes and began to tug them off.
"Your passion." Trying not to stare, she shoved the
fabric over his legs, but found her fascinated gaze
wandering back to his manhood.

She glanced up in time to see him close his eyes
for a moment, then open them and send her a teasing
smile. "My 'passion' is quite overwhelmed by you
as well," he said with a chuckle. Her face, doubtless
flushed red already, grew hotter still.

But she'd not look away.

"And I thank you for what you said," he added,
his voice serious. "It means more than I can say."
He picked up her hand and brought it to his lips. "I'm
glad my body pleases you. Feel free to do with it as
you will."

"Gladly," she murmured. Uncertain where to begin, she sat back on her heels and, taking her time
about it, eyed him from head to toe.

She kissed him while she decided what to do next,
savoring the taste of him, spicy and warm. "Where
did that apple go?"

She found the slice on the sheet and picking it up,
pondered what to do with it. She'd certainly enjoyed
what Rannulf had done, so she brought the fruit to
his lips.

Before she could do anything further with it, he
captured her hand and nibbled at the apple. "You're
not supposed to eat it!" she cried. He snatched the
rest of it from her fingers with his teeth as another
thought came to mind. "You…you smeared that over
my…" she gestured toward her breast.

"I know." He grinned and finished chewing the

fruit. "'Tis the most delicious apple I've ever tasted." He tugged her down onto his chest and kissed her, sweeping his tongue, apple-tart, over hers.

Pulling away, she scowled at him for a moment before deciding that she'd play his game, aye, and beat him at it.

She found the apple on the table beside the bed, then groped under the pillows for the knife, giving Rannulf a close view of her naked torso in the process. The idea didn't disturb her as much as it probably should have—less, in fact, than it had only a few moments ago. After watching him eat the slice of apple with such gusto, she could feel her maidenly reserve ebbing fast.

Catching the knife by the hilt, she slid it free and hacked off a piece of apple, then set it, along with the fruit, on the table. "I might need them again," she told Rannulf, her smile teasing. "Depends upon how much of this you can withstand."

"You may need the whole apple." His expression called her to him, dared her. "What are you waiting for, love?"

If she must be bold, she'd give it her full attention. She reached over and dragged the candle stand on the far side of the bed closer, nudged the bed hangings out of the way. "I want to see what I'm doing," she said when he raised his eyebrow in question.

The slice of apple clutched in her hand, Gillian knelt beside Rannulf on the mattress and leaned over him as though pondering where to begin. He followed her every move with his eyes, amusement brightening his passion-dark gaze when the apple hovered near his manhood. His smile dared her, but she couldn't be *that* bold—not yet, at any rate.

She chose instead to mimic his route, anointing his lips first, bending to sample the taste of him as she grazed her fingernails lightly over his whisker-dark cheek. "I think 'twas naught but a ruse," she whispered in his ear. "All I taste is you."

His laugh was a deep rumble, sending a shiver along her spine. "Perhaps." His tongue darted out and trailed over her lower lips. "Or perhaps you need to try again."

Apple or no, 'twas no hardship to kiss him, to trail the piece of apple on a meandering route from his mouth to his belly, her mouth following in its wake. He didn't touch her with his hands, but he caressed her with his voice, murmured words of passion designed to spur her on.

To build her desire again.

By the time she had kissed and licked her way to his stomach, his comments were interspersed with moans of pleasure—and she'd decided to raise her daring to new heights. Rannulf's eyes, closed now, shot open when she cupped his manhood in her hands.

His breathing ragged, he raised himself on his elbows. "I didn't believe you'd go so far, love." She shifted on the mattress, sending her hair streaming over his belly before she swept it out of the way.

He sat up and caught her to him, his arms hard bands about her, his hands cupping her face. "You win, love. Any more of that, and I'll not last to make you mine." His kiss stole her ability to think, to feel anything beyond the man who held her so tenderly. When he broke off the kiss she found herself sprawled beneath him, his manhood pressing for entrance. "Do you want me?" he asked. He raised himself on his arms to gaze at her face, his eyes dark, intense.

"You know I do," she told him, sounding as breathless as he.

"Then take my love and give it back again," he whispered, staring into her eyes as he joined himself with her.

This made all that had gone before but a game, temptation for a pleasure beyond imagining. Moving together, they found passion, a joy so complete she never wanted it to end.

Together, anything was possible.

Rannulf crept from Gillian's room well before dawn began to lighten the sky. Though they'd barely slept, he still felt wonderful when they met in the bailey a short time later, his body sated with love, his heart full of hope for a future with Gillian.

Perhaps with his family as well, for he'd begun to believe he might resolve his differences with Connor. He'd seek out his mother, too, at the convent near FitzClifford. Perhaps now, with the passage of time to heal her, and the promise of her family together again, she'd be ready to return home.

As for himself, with Gillian by his side he believed he could come to terms with all that had happened these four years past.

To his eyes Gillian had the look of a woman well loved—he'd done his best to see that she was, he thought, hiding a grin—though he hoped that to Nicholas's eyes, she'd simply appear as though she'd just crawled from her bed—alone.

He doubted anyone would notice. In the flickering torchlight 'twas difficult to see clearly.

Will, bundled against the predawn chill, led his mount from the stables and joined them, cutting off

Nicholas's spate of final instructions. "Ready whenever you are, milord," he said, his voice giving the
lie to his words, his expression that of a man ready
to crawl back beneath the covers. Scowling, he
mounted and sat hunched over in the saddle.

"You should have sought your bed a mite earlier,
lad," Sir Henry said flatly. "Look at Lord Rannulf—
'tis clear he got plenty of rest last night."

Rannulf caught the amusement in Gillian's eyes
and nearly burst out laughing. Plenty, aye—but not
of rest, he thought, winking at Gillian. She turned
away, coughing into her cloak. 'Twas laughter she
hid, more like.

Rannulf listened as Talbot finished relaying his orders, handing him a folded parchment with a message
for Ian. "Have a safe journey," he said as Rannulf
climbed into the saddle. "Come back as soon as you
can."

Once Nicholas stepped away, Gillian approached
March and motioned for Rannulf to lean down. "I've
something for you," she said quietly. She handed him
a small, cloth-wrapped bundle. "Don't open it now.
Save it till you're away from here."

He accepted it with a nod of thanks, catching hold
of her hand before she could back away. "Think of
me while I'm gone." Leaning down farther, he
brought her hand to his lips. "Adieu."

Releasing her, he waited only until she'd moved
back before nudging March into motion. Their hoofbeats echoing in the empty bailey, they rode out
through the gate.

Rannulf turned to catch a glimpse of Gillian, compelled to go back lest she disappear while he was

gone. Would it always be this way? Would he wonder, every time he left her, if he'd ever see her again?

Gillian watched Rannulf and Will ride out, then turned to go back to her chamber—and her bed.

Mayhap this time she'd sleep there, she thought, her quiet laughter sounding loud in the silence.

"Gillian, wait," Nicholas said, grasping her by the arm and drawing her to a halt under one of the torches that lit the stairs to the keep.

She glanced around. Sir Henry must have returned to his quarters in the gate tower while she watched Rannulf leave, for only she and Nicholas remained in the shadowy bailey. "What is it, milord? We should go inside if you wish to talk."

He shook his head. "Even at this hour there are too many people in the hall. This suits my purpose well enough." His touch firm, he spun her about so the torchlight fell on her face. Eyes narrowed, he pushed back her hood. "I don't care to see my ward wearing the look of a woman well loved," he snarled. "I don't know what game you and Rannulf are playing, milady—"

"'Tis no game, Nicholas," she said quietly, though she wanted to snarl and rage at him for his words and what they inferred. "Not on my part. Nor on Rannulf's, either, for I trust him to be honest with me."

"Your trust is easily given to a man who is little more than a stranger to you." His expression harsh, he released her arm, but stood close to her, holding her there by force of will alone. "I hope you haven't been foolish enough to give your body as well," he added. Exhaling sharply, he ran a hand back through his hair and gazed intently at her face. "I simply wish to protect you from hurt, Gillian. Not only because you're my ward and it's my duty, but simply because I want to keep you from harm.'' He leaned closer. ''Although he's my vassal, I know very little about FitzClifford. He seems a decent man, but I could not swear to the fact.''

He sounded sincere, appeared concerned for her. She'd come to trust Rannulf again; would she be a fool to risk trusting Nicholas, as well?

''I know less of you, milord, yet you expect me to trust you,'' she said, watching him carefully.

''Unlike Rannulf, however, I want nothing from you.''

''Nothing but my blind obedience,'' she said bitterly.

''Nay, how can you say that? All I've asked of you is to be careful.'' Nicholas appeared genuinely surprised.

Of course, he knew nothing of her unusual upbringing. 'Twould be a mark of trust on her part to tell him of it. ''Unlike most women, milord, I've been taught to defend myself with knife and sword.''

''That won't do you any good if you happen upon a raiding party on your own,'' he said, sounding the stern guardian once again.

She opened her mouth to refute his words, until the meaning of them rang clear in her mind.

He'd not said them to insult her, but because of his concern for her. She worried about Rannulf because she cared for him; could it be that she mattered to Nicholas as *Gillian,* rather than some nameless, faceless ward?

If that was true, she'd been insulting him, though that hadn't been her intention.

She placed her hand on his arm and stared up at his face. "I apologize for my thoughtless behavior, milord. Do you think, if we get to know each other, that we might become friends?"

Chapter Twenty-Two

As the days passed with no word from Rannulf, Gillian's unease mounted. Had something happened to him? Had he and Will ever made it to Gwal Draig at all?

What if the raiders had taken them? Could that explain why there had been no further attacks since the one the day before Rannulf left? But if that were the case, she'd expect to have received a ransom demand, or to hear *some* word about their capture.

At least Nicholas didn't suspect Rannulf of having any part in the attacks—'twas a foolish thought, but not beyond imagining. Besides, the attacks had started long before Rannulf's arrival at l'Eau Clair.

She shook her head. Her mind had become full of such ideas of late, scurrying from thought to thought with scarce a moment's respite—impossible ideas, many of them, but increasingly beyond her ability to control.

Her days were so full, 'twas a wonder she found time to think at all. But the nights...in the dark of night, as she lay in bed wishing Rannulf was nestled by her side, her traitorous mind could believe anything.

Life at l'Eau Clair settled into an uneasy routine of sentries patrolling the boundaries of her lands, of guards dogging her heels whenever she wished to go outside the castle walls for any reason.

'Twas much like being under siege, save for the fact that their enemy remained hidden, unknown to them.

For the most part, she remained within the keep, only venturing to the village every few days to care for the sick. Of late, however, the need for that task had lessened, for the villagers appeared well and happy.

She'd gone to the pool once, accompanied by several heavily armed guards, intending to gather herbs to replace those Rannulf had dumped from her basket of simples. It had been a mistake she'd not cared to repeat, for the place seemed haunted by the memories of everything that had happened there between them.

Everything reminded her of Rannulf, it seemed. She'd become a lovesick fool, for not even the press of her duties could ease her longing.

Or her worried mind.

She told herself her concerns were based on nothing more than the fact that she missed Rannulf, ached for him with every fiber of her being. Having lost him once, she felt he was doubly precious to her now. She missed him far more this time than she had in the early days of his absence four years earlier. Perhaps fear alone accounted for it, the fear that once again they'd shared their passion and he'd left her. The situation was different this time—they were different— yet in the depths of the night when she could no longer distract herself with work or the company of others, she could not prevent her misgivings from rising to the fore.

If only Rannulf's father hadn't died, would Rannulf have returned to her sooner? What would their life have been like? Would they have had children by now? she wondered, pressing her hand to her roiling stomach as if she could drive away another worry come to haunt her.

'Twas no use thinking of what might have been, for all she had any hope of controlling was the here and now. Though from what she'd observed, she'd little chance of that, either.

Surprisingly she found Nicholas's company a blessing. They'd come to an understanding of sorts on the day Rannulf left, and had begun to know each other better. She'd discovered a completely different man hidden beneath the pompous courtier sent by the king to watch over her, a decent man who seemed hesitant and afraid to reveal his true self. She liked the new Nicholas. She would never have suspected the sense of humor lurking beneath his handsome visage, humor directed at himself, often as not. Nor had she realized what a good friend he could be.

He realized how much she missed Rannulf, had come to know some of their story from the conversations they had, yet she'd seen little sign of the overprotective guardian from his early days at l'Eau Clair. His behavior then had been what he thought a guardian should be. Now, though he continued to guard her and her people, he did so with an ease and common sense she found much easier to accept.

She'd even begun to hope he favored a marriage between her and Rannulf.

The question in her mind was whether Rannulf still wished them to be together.

Why hadn't he returned?

But other than a brief message, sent when he reached Gwal Draig, they heard nothing—from Rannulf or from Ian.

Nicholas teased her about her growing malaise, saying she grew sick and wan from pining for Rannulf. If Rannulf didn't return soon, he pointed out with a laugh, she'd dwindle away to nothing. Though he refused to send anyone after them, as the days mounted to weeks, she could see that Nicholas grew anxious as well.

But his words and teasing couldn't cheer her for long, especially once she began to wonder if her sickness was more than longing—and caused by an all-too-likely reality.

Food held little appeal, not that it stayed put for long anyway. It seemed as though everything made her stomach rebel—smells, loud sounds, the mere act of being awake, though *staying* awake had become a challenge, too.

She carried Rannulf's child.

There could be no other explanation for her symptoms. The unremitting nausea, her exhaustion—and her flux had not come since before she and Rannulf had made love.

Add to that the fact that somehow she simply *knew*.... A child, a tangible symbol of their love. How would Rannulf react to the news? Would he be pleased? Feel trapped? Her longing for Rannulf's return became nigh an obsession.

Rannulf had been gone for nearly a month. Gillian

rose with the sun, dressed and descended the stairs to the hall, her heart heavy, her stomach churning.

Nicholas, seated at the table to break his fast, watched her slow progress across the hall. Once she stepped up onto the dais, he stood and pulled out the bench for her, then pushed a loaf of bread and a cup of watered wine her way. He remained silent until she'd broken off a chunk of bread and washed it down with a sip of wine. "I hope he returns soon," he said quietly. He slid along the bench to take her hand, giving it a squeeze. "You won't want to wait too long before you wed."

A glimpse of the concern in his eyes sent the tears she'd held in check since Rannulf left streaming down her cheeks. He slipped his arms about her and simply held her while she sobbed against his shoulder.

Finally, her tears spent, she raised her head. He released her at once, but took hold of her hand again. "You know, I gather?"

He gave a humorless laugh. "'Twould be difficult to miss the signs." He tugged her veil into place. "I was right in my suspicions about you two, wasn't I?"

"Aye." Heat flooded her face, but she held his gaze. At least she saw no condemnation in his eyes, only concern.

And questions she shouldn't put off answering any longer.

"You knew him before—quite well, I'd venture. And he'd been here before," he added, statements of fact, not questions.

"Yes, years ago, before his father died. Everyone believed we would marry." She picked up her cup and sipped at the wine, hoping to settle her stomach. "How did you know?"

"I might have acted like an arrogant fool—likely I still do—but I hope I can see what's before my eyes once I think to look. And 'twas clear to me from the start that there was something between the two of you."

She placed her hand on her flat stomach. "And now there will be something more between us," she said softly.

"FitzClifford will do as he ought, I'm certain." His expression solemn, he added, "If he cannot, I would be pleased to give you my name, my—"

"Nay, Nicholas, you need not do anything rash—or permanent." He'd surprised her, but she knew he didn't want her for his wife. "'Tis good of you to offer, but it's not necessary." Indeed, she prayed it wouldn't be. "Rannulf will be back soon."

Though he tried to hide his relief, she could see it reflected in his eyes. "If they don't return in the next few days, I'll send a party of men to follow their route to Gwal Draig, find out why they've been delayed."

"Thank you, milord," she murmured.

He stood and climbed over the bench. "Sir Henry was supposed to meet me here. I'd best go discover what's keeping him." He made a brief, polite bow and left the hall, calling for Richard as he went.

Gillian turned her attention back to the dry bread that was all she could stomach and tried not to dwell on what Nicholas had said—and what he had not. Did he believe Rannulf would return, or did he think something had happened to Will and Rannulf?

Something terrible.

A woman's scream echoed through the hall. Heart pounding, Gillian tripped over the bench, then stumbled to her feet and looked around to see what was wrong. A maidservant ran toward her from the corridor behind the dais, her gown torn, her face pale as milk. "Welshmen!" she screamed as she dashed into the center of the room. "Run, milady!"

Rannulf rode toward l'Eau Clair at the head of a sizable troop. Ian had been generous in lending them the men they needed; however, because of Llywelyn's prior claim on his resources, it had taken several weeks to bring together an adequate force.

The wait had seemed interminable, although he'd had time aplenty to think—about his past, his family and the life he hoped to have with Gillian.

He'd also taken advantage of Ian's counsel. The talks he had with Gillian's cousin helped him see his life clearly for the first time in many years.

'Twas time to move forward, to stop permitting the past to taint his future. He could not change what he'd done, but he could learn from it, become a better man.

Otherwise, his father had won yet again—from the grave. Wouldn't the cruel old bastard have enjoyed that!

Rannulf refused to let him win this battle.

He'd continue to try to mend the breach with Connor and pry his mother from the convent. 'Twas possible he'd saved their lives by his actions. That must mean something.

Bertram FitzClifford was dead. They need hide from him no longer.

He felt free—free to come to Gillian unhindered, to cease spying for Pembroke. Had he paid his debt for killing his father? He didn't know. But wouldn't the best way to redeem himself be to be a better man, a better father and husband than *his* father had been?

He touched the embroidered ribbon tied around his upper arm. He hoped when Gillian saw that he wore her gift, her favor, that she'd understand all he meant by doing so. She'd given herself to him, had given him so many gifts... Would she accept the gift of himself?

He thought of the bundle Gillian had given him before he left l'Eau Clair, the memory bringing a smile to his lips yet again. Will had looked askance at the apple wrapped in a piece of silk, but Rannulf merely smiled and tucked it away in the pouch on his belt.

Later, alone in his chamber in Ian's manor, he'd savored the apple, and the heated memories of Gillian it brought to mind.

Rapid hoofbeats on the road ahead jolted him back to the present.

Will, who'd gone ahead to scout the area, sped toward him, his mount lathered. Rannulf halted the troop and waited for Will to reach him.

"There's a large force massed along the trail to l'Eau Clair, right before the village," he said with a gasp, bringing his horse to a skidding halt. Surprisingly, he grinned. "They bear your banner, milord."

Praise God! With his men from FitzClifford added to those he'd brought from Gwal Draig, he defied any enemy to elude them.

Smiling himself, he saluted Will as he passed him. "Follow me," he shouted. His heart light, he nudged March to a trot and led the way toward the village.

'Twas an impressive force Connor had sent him, Rannulf thought with pride. His men called out greetings and friendly taunts in equal measure as he rode through them to reach the brawny knight mounted at their head. The man had his back to them as he sat atop a mighty stallion, facing the village.

Whom had his brother sent to lead them?

The man swung about in the saddle when he reached him. Rannulf nearly reeled with shock.

'Twas Connor.

He could not mistake his twin's face—the same as his own, save for the long, narrow scar stretched from his left cheekbone to his jaw.

But he'd never seen his brother like this!

The quiet scholar, pale-skinned and slight of build, was gone. Connor sat at his ease in the saddle, strong and tanned, his well-worn armor glinting dully in the sun. Rannulf waited to see how his brother would greet him—*if* he would greet him. When last they'd met, they'd cursed each other, for their sins, and decided to have no further contact with each other.

'Twas a vow Rannulf had found difficult to keep, but he'd caused his brother enough pain.

"Rannulf." Connor nodded, his dark eyes expressionless, his voice cool.

He'd forgotten Connor's skill at masking his emotions. "'Tis good to see you," he said. Wary, but willing to make the first move, Rannulf offered his hand, reached across the space between them—no longer than a yard, though it seemed a league wide until Connor took his hand in a brief, hard grip.

"I've brought the help you asked for." Connor waved a hand to indicate the twenty or so men ranged behind him. "Your man suggested we wait here for you."

Rannulf glanced past Connor. Sunlight glinted on armor and a battle cry sounded from the wooded hill on the far side of the village. He reached for his sword. "Behind you," he said urgently, and Connor drew his own weapon. "To arms!" Rannulf shouted. "Come on—follow me!"

Mayhem ensued for but a moment, horses milling about until their riders took them in hand and headed through the narrow streets toward the raiders.

Heartbeat pounding, Gillian steadied herself. "Go!" she cried unnecessarily as the people in the hall headed for the door, knocking over benches and tables in their wake. Over the sounds of chaos came the heavy thud of booted feet from behind her.

Behind her, where the only entrance she knew of was the hidden passageway.

She grabbed up her skirts and raced toward the outside door halfway down the hall, the overturned furniture slowing her pace. A sheathed sword lay abandoned on the floor; pausing to tuck her hem into her belt, she snatched up the weapon and drew the blade free as she moved.

"Come on!" A stream of men, armed and armor-clad, streamed into the hall.

A jolt of fear spurred her to greater speed. She jerked open the door as her pursuers clambered over the jumbled furnishings, then slammed it shut behind her.

Damnation! There was no way to bar it from the outside.

One hand pressed to the rough stone wall for balance, sword held in the other, she hurried down the steep stairs. "Nicholas! Sir Henry!" she screamed as she frantically scanned the bailey for them. "There are soldiers in the hall!"

She spied Nicholas near the barracks entrance in

the lower level of the keep, directing their men as they poured out into the maze of people, animals and overturned carts already choking the bailey. The gate stood wide and more villagers streamed in, adding to the confusion.

Were the attackers both inside and out?

Just as she reached the bottom of the stairs the door above her opened and the invaders poured onto the landing. The roar of their battle cries sent the masses milling about her into a greater panic.

'Twas nigh impossible to make any headway, but she pushed through the mob, trying to reach Nicholas. He didn't know about the passageway, and likely had no idea how the invaders had gotten in. They needed to send men to close off that entrance at once.

The thunder of hooves on the drawbridge drowned out everything else. Time seemed to pause in that moment, the sights and sounds surrounding her frozen and still. Standing on tiptoe, she looked toward the gate and saw Rannulf riding at the head of a mounted troop of men, then lost sight of him as the crowd shifted about her.

The Virgin be praised, he was alive!

As she wound her way through the press of bodies, she caught glimpses of him. He dismounted, sword drawn, then turned to scan the crowd.

Even as she watched him, she saw more of the armed men force their way across the bailey, heading for Rannulf, Nicholas and their men.

The fighters met in the middle of the chaos, sending the noncombatants into a screaming, terrified frenzy.

She'd never get through here like this. Shouting, brandishing about her with the flat of the sword, she began to creep ahead.

A path opened up near her. Sword held at the ready, she hastened forward. ''Rannulf!'' she screamed as, blade flashing, he spun to face an attacker.

Hard hands grabbed her from behind, tore the sword from her grasp and tossed it aside and dragged her backward toward the keep. To her horror she saw a man wielding a cudgel race up to Rannulf from behind and club him in the head. ''No!'' she cried when he dropped from her sight. Frantic, she clawed at the mail-clad arms wrapped about her middle, but she could not loosen their hold. When she dug in her heels, her captor lifted her off her feet and slung her over his shoulder, laughing as she continued to struggle.

''Squirm and yell all you want,'' he said in Welsh, his hand on her back pressing her so tightly to his shoulder that he squeezed the air from her lungs. ''Won't make a whit o' difference. You're coming with me.''

Gillian gasped as he carried her up the stairs, each jolting step threatening to force her stomach into complete rebellion. She tried to grab at him, but his mail hauberk proved too hard and slick to catch hold of. She could scarcely breathe, but she tried to call out, to draw attention to herself.

In the melee surrounding them, however, no one would hear her meager cries.

The only thought in her mind was to free herself and go to Rannulf, but no matter how she fought, she could not so much as slow the man who bore her across the hall and toward the passageway.

He couldn't carry her as he'd been doing, so he swung her around and set her on her feet, binding her hands close together in front of her with a length of stout rope. "Master told us you weren't to be harmed," he said, unbuckling her belt and slipping her sheathed eating knife from it. "But I can't have you trying to get away, either."

"Don't you know who I am?" Her voice shook from fear and anger. Taking a deep breath, she tried again. "I am lady of this keep. I'll reward you well if you let me go."

"'Course I know who you are—I wouldn't be haulin' you out o' here elsewise," he muttered. "But I got my orders, milady. You're comin' with me." He nudged her down the ladder into the passage, caught her by the end of the rope where it trailed between her hands, and towed her after him down the dim, narrow corridor, a stream of men following hard on their heels.

She couldn't see any way out of this coil. Fear threatened to overcome her, but she beat it back, willed herself to an outward calm. Inside, however, she quivered with terror. The image of Rannulf, falling beneath a crushing blow, replayed itself in her mind. That vision, coupled with concern for her people, left her little energy to fear for herself.

Besides, if they wanted to take her hostage, they clearly didn't intend to harm her—not yet, at least.

It seemed that Nicholas was right after all. Taking her captive *was* the reason for the raids.

But who was behind it all?

Chapter Twenty-Three

Once her eyes had adjusted to the bright sunlight after she emerged from the cave, Gillian stared at her cousin, who stood, outfitted and armed for war, at the head of the path. Unlike his men, he looked clean, unsullied by the filth of battle. "Steffan, you always were a cowardly bastard," she muttered.

A scowl marring the handsome lines of his face, he shook his head. "Is that any way for a lady to speak?" He motioned her captor away and reached for her leash himself, his mouth quirked into a mocking smile. "I expected better of you. I'll forgive you this time, for I'm sure you've had a difficult morning."

How she'd love to slap that taunting expression from his face!

But since she could not, she'd have to be satisfied with meeting his covetous gaze with her own stubborn hatred.

"My lady, I trust your mood will improve soon," he said, his tone a warning. "Come, we cannot tarry here." He tugged her at a headlong pace down the rocky hillside toward the horses tethered by the pool, frowning when she stumbled. He pulled her onto her feet and into motion again. "Don't worry—I'll return you to your home soon, I promise you. I hadn't planned on FitzClifford and Talbot amassing so large a force, or on them arriving this soon. Otherwise I'm sure you and I would already be happily settled within, without all this bother your Norman captors have caused me."

She'd have liked to throttle him, simply to stop his chatter. She went cold inside when his words sank into her fear-dulled brain and she realized how much he knew about their business. How did he know?

Who was the spy?

Steffan stopped near his showy stallion, stepping out of the way when another man came forward and hefted her into the saddle of a horse beside her cousin's. "I cannot risk overburdening my mount," he told her. "Though it means I will have to wait before I'm able to enjoy your company more... intimately."

She would gladly wait forever before that day arrived, though she doubted she'd have that choice. Her flesh crawled from the mere thought, however. Squirming, she tried to untwist her skirts and settle them to cover her legs, a difficult task since her hands remained bound tightly. When she'd done what she could and looked up, Steffan sat atop his mount, struggling to bring the restive animal under control.

The line of men streaming down the hillside came to an end, the last man hauling along a woman in his wake. "Marged, are you unharmed?" Gillian asked when they stopped at the foot of the hill and she recognized the woman.

Why had they brought her from the keep, and no one else?

"Help me, milady!" the maid pleaded, her eyes full of terror. And betrayal?

"Kill her," Steffan ordered before putting spurs to his mount and riding into the forest.

"No!" Gillian tried to guide her horse with her knees and her weight to reach the maid before they could carry out Steffan's command, but all she managed was to send the animal edging sideways. The man behind Marged slashed his knife across her throat before she'd a chance to struggle, then left her crumpled on the grass, her body spattered with her own blood.

The sight proved too much for Gillian's already-churning stomach. She turned away, leaned over the side of the horse and vomited.

Head hanging, she closed her eyes and tried, unsuccessfully, to will away the sick feeling.

"You through?" a man asked.

Still bent over, she opened her eyes, turned her head and saw him standing beside her mount. "I don't know," she whispered, not daring to risk sitting up straight quite yet.

"You'd better be, because we have to go. I don't intend to stop every few feet for you," he warned her. "I haven't the patience, and we don't have time for it. You'd better not be sick on me, either." He shoved her upright, swung behind her in the saddle and gathered the reins in one hand. "From what I've heard of you I thought you'd be stronger than that."

She'd thought so, too. She used to be. Would carrying a child turn her weak, she wondered?

Assuming she lived long enough to find out.

His words had sounded as though they came from far away. Gillian swayed until he caught her and pressed her back against his brawny chest, then surrendered to the wave of blackness washing over her.

Rannulf came to his senses in the gatehouse, his brother and Sir Henry kneeling by his side. "Never would have believed a little tap like that would put you out cold," Connor observed. "Perhaps you're not as tough as I thought."

Narrowing his eyes, Rannulf glared and sat up, leaning against the blessedly cool stone wall until his head stopped whirling. "'Twould scarce have made a mark on *your* head, you brawny fool—no doubt you've developed that as well as the rest of you."

"Are you all right, lad?" Sir Henry asked.

"He must be, if he can bait me," Connor said. He grinned—an expression Rannulf hadn't seen on his brother's face since they were young boys—and clapped Rannulf on the shoulder. "I've changed a bit."

Rannulf grunted as the echo of Connor's meager blow reverberated through his head. "That you have." He reached back and gingerly touched the lump at the back of his neck. It hurt like the devil, but it wasn't the first bump on the head he'd received, and he doubted 'twould be the last. "Is the battle over?"

Connor nodded. "Aye. They cleared out fast shortly after you fell." He motioned for Rannulf to lean forward, and slapped a cold, wet cloth on the bruise. "It's a wonder they didn't break your neck. You should have worn your helm."

"I doubt it would have made much difference."

Rannulf looked past his twin and saw Nicholas heading for them, his expression grim. He stood, somehow managing not to sway. "How did we fare?"

Nicholas halted in front of him. "They've got Gillian," he said, his grim tone matching his expression. "Other than that, we've come through surprisingly well."

"By Christ, I'll—" Rannulf's knees felt ready to collapse. He wavered on his feet; Nicholas took him by the arm and eased him back to lean against the wall. "Sit, you fool, so you can focus your energies on planning how we'll get her back."

Keeping his back pressed against the rough stones, he slipped down to sit. "Do we know who took her?"

"Aye, milord," Sir Henry said. "Though we never saw the coward behind all this—not that I'm surprised." He shook his head. "He's too fainthearted to put himself at risk, the bastard."

"Who is it?" Rannulf demanded.

"Steffan ap Rhys." Sir Henry spit out the words as though they left a foul taste in his mouth. "Many's the time I warned her about him, told her not to tease him—" He looked away, his face old suddenly.

"Why are you still here, then? Shouldn't you be out chasing him down?"

"Calm yourself," Nicholas said sharply. "If we'd a chance in hell of catching up to them, the rest of us would have left even before you came to your senses. But we didn't realize she was gone until after the attackers had retreated. We couldn't find her. Once the villagers calmed down, a young woman said she'd seen a Welshman dragging Gillian through the bailey and into the keep. Seems she tried to get to her to stop him, but in the press of things, all she got for her pains was trampled in the crush. She's not like to survive," he added, his voice grim. "But she managed to tell Ella what happened when they were treating her injuries."

Rannulf said a silent prayer of thanks for the woman's loyalty—and that she might recover.

"My apologies, Nicholas," Rannulf said. "I should have realized you'd not leave Gillian in Steffan's hands any longer than necessary without a reason."

Desperation filled him. He cudgeled his already battered brain for information, to recall what he knew, what he'd seen in the thick of the fighting. "How did they take her? She should have been safe inside the keep." He closed his eyes, remembered hearing her voice screaming his name. "Was she in the bailey?"

"Aye. Some of them came into the keep through a certain passageway." Nicholas's grim expression turned cold. "Seems my servant, Richard, knew of the route to the pool from his whore. I gather she must have seen you—and Gillian—come through it at some point. He'll not betray us again, I vow—nor will she," he added. "It seems they outlived their usefulness."

By the rood, had his carelessness led to Gillian's abduction? To the carnage, the dead and wounded he could see out in the bailey?

Telling himself his own injury was no more than he deserved, Rannulf rose to his feet and walked out into the bright sun. "Do we know where he took her?" he asked, squinting when the light threatened to cleave his head in two.

"Back to his lair in Wales, I would guess," Nicholas said. "Likely he doesn't believe we'd follow him there.'' He gazed into the distance for a moment. ''He'd be right about that, too, for we can hardly lead an army through the area.''

''Why not? I just did,'' Rannulf pointed out. ''We cannot leave her with him!'' Frustration made him want to snarl and snap, but that would help nothing, might even harm their chances of freeing Gillian.

''Come with me,'' Nicholas suggested, and led the way to the room that sat on top of the gatehouse tower. ''There's naught but chaos everywhere else,'' he said, motioning for them to sit on the benches lining one wall. ''You led a troop of men, true, but there weren't many, and they weren't traveling as a war party.'' He leaned against the wall and sighed. ''The situation between the king and Llywelyn is unsettled as it is. I cannot drag an army into Wales and attack one of Llywelyn's kinsmen. Not even to save Gillian,'' he added when Rannulf opened his mouth to protest.

''Can't you go to Llywelyn, ask if he'll order the man to release her?'' Connor asked. ''It hardly seems right that he could remove a noblewoman from her own castle without some punishment for it.''

Restless, Rannulf stood and gingerly paced the confines of the small chamber. ''It would take too long,'' he said. He stopped by the window and gazed down into the bailey, the destruction he saw angering him anew. ''Besides, Ian—Gillian's Welsh cousin who sent some men to help us,'' he told Connor. ''Ian said that Llywelyn wouldn't help Gillian before we arrived, didn't even reply to her request. I don't know that we could trust him to favor Gillian over Steffan.''

''Then we need some way to get into Steffan's holding and rescue her ourselves,'' Connor said.

Rannulf turned to his brother. "We?"

"Of course. You don't think I'm going to go back to my placid existence at FitzClifford when there's adventure to be had here, do you?" Connor asked. "Besides, I'm assuming *this* Gillian is *your* Gillian, the woman you told Mother and me you intended to marry years ago."

"Aye." Rannulf stole a wary glance at his overlord, whose expression of mild interest looked at odds with the curiosity in his eyes.

"I cannot, in all conscience, permit my future sister by marriage to languish in captivity," Connor assured him.

"He's right. We cannot leave her in Steffan's hands for long," Nicholas said. He pushed away from the wall and crossed to stand before Rannulf. "There are many reasons we need to get Gillian away from Steffan, reasons I'm sure you realize, but there's another you don't know about." He stared out the window for a moment before fixing Rannulf with a stern look. "A most important reason. Gillian is carrying your child."

Gillian came to her senses soon after they rode into the heavily wooded hills beyond the northern boundaries of l'Eau Clair. She recognized the area, having passed through it the one time she'd traveled to Wales to visit Catrin. Steffan's manor lay close to Ian's keep at Gwal Draig, she thought, though she knew nothing about it.

She prayed 'twas a manor house, and not a walled keep or some other fortification. Otherwise, she couldn't imagine how she'd manage to escape from it.

Or how Nicholas could rescue her.

She still held out hope that Rannulf had survived that brutal blow to the head, but she couldn't imagine he'd be in any condition to fight.

Her stomach gave an ominous shudder. "Stop, now," she blurted out. "Please."

Her captor took one look at her face and leapt from the saddle, pulling her down after him just in time for her to be wretchedly ill in the bushes.

"Thank you," she said weakly once she was able to stand. "I'm sorry—I cannot help it."

Steffan trotted back along the trail toward them, his face dark with anger. "Why did you stop?" he snarled.

"'Twas my fault," she said. "I'm…my stomach is not well," she told him. Should she tell him why?

Another glance at his expression convinced her that the less Steffan knew, the better. She saw such malice in him, worse than in his youth, that she feared his reaction if he knew she carried a child.

Considering the plans he'd made for her, plans that included their marriage, she'd not put it past him to try to rid her of the babe somehow.

Or to punish her for its existence.

"Are you better now?" Steffan asked, his gaze narrowed as he stared at her face.

"Yes. I'll be fine, milord," she assured him. "Please go on. I'll not delay us any longer."

She scarce dared to breathe until he rode back to the head of the column. "I'm ready, sir," she told her captor.

He hefted her into the saddle. "I'm no 'sir,'" he said, laughing. "Huw is my name, milady, and I make you free of it."

Huw proved a silent companion, a blessing when it took all her resources to maintain control over her stomach. They left the main trail and followed a path so rugged they had to dismount several times to lead the horses.

By some miracle she survived that jolting, exhausting trek without disgracing herself with further sickness, but she could not fight sleep. They pushed on through the night beneath the light of a nearly full moon; she slept through most of the night pressed against the coarse surface of Huw's mail hauberk.

Two days of this made her so limp she couldn't stand when they finally rode through the gate of Bryn Du. While 'twas not a keep, the large manor house and outbuildings sat in the midst of a fortified wall surrounded by a ditch filled with stakes.

Her desire for independence wouldn't matter here. It didn't appear she'd be able to get herself out of Steffan's grasp without outside help.

She'd considered trying to convince Huw to help her, but after two days in his company, she could see that Steffan held him deeply within his grasp. Huw hated Steffan—how could he not?—but he obeyed his every command, no matter how monstrous.

By the time Steffan ushered her into a chamber on the far side of the house from the gate, the effort of pretending to have recovered from her "illness" had taken its toll. Tired past exhaustion, her spirits low, her belly rumbling to be fed, she permitted her cousin to tether her to an iron ring on the bed frame with nary a complaint and settled back against the pillows with a sigh.

At least her hands weren't tied together any longer. Steffan sat in the chair beside the bed and took one of her hands in his. A frown crossed his lips as he laid her hand on the coverlet with insulting haste. "I see we should have cared for you better on the journey," he said. He rose, went to open the door and shouted for his maid. "I'll visit you again once you've had a chance to bathe."

She nearly laughed. Afraid of a bit of dirt, was he? In that case, she'd not wash unless forced into it.

And perhaps the time had come when she could allow her malaise full rein, as well—not that she enjoyed the sickness, but 'twould be easier for her if she need not pretend to be well.

Anything to keep that expression of distaste on Steffan's face, to keep him away from her a little while longer.

Until help arrived.

Rannulf, Connor and Nicholas made the journey to Gwal Draig, Ian's keep, in record time. Though Rannulf's first instinct was to run Steffan to ground and then do his best to put the bastard *under*ground, he knew he'd never get the opportunity. He couldn't lure Steffan out when he had nothing Steffan wanted.

While Steffan had everything Rannulf held dear within his grasp.

Despite the fact that all they had were a number of half-formed plans for releasing Gillian from captivity, those plans involved Ian. Rannulf could have screamed in frustration when they learned that the Dragon wasn't at Gwal Draig.

Nor did Catrin know where to find him.

"Llywelyn sent for him," she told them as soon as they were shown into her solar. "Why do you need him? Is it important?"

"Your kinsman, Steffan, took Gillian," Rannulf said, his voice devoid of emotion. Refusing to permit himself to express his fear for her was the only way he could survive this hell.

He could not lose Gillian again.

The mere thought of her—and their child—in the hands of that madman struck deeper than any other loss in his life. Regaining Gillian's trust, and now the promise of parenthood, gave him a new perspective on many things in his life. His guilt for his father's death was gone. He'd made amends for his unwitting sin, served his country through his work for Pembroke, and vowed to care for his family—both Connor and his mother, as well as Gillian and their children—for the rest of his days.

'Twas time to move on with his life, but to do that, he needed Gillian by his side.

Catrin leapt from her chair by the fire. *"What?"* She paced the floor, stopping in front of Rannulf. "The why is easy enough to see, for Steffan has always desired what he could not have. But how did he get her?"

Nicholas explained about the attack, and their hope that Ian would help them find a way to remove Gillian from Steffan's clutches.

They sat in silence, sipping mead while Catrin resumed pacing. Rannulf felt ready to jump up and run from the room. Simply to run, to do *something*.

"Is there any way we can find Ian?" he asked Catrin.

She shook her head, then held up her hand to stop him when he started to speak again.

Finally she halted, reached out and took his hand and held it tightly. "I believe I know how I can get you into Bryn Du,'' she told them. ''You must be patient, for it could take several days to bring my plan to an end, but I think—nay, I know—we can make it work.''

She poured herself a drink and sat down again. ''Listen carefully, for this is what we'll do....''

Chapter Twenty-Four

Rannulf gazed at himself in the mirror Lady Catrin held before him, wondering yet again if he had the skill to carry off his part in this ruse. He believed the scheme could work. He'd had plenty of opportunity to think it over, and they'd discussed the plan endlessly in the two days since Lady Catrin had suggested it. A bit of polishing, and what had sounded completely impossible took on the sheen of a workable strategy.

Despite Ian's continued absence, he was glad they'd come to Gwal Draig. All of his own ideas involved bloodshed and battle, and presented an unacceptable risk to Gillian and the babe.

Lady Catrin's plan might allow them to avoid any of that.

She'd sent several maidservants to Bryn Du with the offer of helping Lord Steffan with some housekeeping chore. As Catrin expected, they'd returned full of gossip about the sickly woman their master had shut away in his manor. Rumor had it that she was to be his bride as soon as she recovered from her malady.

Not if he had anything to do with it, Rannulf vowed, sneering at his brown-stained face in the mirror before handing it to Lady Catrin. "What do you think?" he asked, turning so that Nicholas and Connor could view his disguise.

"Mother would scarce recognize you," Connor said. "If she hadn't already decided to remain at St. Anna's, without a doubt the sight of you thus would send her there."

Rannulf scowled at his twin. He'd rather not be reminded that their mother had decided to take the veil and live out her life within the peaceful and safe confines of the convent. He had hoped she might consider coming to live with him and his family, although he could understand her decision.

And he was glad that she'd finally found a peaceful existence.

Nicholas stared from one brother to the other and shook his head wonderingly. "You've performed a miracle, milady," he told Lady Catrin. "No one will realize that FitzClifford isn't a Saracen in that guise." He merely smiled when she sent a scowl his way, making Rannulf wonder where Talbot found the patience to endure her continual slights.

"But will I be able to convince Lord Steffan?" Rannulf asked. "I know nothing of how to heal the sick, nor—"

"You won't need to actually treat anyone," Lady Catrin said dryly. "You can pretend, can't you?"

"Aye." He'd dare do no less under her watchful eyes, even if Gillian's and the babe's safety didn't depend upon it.

"'Tis time to leave." She led the way to the stables and permitted Nicholas to lift her into the saddle.

Rannulf felt as though he were watching everything from a distance. He'd never been this nervous before a battle—but never had the stakes been so high, either.

They rode through the forested land that separated Gwal Draig from Bryn Du, halting beyond sight of Steffan's manor. "You'll be ready for them as soon as they leave?" she asked Nicholas yet again.

He dismounted and handed the reins to Connor. "Aye, milady—you've laid out our duties clear as glass." He sauntered toward her. "Can't you trust, just this once, that I might do something right?"

"You've shown so little skill in that regard," she said, peering down at Talbot from her perch atop her mare. "This is important. I don't want anything to go awry."

Talbot stopped beside her and, snatching her from the saddle, kissed her hard.

She slapped him. It deterred him not at all.

He took his time settling her back onto her mount. "Godspeed," he said, then slapped the mare on the rump, sending her leaping onto the road.

Chuckling despite his uneasiness, Rannulf urged his palfrey into a jarring trot and followed Lady Catrin toward Bryn Du.

The sound of footsteps in the corridor outside her chamber—her prison, more like—jolted Gillian from sleep. Moaning as her muscles throbbed, she sat up and swept the tangled fall of her hair out of her face.

What she wouldn't give for a hot bath and the security to immerse herself in it! She'd held firm to her resolve not to bathe or groom herself since she'd arrived here two days ago, but she hoped she wouldn't have to do so for much longer. It seemed such a petty thing under the circumstances, to wish she were clean, but she felt so miserable from head to toe.... And it gave her something to dwell upon besides the untenable situation she'd landed in.

The footsteps stopped outside her door; she clambered off the mattress and tugged her gown into place as Steffan entered the room.

"Good morning, my dear." He set down a tray of food on the table next to the bed and nudged the door closed with his hip.

The scent of hot bread and sharp cheese, usually a welcome aroma, sent waves of nausea hurtling through her. Feeling faint, she sat abruptly on the bed.

"I'd hoped you would feel better today," he said. He lifted the lid from a trencher, watching her with an intensity she found difficult to ignore. The smell of mutton rose from the dish; hand over her mouth, she dashed off to the far side of the bed and grabbed the chamber pot.

"Whose child is it, cousin? Who dared sully your purity and spoil my plans?"

Her stomach calmer for the moment, she wiped her face on a towel and rose slowly from the floor.

Steffan's face twisted with rage. "Who, Gillian?"

He circled the bed and yanked her close. "By Christ—why haven't you washed?" he snarled, tossing her aside to land hard upon the mattress. "I'll have answers from you, Gillian, as soon as the servants bathe you."

He hauled open the door, then spun on his heel to face her again. "Remember one thing, cousin—you are mine, and I shall have you just as soon as I've found a way to rid you of that Norman brat."

Frantic with fear, the moment the door closed Gillian forced herself to sit up and examine yet again the shackle locked round her wrist. The chain tethering it to the bed was sturdy—she knew she'd no way to break it—but perhaps in time she could loosen the shackle and break free.

Of course, she had no idea what she would do in that case, but 'twas a beginning.

She could not wait for help to come, not if she wished to protect Rannulf's child.

A servant led Lady Catrin and Rannulf—in his guise as a physician—into Steffan's hall. "I hear you've my cousin Gillian visiting here," Lady Catrin said as soon as she'd introduced the "physician" to Lord Steffan. "I came to see her." She strode past them toward a doorway across the hall. "Since I also heard she was ill, I've brought this esteemed healer to see if he can cure her ills. He's come here from the court of our kinsman, Llywelyn."

The Welshman scowled at his cousin and said nothing.

Rannulf huddled deeper into the enveloping robes he wore, as much to hide his hatred for the man as to maintain his disguise. This preening popinjay was the cause of the raids? This *fool* stole Gillian away and believed she would wed him?

His mind must be lacking in sense and intelligence, to mislead him so thoroughly.

"Steffan, may I take him to her?" she asked, moving to wait near the doorway. "Ian will be so pleased to know I've seen her."

At the mention of Ian, Steffan's frown deepened. "A moment," he said, then motioned forward the maid who'd been standing silently near the main entrance. After a whispered conversation he handed the woman a ring of keys and sent her away. "Catrin, you may go with Maud," he said. "But I wish to speak with the healer before I will permit him to examine Gillian."

They watched Lady Catrin follow the servant, then Lord Steffan turned to him. "What do you know of ridding a woman of an unwanted child?"

Rannulf's hands clenched into fists within his long sleeves as he fought the urge to throttle Steffan where he stood. Rid Gillian of her child? *Their* child!

Never.

Why try to steal Gillian out of the chamber and lock Lord Steffan in, running the risk of his calling in the guard? He could eliminate him now, he thought frantically. He glanced about the hall. They were alone; he could hear no sounds of servants anywhere about. There would be no better time than this.

He moved closer to Steffan. "What do you mean, milord?" he asked in a low, accented voice.

"She carries another man's child," Steffan explained slowly, perhaps believing Rannulf hadn't understood. "I would be rid of it before I make her my wife."

A few more steps, past Steffan, then Rannulf whirled and thrust back the sleeves of his robe to free his hands.

He closed his fingers about Steffan's throat, squeezing hard, ignoring the other man's muffled attempts to speak, to breathe. He grabbed at Rannulf's hands and tried to pry them loose, but he could not budge them.

He kicked at Rannulf's shins, his movements less

lively now, so Rannulf lifted him until his feet left the floor. "You craven bastard," he muttered. "'Tis *my* child you wish to kill, *my* woman you stole away." He cast another look about to make certain no one was coming. "I—don't—share." He punctuated each word with a shake, until Steffan hung limp from his grasp, unresponsive.

He didn't believe he had killed him, but he wouldn't be chasing them any time soon in his present condition. He tugged a length of rope from beneath his robe and bound Steffan hand and foot, then ripped a strip of fabric from Steffan's elaborate tunic and gagged him with it.

This could work just as well as their original plan, he told himself. And it had the added reward of removing the man from access to his men and weapons.

Not wanting to waste any more time, Rannulf rolled him beneath a long cloth-covered table and hurried down the hall where Lady Catrin had disappeared. Knocking lightly, he slipped into the chamber and closed the door quietly behind him.

Gillian sat on the bed, pale and wan, but her eyes glowed with an emerald fire. He crossed to her in two strides and wrapped her in his arms. "Are you all right, love?" he murmured into her hair. "He hasn't harmed you?"

Gillian clung to Rannulf as tightly as she could, drawing strength from him. "I'm fine," she assured him. "What of you? I saw you fall during the battle."

"I'm fine now that we've got you."

"This is very touching," Catrin said. "I do mean that, Gillian," she added when Gillian glared at her cousin's tart tone. "But we're far from safe." She gestured to the maid, trussed up on the floor on the other side of the bed. "I thought you were bringing Steffan in here so we could lock him up, too." She stood by the door, listening. "What is he doing while you're in here?"

"I choked him till he swooned," Rannulf said dryly. "I didn't like what he said, and it seemed the best way to silence him. I left him under a table in the hall for the moment, awaiting your pleasure, mi-lady."

Gillian looked from one to the other, uncertain what they planned to do next. "Could we leave?" she asked. "My stomach isn't too bad right now, but I've no way of knowing how long my good fortune might last."

Rannulf bent and kissed her brow. "I'm sorry, love." He turned to Catrin. "What shall we do with him—take him with us as a hostage or a shield, or leave him locked up in here?"

"Take him with us, at least to leave the manor," Gillian suggested, though they hadn't asked her advice. "His men won't harm us if it might put him in danger. If we leave him here, they'll just come after us and follow until they catch up."

Rannulf nodded. "So be it."

Another concern rose to mind. "I doubt I can ride far," Gillian told them. "The journey here was pure torture, I felt so ill."

Catrin reached over and gave her hand a squeeze. "Do you believe I'd allow them to drag you through the Marches in your condition? We're taking you to Gwal Draig. You might need to stay there for a bit, until Ian returns and can help smooth over this situation with Llywelyn, but you should be safe from Steffan there."

"Should we bring him with us to Gwal Draig?" Rannulf asked. He loosened his hold on Gillian and went to open the door.

"Nay," Catrin said quietly. "'Twill be difficult enough to talk our way out of this, for I warrant Llywelyn won't be pleased. For some reason, he seems to like our weaselly cousin," she added with a frown. "Though I have no idea why."

"No one's about," Rannulf said. "Let's go."

They strode boldly out of the chamber and into the still-empty hall, where Rannulf collected Steffan from beneath the table and slung his deadweight over his shoulder. They made it halfway across the small courtyard before anyone tried to stop them, but the sight of Rannulf's knife pressed against their master's throat deterred everyone from approaching them.

Gillian rode with Catrin, while Rannulf draped Steffan over March's withers and leapt into the saddle behind him. They raced out the open gate and onto a trail into the forest, no sounds of pursuit following them.

But their good fortune couldn't last for long.

"We're going the wrong way!" Gillian told Catrin as she clung to the saddle and prayed her stomach would remain calm.

"We're meeting Talbot and Connor FitzClifford," Catrin said.

"Connor's here?"

"Aye—he came with Talbot and Rannulf."

Gillian reached up to brush her trailing hair from her eyes. "Why aren't they at Gwal Draig?" Connor's presence must mean he'd forgiven Rannulf. She hoped their mother had come from FitzClifford as well.

"They were supposed to escort the two of you back to l'Eau Clair," she said as she tugged on the reins to slow her mount as they entered a thick stand of trees. "This new plan will be better, though, for you'll be safe with us, and you'll be able to rest."

They stopped, and Nicholas and Connor stepped out from behind the trees, leading their horses. Connor looked nothing like she'd expected, for Rannulf had described a very different person than the healthy-looking, brawny man who approached them.

"I'll take him," Connor said, lifting Steffan's still body easily and setting him on the ground.

I hope there's some poisonous plant growing there, Gillian thought with a burst of anger. He deserved any torment she could devise.

"Will you take him and leave him someplace where he won't come to too much harm?" Rannulf asked Nicholas.

"Why not kill him?" her guardian asked, making the scheme sound reasonable.

Catrin strolled closer to him. "Because 'twould be a fleeting pleasure, milord—appealing, over too swiftly, leaving naught but regrets. You're familiar with that feeling, I'd imagine," she added with a smug smile.

Nicholas's face reddened and he turned away. "Give me the bastard," he told Connor. "We can take care of him—you go on to Gwal Draig. We'll meet you there."

Catrin set about pampering Gillian as soon as they arrived at Gwal Draig. Gillian climbed into a tub of warm water with a moan of pleasure and didn't climb out until she'd scrubbed from head to toe. Now she sat drowsing by the fire as her hair dried, her belly full of dry bread and mead. If Rannulf would join her, her happiness would be complete.

It would take a while, she'd imagine, to remove whatever paint he'd covered his face and hands with. Though Catrin had warned her of how he'd appear, she'd been surprised by how different he looked.

But she'd have known him anywhere, no matter how he was garbed.

She heard the door open and close behind her. Smiling, she didn't bother to turn, for she knew it must be Catrin, come to bully her into something.

The smell of sandalwood warned her of her mistake; the withered apple that dropped into her lap confirmed it. "Rannulf," she murmured, rising half out of the chair before he gently pressed her back down onto the cushioned seat.

"My love," he whispered. He moved around the chair to sit on the floor by her feet. He rested his cheek on her knees and settled his palm on her belly. "Did you swallow an apple seed?" he asked her, his voice alight with laughter.

She giggled. "Is that what happened?"

He raised his head and met her gaze, his dark eyes warm and full of love. "I do believe an apple was involved," he said seriously.

"I believe you're right."

He rose on his knees and wrapped his arms about her. "I'm so glad you're all right," he whispered, his voice shaking. He buried his face in her hair and held her. "So glad you're finally mine."

She savored his touch, the wave of love and contentment that flowed from him to her and back again. "As you are mine, milord." Framing his face in her hands, she drew back and pressed a kiss to his lips. "And don't you ever forget it, my love."

"I'd sooner forget how to breathe."

In one swift motion he stood, scooped her into his arms and sat down with her nestled in his lap. "We've so much to talk about." She snuggled deeper into his hold and rested her head against his chest. "Your family, my guardian, my cousins, l'Eau Clair, my father's wishes..."

"Aye, love—I've much to tell you," Rannulf murmured. "Though I hardly know where to begin."

"Is everyone at l'Eau Clair safe?" she asked, not bothering to disguise her sense of urgency. Her concern for her people and her home had been nigh as strong as her worry about Rannulf the past few days, haunting her thoughts.

His eyes darkened. "Most everyone. Several of the villagers were killed in the crush of battle in the bailey, as were a few of our men, God rest them." He took her hand in his after she crossed herself and pressed a kiss upon her fingers before placing it palm down against his chest. "But considering the intensity of the fighting, we suffered little harm."

"Will and Sir Henry?" she asked, her gaze fixed on his face.

A faint smile brightened his expression. "Those two? 'Twould take more than a few Welshmen to best them." His smile deepened. "A bit battered and bruised when we left, but nothing serious."

Despite her pleasure at the welcome news, a chill passed through her. "I saw Marged killed," she whispered, the image etched in her memory tainting her joy at her friends' survival.

Rannulf's expression sobered. "Aye, she's dead—

and Richard as well. 'Tis a just payment for their treachery.''

"Treachery?" Gillian shifted in Rannulf's lap so she might see his face more clearly. "Richard's hatred of me was clear enough, but Marged—"

"It seems that Marged was Steffan's spy, my love, and Richard her willing accomplice. Nicholas gleaned that much from Richard before he died of his injuries soon after the Welsh fled l'Eau Clair. One—or both— of them must have seen us using the passageway, and passed the information on to Steffan."

She thought back over the two servants' behavior; if they'd been in Steffan's employ it explained a great deal, for she'd noticed several times that their actions and expressions had seemed odd, furtive. Wrapping her arms about Rannulf's waist, she laid her head against his chest and held him tightly. "Should we have recognized what they were doing? Were we so distracted by our pleasure that it blinded us to their schemes?"

He stroked her hair and nestled her closer. "Perhaps." He brushed a kiss along her cheek. "We'll never know, love. But there's naught we can do to change the past. I realize that more than ever now. All we can do is to learn from our mistakes, and vow to do better. I've made that promise to my brother, and I intend to keep it." He eased her away from his chest and framed her face in his hands. "And I make that vow to you, Gillian, and to our child. I'll never stop regretting that my father died by my hand, but I see now that there's nothing to be gained by punishing myself for the rest of my life."

"I refuse to allow you to," she told him fiercely. "'Tis time to look to your future, to *our* future—ours and our child's. Your responsibilities have changed.'' Her gaze holding his captive, she asked. ''Does this mean you're finished with your work for my godfather? Will he allow you to stop spying, to lead a normal life?''

Rannulf drew in a deep breath and let it out slowly. ''My task is complete, and I shall not seek another from Pembroke. I know now that Nicholas Talbot is no close friend to the king, and is not deserving of Pembroke's distrust. Nor do I believe him any threat to you, especially since he's given me permission—nay, he's ordered me, as your guardian and my overlord—to make an honest woman of you,'' he added, his smile brightening his face and eyes.

Gillian's heart thumped harder in her chest, sending a wave of anticipation thrumming through her. ''Has he indeed?''

''Aye. You're free of Talbot's hold, but I hope you'll soon be caught firmly within mine.'' He tightened his hands about her middle. ''I feel as though the weight of the past has been lifted from me. All I desire from life is simply to hold you, to show you all I've held hidden in my heart these many years.'' He kissed her lips slowly, reverently, in a solemn vow. ''Will you marry me, Gillian? Will you help me make a life for us, allow me to make up to you for the pain I've caused you?'' He laced his fingers with hers and traced his tongue over her palm. ''Let me care for you, for our babe,'' he added, placing their joined hands on her stomach.

''We say yes, milord. *I* say yes.'' She turned his hand and pressed her lips to his callused fingers. ''With all my heart.''

* * * * * *

This season,

is proud to introduce four very
different Western romances that will
warm your heart....

In October 1999, look for

COOPER'S WIFE #485
by Jillian Hart

and

THE DREAMMAKER #486
by Judith Stacy

In November 1999, look for

JAKE WALKER'S WIFE #489
by Loree Lough

and

HEART AND HOME #490
by Cassandra Austin

Harlequin Historicals
The way the past *should* have been.

Available at your favorite retail outlet.

Makes any time special ™

Visit us at www.romance.net

HHWEST4

This season, make your
destination Great Britain with
four exciting stories from

Harlequin® Historical

In October 1999, look for
LADY SARAH'S SON #483 by **Gayle Wilson**
(England, 1814)

and

THE HIDDEN HEART #484 by **Sharon Schulze**
(Wales, 1213)

In November 1999, look for
ONE CHRISTMAS NIGHT #487
by **Ruth Langan, Jacqueline Navin and Lyn Stone**
(Scottish Highlands 1540, England 1193
and Scotland 1320)

and

A GENTLEMAN OF SUBSTANCE #488 by **Deborah Hale**
(England, 1814)

**Harlequin Historicals
Where reading is truly a vacation!**

HARLEQUIN®
Makes any time special ™

From the bestselling author of
THE CHARM SCHOOL

Susan Wiggs

When Hunter Calhoun's prized
stallion arrives
from Ireland crazed
and dangerous, he is
forced to seek out the
horsemaster's daughter....

Eliza Flyte has been raised far
removed from the social world of wealth and
privilege, but her talent for gentling horses draws
her into Hunter's life and into the heart of his
shattered family. She can tame his horse, but can
someone from her world teach someone from his
what truly matters in life?

The Horsemaster's Daughter

On sale mid-October 1999 wherever paperbacks are sold!